SHIP OUTTA LUCK

Published by Brittany Kelley

www.brittanykelleywrites.com

Copyright © 2024 Brittany Kelley

Cover by Yummy Book Covers

Edited by Happy Ever Author & Waddle Editing

For sub-rights inquiries, please contact Jessica Watterson at Sandra Djikstra Literary Agency.

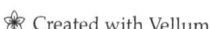 Created with Vellum

For all the girls who were too stubborn to give up and grew into women who know what they want

AUTHOR'S NOTE

Eagle-eyed readers will find dramatic liberties have been taken with football, dance, and cheerleading for the sake of the story. Furthermore, some readers may find themes in this book troubling. For a full list of content warnings, please visit my website.

www.brittanykelleywrites.com

CHAPTER
ONE

JUNE

I BLINK TWICE, my best polite smile starting to slide, much like the sweat dripping down my collarbone. The fan clicks lazily overhead. It doesn't so much cool the room as simply push the stagnant South Texas air around.

A white silk button-down? In the summer? No deodorant could make this right.

I chose... *poorly*. Though at this rate, I wouldn't mind disintegrating à la an Indiana Jones enemy if it meant relief from this heat.

The mere thought of Indiana Jones sends a shockwave of grief cresting through me. It was my dad's favorite movie franchise. There were so many late Sunday nights spent watching them with him on the couch, but they'll never be enough.

It's been three weeks since my dad's funeral. Three weeks of trying to piece myself back together, only to find everything crashing down around me.

I fan myself, rewarded with puffs of stale air as I try not to cry.

"Dr. Legarde, are you paying attention? You look like my undergrads when I ask if they've read the syllabus." Dr. Weaselton, my boss, snorts at his own joke. As the history and archaeology department chair at our small state university, he holds the future of my research in his hands, and he regards me over horn-rimmed glasses that went out of style three decades ago.

A faint smile stretches my lips at the joke, my throat bobbing as I nod once.

"Yes, sir," I say, stretching my fingers across the hem of my skirt. "But I fail to understand your reasoning. My research is airtight, but to continue it, I need assistance. Financially."

The wooden chair creaks as I try to scooch forward, my thighs glued to the seat.

Dr. Weaselton narrows his eyes at me, and I half-listen as he drones on about budget cuts.

"I understand," I finally bite out.

I'm not an idiot. I don't need my hard-earned PhD to understand he isn't going to sign off on my grant application. That there are other professors that have much less risky research projects. That they need the meager funds just as much as I do, if not more.

Hunting for a long-lost sunken treasure might sound exciting, but the chances of finding it are slim to none, and my colleagues' chances of finding the texts they need in libraries overseas are much, much stronger.

Awareness prickles the back of my neck, and I glance over my shoulder. Unless the ceramic bust of Herodotus sitting on the bookshelf is staring daggers at me, I'm imagining it. Again.

Still. I can't shake the feeling someone has been watching me for days. Other than Herodotus, that is. And my father taught me to never ignore my gut.

"Dr. Legarde, I hope you can understand that this isn't personal, although I know your current focus is personal to you. We were all saddened by your loss, and we do wish you the best."

A tart reply sits on the tip of my tongue, but I swallow it.

I sigh as my Dr. Weaselton closes the manila folder with my paper application in it, unsigned. Paper, of course, because even kind dinosaurs like Weaselton are nothing if not set in their ways.

"The university simply will not accept the risk of funding such a venture, and our department has other priorities."

The curt dismissal hurts, and my fragile porcelain façade cracks.

"It's not a risk." My eyes sting with stubborn tears as I lean forward. "I know the *Santu Espiritu* is out there; you have all the research and proof anyone could ask for in front of you. I just need the money to continue looking for its final resting place." My voice grows jagged the more I talk, and I know it's not helping.

I know, and I can't stop it.

Years of research, nearly a decade of charting currents over the past four centuries, years' worth of weekends spent digging through archives, and untold hours splashing down on dives all over the gulf. It had all been fruitless—until I'd stumbled upon docking logs challenging the ship's assumed departure date, setting it back by a month… and placing it in the Gulf of Mexico during one of the worst hurricanes on record.

"I can go over the data again, if you'd like." I motion to the closed folder, somehow maintaining a calm, even tone. "I have strong evidence indicating that hurricane in 1554 knocked the ship off course."

"You went over that source already," he says shaking his head. "It's not incontrovertible proof, Dr. Legarde. And I can't sign off on this. It would be like looking for a needle in a haystack, if you'll excuse such a puerile cliché." His tone is gentle, but the words are a slap in the face.

I wish I could shake him, make him see reason. But shaking him wouldn't get me the money; he isn't the stuck vending machine outside my office. So I take a deep breath, my smile sharpening.

"Even if I knew beyond a shadow of a doubt it was there… an underwater exploration of this size?" He sighs heavily, pinching the bridge of his nose. "Dr. Legarde, we simply do not have the funds we once had. If we had the money, we would give it to you." Despite the incontrovertible no, his eyes are kind as he pushes my application to the side. "As always, you're impressive. Publish what you've found so far in one of the academic journals. I can see a lot of promise in your research, and I'd enjoy looking over any papers you produce."

Uncurling my fists, I smile faintly at the praise. Relaxing slightly against the hard chair-back, my smartwatch buzzes; it manages everything from my breathing to my calendar.

"But this is coming from above." He shakes his head. "The university simply won't fund your search." He smiles sadly, and I recognize the look.

He wanted me to get the grant.

Stomach sinking, I close my eyes.

I'll find the Santu Espiritu *without their help.*

Though how I'm going to come up with the money…

The prickling sensation returns, and I cast my gaze out his office window, to the bay glistening under the blazing sun.

"I understand. Thank you for your time and consideration." Somehow peeling my legs from the chair, I stand, resolving to leave with my dignity intact. "I'll consider your advice regarding the paper."

Ha. No way I'm writing that paper, all so some jerk treasure hunter can find the *Santu Espiritu* first.

I head for the door, blinking back tears threatening to ruin my 'I've got my life together' professor vibe. Straightening my shoulders, my hand closing around the cool metal doorknob, I swallow back an undignified sob until Dr. Weaselton's voice brings me up short.

"June, do you really think it's out there? This close to the Texas shoreline? Wouldn't we have found it with all the oil drilling?" Even now, he is incredulous.

Not trusting myself to turn around, to make another plea for the grant, I take a breath. "I would stake my entire career on it, Dr. Weaselton," I say, finally stepping into the blessedly cool hallway. The sticky hair on my shoulders practically floats as the AC blasts it.

The door snicks shut behind me as goosebumps prickle my skin.

Maybe it's leftover adrenaline from the meeting. The *failed* meeting.

My shoulders sag.

Yeah, adrenaline… or maybe I'm getting even more paranoid these days.

My watch buzzes, congratulating me on standing up.

At least I accomplished that.

My heels clack against the empty tile floor as I barrel down the hallway, thankful classes ended last week and summer semester won't start for another week.

I'm ready to escape, to rip off the sweaty silk shirt and heels and replace them with a swimsuit, cutoffs, and flip-flops. Then make a new plan to find the *Santu Espiritu*.

The ship my father spent a lifetime looking for.

Like I'm going to now—with or without the sanction of my employer. I don't need them, not necessarily.

Nope.

All I need is cash-flow. Resolve stiffening my backbone, I inhale deeply, trying to shake off the disappointment.

I'm better than this.

When a door closes, a window opens.

With any luck, a window that leads directly to a pile of money and the GPS coordinates of the *Santu Espiritu*.

You know, lightning strike, lottery winning luck.

Outside, the sea breeze dulls the stuffiness of the small, under-funded liberal arts building. My shoulder blades itch, and I glance back at the Brutalist concrete building, completely out of place in the flat salt marsh landscape. Its small slits for windows, the only reprieve from the dun-colored cement blocks.

Unable to shake the distinct sense of being watched, I look around. But find no one.

"Fudge."

I savor the euphemism, the shape my lips make around the f

as it rolls from my tongue. But it isn't as satisfying as the real thing, and my lower lip curls down.

Control is satisfying though. Control, with my carefully scheduled days. My constant reminders to stand, breathe, and exercise… routine and control are the only things keeping me from a complete meltdown.

"Fudge."

Unbuttoning a few of my top buttons, which doesn't make a difference at all, I stride towards my old, beat-up truck. The red paint peeled and pebbled in places, a victim of the same salt air I taste on my tongue. Another relic of my father, of our shared past.

My throat swells, my tongue thickening in my mouth.

The *Santu Espiritu* was our thing; the hobby we shared. Then the mutual obsession we shared, hours spent tracking tides and histories and leads that would go up in smoke. Just because I don't know *exactly* where it's collecting silt and sea creatures doesn't mean it isn't out there, waiting for me.

It should be waiting for *us*.

And now?

Now I go home, to no one. No boyfriend, no roommate.

Just the constant glow of my laptop, the endless cataloguing of historic tides and possible historic sandbar locations. Primary sources and spreadsheets. And checking my scuba gear. Cleaning the boat. Working on the boat. Remembering to eat, thanks to the reminders in my schedule.

Alone.

Maybe I should make time for something else—someone else.

I shake the thought off.

No.

The wreck—it's my life's work. I won't give up now, not with success so close I can taste it. There isn't time for anyone. And it's selfish to expect anyone else to understand how much the ship means to me.

The hair suddenly rises on the back of my neck. That feeling's back—that I'm being watched. Did I hear something? I stop walking, listening intently.

The calls of seabirds replace the crunch of caliche under my heels, but there's nothing else to hear.

I inhale deeply.

I could have sworn I heard something.

Another rustle.

My eyes dart to the massive plumbago border of the parking lot, its powdery blue blooms swaying gently.

Nothing. It's nothing.

I need sleep. *Mmhmm.* And maybe a really big, salty margarita.

Still, despite the heat, I shiver. Reflexively, I palm my car keys, turning them into a weapon. Just like my dad taught me.

Along with plenty of other tricks.

"June?" A voice pings off the truck, and I levitate briefly before regaining my balance, clutching my chest.

A tall blonde strides around another car.

"Charlie." I press my hand to my heart. "You nearly scared me to death."

It's just Charlie. There's no one hiding in the plumbago. God, sleep deprivation is making me slightly insane.

"There you are," Charlie chirps. "I've been looking for you. How'd it go?"

"Not good." I swipe my hand across my forehead. Sweat clings to my skin, and I scrunch my nose. "I didn't get the grant."

"Oh, shit, June. That fucking sucks. Fuck Weasely Weaselton. You okay? You look… not great. Hot, but not in a good way." Charlie pushes her white-blonde hair back, tying it up with a ponytail holder, pinning me with an appraising look.

"Wow. Thanks." I snort.

"Sorry, that was rude." Charlie grins, and it's full of sympathy. "You seem off. Jumpy." Her blue eyes narrow, and I can practically see her brain working behind them.

"Just wound up." I'm not about to tell her I might be paranoid about being followed. I like Charlie, but I think it's better to keep that little tidbit to myself.

"Sounds like you need a drink. And hey, guess what?" She smirks. "So do I."

The plumbago bush rustles, and we swivel towards it as a rabbit bounds out, racing off to another clump of bushes.

"Did that sound like a bunny to you?" I ask, clenching the keys tighter.

"It looked like one." Charlie shrugs, but she stares at the bush for a beat longer than she should, too. "Come on June, first round's on me. I'll drive. But we take your truck."

"Okay, that sounds—" I pause, staring at the plumbago's non-threatening flowers, despite the massive bumblebees swarming the fragrant blooms. "Let's get out of here."

I try not to jog to the truck, but by the time I get there, I'm slightly out of breath.

Better safe than sorry.

With an apologetic grin at Charlie, I toss her the keys and climb into the passenger's seat. Shucking my heels, I toss them and my work bag into the back seat. I sigh in relief, wiggling my toes as I slip on my sandals.

"That was fast. You must really want that drink." She laughs, the sound slightly manic.

Is paranoia contagious?

The old Toyota roars to life as Charlie slams it into reverse.

Into *something*.

Something that screams.

"Was that the bunny? Did you hit the bunny?" My voice is a high-pitched squeal. I glance into the side-mirror, my brain not quite catching up to what's just happened.

White dust partially obscures a man, lying on the ground.

He moans.

"Whoops," Charlie breathes. But it's barely audible over my high-pitched screams.

"Oh my god. Oh my god, Charlie. I think you hit someone, oh

my god." I fumble with the button on my seatbelt before the dilapidated thing finally releases.

"That's not a bunny," Charlie finally manages, her nose scrunching. "Oops. Shit. Is he okay?"

"Oops? That's all you have to say?" Cold sweat breaks across my skin, my heart threatening to leap out of my chest. "What the hell, Charlie?"

"I *did* ask if he was okay. But, yeah, I'll go check on him. Big yikes." Charlie jumps out of the car, her huge eyes looking to me one more time before she heads to the back of the car.

"We were barely moving. He has to be okay. *Is* he okay?" I scream at her. My legs are shaking so bad, I'm not sure I can get out of the car.

Will insurance cover this? Did I pay my insurance?

Of course I did. It was on the calendar.

Where the hell did he come from?

My nails scratch against the door handle before finding purchase, and I leap from the car. Some part of my brain registering gratitude for abandoning my heels in favor of sandals.

I cover my mouth, taking in the sight.

Clutching his head, the man grabs at something lying on the ground next to him. Looking more pissed off than anything.

"Holy shit," Charlie says, crouching next to him. "Oh no." Her voice is oddly flat.

His eyes narrow as I approach, and for some reason, he's scooting back from Charlie, eyes darting between us.

"Are you okay, sir?" Frantic, my voice escalates to a pitch probably capable of breaking glass. "Are you hurt?"

Stringy blond hair pulls back from the man's face, and I wince at the scrape on his head, blood trickling from the wound. His pants are ragged where his hip hit the crushed-shell parking lot.

"Sir, may I render aid?" I crouch, trying to help the man to his feet, but he swats my hand away.

"Fuck you," he spits out, a thick Russian accent nearly rendering the words incomprehensible. He presses up onto his hands, sitting up. The man mutters something in Russian that I don't understand at all. Obviously, seeing as how I don't speak Russian.

"May I render aid?" Charlie snorts. "What the hell, June? Who says that?" she says covering her face with a palm.

"It's not funny." I glare at her. "Stop laughing. Nothing about this is funny, Charlie. It's what they taught us to say in that safety training. Remember? That weekend course with all the liability stuff?"

She laughs at me while I turn back to the man. "Sir, would you like me to call 911? May I administer first aid?"

Another snort erupts behind me, and I shoot a disbelieving look at Charlie's silently shaking figure.

How is she laughing at a time like this?

Still covering her face, Charlie holds a hand up. "I'm sorry, I don't know what's wrong with me."

"Hitting this guy must have been too much for you. I think you're in shock, Charlie." I shake my head, glad one of us is at least trying to help.

"Get away from me, you bitch." He barks something else out in Russian, stumbling and wincing as he stands.

"Sir," I gasp. "I understand you're upset, but it's good that you are talking—"

"June, June, stop it," Charlie says, and I turn back to her. "He's being so mean to you." A tear runs down her cheek, eyes crinkling in the corners.

Is she still smiling?

I glare at her.

"Charlie, I am pretty sure you're in shock." My hands shake at my sides, my heart doing its best impression of a hummingbird trying to take flight. Heck, I think I might be in shock. "I'm going to go get my phone and call 911. Sir," I call over my shoulder. "Stay where you are. Help is on the way."

"You stupid *fucking* suka."

Surprised at the venom, I turn back to him, only to see him

running away. Well, more hobbling at a high speed, something shiny and black dangling in his hand.

"I thought hit-and-runs were where the driver ran away," I say, cocking my head.

"June, stop it." Charlie snorts, pulling me back toward the truck. "Come on, he's fine. Those margaritas aren't going to drink themselves."

"Seriously, what the heck is wrong with you? How can you think about margaritas at a time like this?" I spin back to her. "You hit a man. You ran him over."

Charlie's hand is firm on my shoulder though, and she just shakes her head as she guides me back to the truck. She holds the door open for me, gesturing to it, and I relent, climbing into the truck.

"Answer me," I demand, though. "We can't just run people over," I reason with her.

She shuts the door, but it doesn't drown out the gale of laughter she lets out.

"What?" I ask as she plops down in the driver's seat, gratified to see her hands are a little shaky. "What is so funny? We need to find him and get him help."

"You're talking to me like I'm one of your freshmen. 'We can't just run people over,'" she mimics.

"Are you for real right now?"

"I didn't really run him over. I just bumped him a little." Charlie shrugs, helping me buckle the seatbelt, which I'm grateful for. My own incessant shaking made it impossible to do myself.

"How can you be so calm about this?" I'm screeching. I take a deep breath, but it doesn't really help.

"Probably all my years of training," she says, buckling her own seatbelt. Seems a little late for safety first, but what do I know?

"Training?" I echo.

"Yeah, you know, liability training."

I shake my head, dizzy with adrenaline, shaky and sick. While

Charlie takes the most bizarre hit-and-run *ever* completely in stride, and despite the odd strangled laughter bubbling out of her, she seems almost fine.

I'm not. Not by a longshot.

No grant, no search for the *Santu Espiritu*, and Charlie hit a man. With *my* truck.

"Fuck," I finally say.

CHAPTER
TWO

DEAN

THE BINOCULARS ARE TOO small in my hands. I hate using other people's equipment, and I make a mental note to budget for my company's own supplies as soon as we collect on this job. I grunt, my elbows digging into the roof of the science building, where I lie sprawled on my stomach, sweating through my jeans.

At least at this height we can catch a bit of cool ocean breeze.

The ocean momentarily distracts me, glittering in the late afternoon sun. The siren call of the water, the ability to float, to forget. The ocean is the only perk of this job, and it's the only place that feels free these days. Safe.

Feeling safe is a trick.

"She should be out here by now," Pierce mutters.

"Yep," I agree.

Angling the nocks lower, I sweep the parking lot. Some instinct nagging at me to keep watch. Maybe it's training. Or, as my government appointed therapist likes to say, trauma response.

"I told you I don't like this kind," I mutter, flicking the binoculars' magnification with unnecessary force, speeding past the setting I need.

Unnecessary force. That's been my life to a tee lately.

"What's not to like?" Pierce makes a small noise of disgust, barely shifting next to me. "Under nineteen ounces, easy to transport, military standard. You're such a princess sometimes," he snorts. "Would you rather have those fancy crystal ones?"

Yes. Swarovski.

"Nothing wrong with princesses."

"If you say so." Pierce shrugs, the derision in his voice clear.

I scoff under my breath. Hoping Pierce doesn't hear. Can't let the 'man in charge' know I'm not impressed.

You're just a contractor. You're not here to pick the equipment.

Nor was I able to give Pierce a detailed list of exactly what was needed for this op.

This is the DEA's business. They only brought me in for support. Muscle.

Despite my misgivings towards government agencies these days, Pierce isn't a terrible partner. At least, there's nothing wrong with him I could find. I read up on him, asked around—at least as much as a contractor can. Everything I got my hands on said Pierce was clean, and at the very least he didn't raise any red flags with the DEA.

But still, I would have preferred my own team, especially on a job that could make or break my fledgling company. A grim smile turns up the corners of my mouth.

Not like my team's far away, though.

Shifting, the black roof wickedly hot, I glance over at Pierce again. Something about the man bothers me.

He handpicked me for this job, despite my quick and dirty departure from the military. And that black mark cost me a dozen bids for other work. It kept a lot of guys from picking me. Yet here I am.

Trust issues.

My therapist would love to explore that at our next meeting.

Again.

Sighing, I flick my eyes to the slick black gun propped next to us.

Guess we do have everything we need.

The rifle my therapist dubbed a *troubling safety blanket* sits there, waiting should the need arise. Troubling or not, the government hasn't sidelined me, not when there are fish this big out there. Not that they would. Contractors with my resume aren't exactly easy to come by. No matter *how* I left the military.

Grunting, I refocus on the task at hand.

Mission first.

Dark brown tendrils of hair halo the target's face as she steps out of the shade of the building.

"Heads up." I swallow as Pierce goes quiet.

Perfect body, ten out of ten. Curling hair down to her slim waist, shapely legs I've been tasked to watch all week. Eyes like chocolate, long lashes. High cheekbones and full pink lips.

The black and white faculty photo the analysts provided with her profile didn't do her justice.

So she's pretty. Doesn't mean she isn't neck deep in this shit with the fucking Russians. If anything, her beauty makes her doubly suspicious.

"Target on the move," Pierce says, shimming closer to the rooftop edge, bringing his own tiny pair of binoculars up. "She looks pissed."

June Legarde, PhD, pauses, looking around.

"She's spooked. Goddamnit Pierce, I told you we should've stayed in the car."

"I'm sick of sitting in that thing," Pierce mutters. "It's hot as balls. Besides, you know we don't have the go-ahead to make contact."

"Fucking stupid," I mutter.

Working for this new org comes with endless bureaucratic catch-up for one of the alphabet soup agencies, the steep learning curve of figuring out when I can push them to my timetable and where they might budge.

But I grin and do it. I'd do it all to get back in the intel community's good graces, to carve out a spot for my new company.

And once I figured out the stakes of this op, no one could talk me out of taking the job. Not even my team.

"We need approval to make contact." I keep my focus on Legarde. "I don't like it. If she runs, with all the info her dear old dad left her, you and I both know this job is fucked." The mere thought of this op going sideways makes my stomach churn.

I need this. I need this win.

"I swear to god, if you tell me that one more time, I'm going to lose it." Pierce growls, kicking me in the shin.

Ten, nine, eight… I grit my teeth, gluing my attention to the parking lot below us.

A second woman bursts into our field of view, scurrying between the cars, platinum hair waving behind her.

"Who's that?" I ask, keeping my voice even, knowing for all my trust issues I might be the biggest liar of all.

Because I know damn well who she is, but Pierce doesn't need to know that.

Pierce scoots even closer to the edge. "It's that other prof in Legarde's department, the newer one. Charlotte Abbot. Goes by Charlie. Teaches Texas history."

I briefly cut my eyes to Pierce. He sounds… interested. That little teaching fact sure rolled off his tongue real quick.

No time to wonder at that—it's time to focus. Shit's heating up on this op.

This op, that's nothing like the one five years ago.

Seven, six, five…

Nope, to repress *that* memory, I'd have to start counting down from ten thousand.

"What do you have on her?" I make myself ask, just to give my brain something else to do.

"Not much," Pierce says. "Friends with the target. Girls'

nights, wine nights, whatever. A shoulder to cry on after Legarde's old man got popped. There was an opening at the beginning of the semester. She got lucky, scooped up a job like that," Pierce says, snapping his fingers.

I stop myself from rolling my eyes. *Lucky* isn't in my vocabulary, shouldn't be in Pierce's, either. Nothing about how Charlie got that job was luck, but what Pierce doesn't know won't hurt him.

The two women are talking now, Legarde scanning her surroundings. Like she knows we're watching.

Unlikely. Everything has been smooth as silk so far.

"Allegedly popped," Pierce smirks, correcting himself.

"Allegedly my ass," I growl.

The circumstances surrounding Legarde's father's death were shady at best.

"Agreed. Everything was a little too neat for someone *that* useful to the Russians to up and die." Pierce tells me this like it's brand-new information.

I grunt, annoyed at him all over again.

"We just gotta find his drug sub before the Russians do and close this case. Then we can spend a day at the beach. Easy."

"You talk too much," I growl.

I blow out a breath, frustration making my hand twitch. The intel is as murky as the missing drug sub's watery grave. There's too much chatter, too much noise about the shipment. And the cartel is constantly increasing their reach, ramping up their interest in additional revenue streams. Running weapons, human trafficking, even working with domestic terrorists.

Well, if the DEA's now missing informant is right.

Why couldn't fucking assets stay fucking put?

Thanks to them and the fucking analysts, I'm sweating my balls off watching a bombshell I can't approach. They suggested Legarde would be the easiest to leverage, the key to the whole damn thing.

Suggested. I snort, keeping my eyes on our best bet to find the sub.

Damn analysts, always hedging their assessments. But the cube jockeys *just* so happen to be right this time. And not because there are worse-looking targets to surveil.

Legarde's key ring flashes in the sunlight as she dumps it in Charlie's outstretched hand.

"I don't like this." I move to get up.

Charlie piles into the driver's seat of Legarde's beat-up truck.

"I checked the work-up on the blonde myself," Pierce says. "I think she's clean."

A rangy blond man, dressed in black, moves out of the bushes. Directly behind the target.

"Son of a bitch," I murmur. "Russians are here."

"Gun." Pierce points like I don't see the man with a gun.

With lightning speed, I replace the nocks with the long-range scope of my rifle.

"You know we're not cleared for wet work," Pierce says lazily.

"Fuck me sideways." Legarde is our only lead. "We have got to get down there. Call it in." I line the man up in my scope. "*Now.*"

The man approaches the vehicle, raising his gun, and I suck in a breath, holding it, steadying the shot.

The truck roars to life, plowing the gunman down.

Good job, Charlie.

"Oh shit." Pierce sounds genuinely shocked. "The blonde mowed him down."

My eyes narrow, waiting for the gunman to try again as the two women go to his side… but he gets up and runs, well, limps away.

What the hell? Did Charlie say something? Did she blow her cover? Fuck. Fuck!

"She just ran him over," Pierce repeats, clearly confused.

Lowering my rifle, I turn to face him.

"I ran the check on her myself." Pierce wipes a hand over his sweaty face, standing and collecting the fallen equipment. "She's a civilian."

"Hmmph." I grunt, hefting the rifle, following Pierce to the ladder leading from the roof.

No matter how much I *should* want to trust Pierce, I don't.

I learned the hard way that sometimes it's better to keep my mouth shut.

CHAPTER
THREE

JUNE

MONOTONOUS LANDSCAPE FLIES past the window, green-brown marsh grass and low, scrubby trees.

It should soothe me. Familiar. Home.

It does not.

My eyes dart from Charlie's thin-lipped expression to the road and back again, fingers tightening around the pebbled plastic handle in the ceiling.

"I'm sorry about that." Charlie glances over, the rictus grin she wore after backing into the poor, poor pedestrian finally sliding off. "He's probably okay, right?"

"Sorry about hitting that guy, or about laughing at the fact that you hit him?" My voice creeps up a pitch. "What the hell is wrong with you, Charlie? I thought I knew you better than this."

I never pegged Charlie for the type of woman to drive over a human and barely hold back laughter over his groaning form. And it's only adding to my anxiety for the unfortunate man, bringing it to a boiling point.

"Do you think he ran away because he doesn't have health insurance?" She shrugs, keeping her eyes fixed on the road.

"I think we should try finding him," I say for the hundredth time.

"Nah. I'm sure he's fine."

Is she… still smiling?

Concern for her trickles through me. "Are you okay? Like, do you feel cold? Are you experiencing—"

"I'm not in shock, June." Her voice is flatter than a can of La Croix left open in the car all afternoon, and it makes me wince.

Denial. Charlie is absolutely, one hundred percent in shock. Has to be. No way any normal human could be unshaken after that. Even I'm in shock, and I didn't hit the guy.

"Uh-huh." My voice is calm, even. "I think you should let me drive. Huh? How about that? Would it make you feel safe if I drove?"

Charlie narrows her eyes, shooting me a look I recognize. The one from tense department meetings where our resident mansplainer tries taking over the agenda.

"Will it make *you* feel better to drive?" she asks.

No. I do *not* want to drive after that. All I want is a double-shot margarita, hold the margarita part, and to call the cops. My lips purse.

"I didn't think so."

My grip on the bar tightens and I can't help but feel Charlie's voice is… off. A coldness in it. A tone she uses on idiots in meetings, or students who cross the line in lecture, and I usually love it. But it's not a tone she's ever aimed at me. Like this is somehow my fault.

Which is entirely ridiculous.

"You know what? I *would* like to drive. Seeing as how this is my truck, and you just ran someone over with it."

"You going to be able to let go of the Jesus H. Christ bar long enough to get out of the car right now?"

Tilting my head, I glance up to where I'm white-knuckling the plastic. "Huh, is that what it's called? I always thought it was 'Jesus, take the wheel,' not, 'Jesus, hold the handle.'"

Charlie snorts out another laugh, and heaven help me, I join her.

The palms and beach scrub on either side of the highway give way to a glimpse of sparkling ocean. The smooth water is serene, and my eyes close, momentarily allowing the surf to take away some of my anxiety.

"We're almost there, anyway," Charlie says, breaking my small moment of peace. "Tell you what, if it makes you feel better, I'll call us an Uber after we eat and drink, my treat. And I'll pay to get the blood cleaned off your front fender, too."

My mouth falls open, turning to the back of my truck. "Wait, there's blood on the fender? When did you even look at the fender?"

I hadn't even considered possible damage to my car. No, being the normal one of the two of us, I'd been too caught up worrying for the man on the ground cursing me out. To busy focusing on the fact she hit a guy holding a gun—

"Oh my god."

"Are you gonna puke?" Charlie shakes her head, like this is a common occurrence. Like she often sees people puke after running over fellow humans.

I blink at the odd thought. Why would she have experience running over people?

Charlie is a professor of Texas history; she is my friend. She is not a serial people-runner-overer.

She's just trying to shrug it off like it's nothing. That's all.

We're both in shock.

It's the only logical conclusion.

"No." My stomach roils noisily. "Maybe." I swallow. "No." I take a breath.

"Uh-huh," Charlie says, glancing sidelong at me. "Cleaning up your puke in the car wasn't part of the deal I was offering."

"No, Charlie, listen…"

I trail off, and she slides another meaningful look my way.

"I just figured out what he was holding," I squeak out. I glance down at the hand in my lap, pretending to cradle something in it. "Did you see it?" I look back to her. "He was holding a gun. Oh my god. He had a gun? Why would he have a *gun*?"

My nerves fray, crackling like a downed live wire after a bad storm.

"Why *would* he have a gun?" Charlie repeats the question in a sing-song voice. Her fingers thrum against the steering wheel.

The rippling ocean comes into view, reflecting the late afternoon sun as we round a corner. I take a steadying breath as we get closer to the marina and bar.

"I felt like someone was watching me all day. What if…" I push my hair back with one hand. "What if he was watching me?"

Charlie makes a non-committal noise.

Now that I'm talking about it, I can't seem to stop, the words rushing out of me.

"You saw the gun too? Didn't you? Is that why you didn't care that he was hurt?" As soon as the words leave my mouth, my brain catches up to the facts. "Is that why you hit him?"

I stare at her, uneasy. How well do I really know Charlie?

"I don't make a habit of running people over." Reaching over, she cranks my window down noisily, filling the car with the salt-heavy tang of ocean air. "If you're going to barf, do it outside your truck, please."

I hang my head out the window, willing myself not to be sick.

This is a nightmare come to life, feeding on memories from the week leading up to my thirteenth birthday. A week I'd done everything in my power to forget.

This might not be anything at all. We're in South Texas. Open carry is practically a given at any time.

Still. *Still.*

I'd spent the last fifteen years thinking about what would happen if I encountered the people who inspired my nightmares again. The people who caused my paranoia—who'd earned it.

Charlie glances over at me as the speedometer inches past

seventy. She guns my old truck over the speed limit, singing at the top of her lungs.

Doing her best to act like nothing just happened.

I turn back to the ocean. It can't be related to what happened to me when I was a child.

Clenching my jaw, I banish the thought.

The man could've been a random carjacker, deciding it was easier to run away after getting, well, run over. Could be he was just out taking his gun for a walk.

I blow out another breath, watching the sun ripple off the water. Searching out the shrimp boats heading back home to the shelter of the bay, specks of white against the endless blue.

It's just a coincidence.

All kinds of people flock to the South Texas beaches for relaxation, especially during the summer. Maybe he was a student enjoying the solitude of the empty campus.

I should alert campus police.

Letting go of the handle, I reach back for my purse, determined to do the rational thing and tell the authorities.

Very adult.

Not paranoid, but smart.

Calm, cool, collected. Or, at the very least, one of those adjectives.

The purse is cool against my lap, a victim of overactive floorboard air conditioning, another problem I put on the back-burner after my father's death.

Phone, phone, where's my phone? Aha.

My clammy fingers finally find it. I tap through the university's website until I find the campus services number. It rings several times before a bored voice finally answers.

I open my mouth to reply, to get the weight of Charlie's hit-and-run off my shoulders, but let out a wheeze of surprise instead.

"We're here," Charlie sings out, yanking the wheel left, skidding into the parking lot.

The force of the turn has me scrambling for the Jesus-take-the-wheel bar, grappling for purchase. Charlie slams on the brakes, sending my phone flying out of my sweaty grip, out the open window.

"That's it," I scream.

There it goes, my last straw, flying right through the open window along with my phone.

I don't have the time and *certainly* don't have the cash to replace it right now.

I barely glance at a group of people outside the restaurant and bar, ignoring shocked expressions on their faces in favor of searching for my phone on the ground.

Charlie slides to a halt in a parking spot near the restaurant entrance. The phone sits, screen up, glowing from the still-connected call. Dirty, and beat to hell, but not ruined.

"It's okay, my phone's still intact," I tell Charlie on an exhalation. "Finally, one piece of luck in an absolute trashcan of a day—"

A massive, macho-man Jeep pulls into the spot, crushing my phone under the lifted wheels.

The group of bystanders let out a collective gasp. A few shake their heads, throwing me pitying looks as I bite back a shriek of rage.

Charlie's saying something. "Don't start something you can't finish, June."

"I'm so *done* with caring at the moment." All I wanted to do was the right thing, to call the university. To help the man Charlie ran over. And before that, get the grant. Find the *Santu Espiritu.*

But *nooooooo*. I get the day from hell instead.

"June, wait—"

I ignore her.

"All I want is to pick up what's left of my phone, scream at the driver of the Jeep, then forget about this awful day with as much tequila as possible," I ramble under my breath.

A three-point plan never fails.

The car door slams behind me, flip-flops smacking against the uneven pavement as I storm across the parking lot to the shards of my phone, may it rest in peace. Or pieces.

The Jeep driver's door opens, and a Dorito of a man steps out. A tight black athletic shirt calling attention to broad shoulders and ridiculously muscled arms setting off his narrow hips in form-fitting black cargo pants.

Probably way too big to start arguing with.

But I'm in no mood to let a little detail like that stop me. I've got enough steam building to power an angry freight train.

The man runs a hand over his stubbled chin as I bear down on him. I stop a few millimeters away and poke him right in the chest.

Damn. It's a hard chest. I draw back and clear my throat. Where was I?

"You ran over my phone." Fresh irritation flares, and I crane my neck up to make eye-contact.

He's so tall I have to step back, which, frankly, is rude as hell of him.

His mirrored aviator sunglasses reflect my irate expression, not to mention how snarled my hair is, thanks to the open car window.

What a douche.

I try combing it back in place, and the man removes his sunglasses… and my mirror. His eyes are a warm whiskey brown, fringed in long dark lashes.

"My phone." I point at where my phone lies shattered on the ground. Way to go, June, really helpful declaration. "You ran it over."

"That explains why you're looking at me like that." His voice is deep. Gravelly.

"Yeah, it does," I say, poking him in his rock-hard pecs a second time before looking back up.

Oh. *Oh*.

The Douche Edition Ken Doll is *hot*. Stubble lines a defined, square jawline, dark brown eyes set off by a fringe of lashes and thick black eyebrows. For a second, I forget why I was mad at all, my brain stuttering to a bit of a halt as it registers that this man is fine. Like, really fine.

Built and pretty?

Probably has the personality of my dead grandmother's floral couch, with a face like that. Perfect for sitting on.

No, wait, that isn't right.

Clearing my throat, I wait, placing a hand on my jutted hip. As good a way as any to hide the way I'm now irritated with myself for finding this absolute douche nozzle hot.

"I'm Dean, and I'm sorry about your phone." He grins, white teeth flashing, a dimple appearing in his cheek.

It must be a magic dimple, because my irritation vanishes. *Poof.*

"Hi," I breathe.

My finger bends now, lying against his chest, not at all pokey. More stroke-y. Embarrassed, I move my hand away, now worried its clamminess has stained his shirt, only to have him catch it. His hand rough against mine, warm and powerful.

"And you are?"

"June."

He shakes my hand once, somehow firm and delicate, all charm and danger, and a thrill shoots through me. Then, just as abruptly as he clutched at my hand, like it was a lifeline, he drops it.

Charlie sidles up as the other man from the Jeep walks around the front of the it.

"We were about to go in for drinks. And dinner." I smile, rewarded by another dimple sighting.

Well, mostly drinks, but maybe I'll eat if he eats. Maybe he's in the mood for a taco. *A special taco.*

I blush. What the actual hell is wrong with me?

"This is Pierce," Dean says, pointing to the guy now checking out Charlie. "And what a coincidence, we were going to have drinks too. And dinner. Maybe I can buy the first round, since…"

He trails off, gesturing to the phone, and a fresh wave of irritation surges over me.

I welcome it. Better irritated than trying to jump this dude in the bathroom as a distraction from my hell of a day. That would be gross.

Probably.

"Since you crushed my phone with your monster truck?" I make myself say. It comes out breathy though, not at all pissy like I was aiming for. I tilt my head, a wayward tendril tickling over my cheek. "That seems like the least you could do."

"It's a Jeep, ma'am."

His formal tone screams *military*, but the heat in his eyes, the way they travel up and down my body—triggers an instant response.

Nobody has looked at me like that since... Well, nobody I *wanted* to look at me like that, at least.

Like he wouldn't mind having more than dinner with me.

Like maybe I'm on the menu, too.

CHAPTER
FOUR

DEAN

JUNE LEGARDE, PhD, stands in front of me in a blazing fury. Deep brown eyes narrow in anger, going wide as I introduce myself. Her face softens with a smile, and my breath catches. Vibrant oranges and pinks halo around her, the sky purpling into dusk in a blaze of glory.

She's even more gorgeous up close.

I swallow, my lips curving in an automatic grin, needing to play nice. Needing to convince her to trust me, even if she puts me on edge. No, her beauty puts me on edge. My last girlfriend taught me that lesson.

June Legarde is the target. Don't forget that.

"Well, June, what will you be drinking tonight?" I offer my arm with a wink, like leading her into the building will give me some kind of control. But when she slides her hand into the crook of my elbow, it doesn't feel like control.

My chest aches.

Why can't the past stay buried?

We walk through the door, and the sounds from the highway

fade. Jimmy Buffett croons about a lost shaker of salt over the raucous noise of people having a good time.

The occasional too-loud laugh, the clatter of forks on plates and the smell of salty, fried food invade my senses as I take in the surroundings.

Two visible exits.

One in back, to what looks like a marina, and the one we walked in. Probably at least one more, out the back of the kitchen. People mill around, light from their phones illuminating their faces as they wait to be seated.

We head to the hostess stand, and I try not to notice June constantly sneaking looks up at me. It shouldn't leave me weak in the knees.

Two hundred and fifty pounds of hard-won muscle, towering at six foot five, and I'm KO'd by this woman's casual touch.

Fucking hell.

Gritting my teeth, I chance a backwards glance at Pierce. He animatedly chats up Charlie, who, as usual, looks completely unimpressed by him. She definitely doesn't seem rattled by the fact she just ran over a would-be gunman.

June squeezes my forearm, slightly startling me.

Shit, what did she just ask? "I didn't catch that, princess."

"I said you better be buying." She leans in, her soft curves in all the right places, pressing against me. Thank fuck HQ okayed contact with her on our way in, because now all I can think about is how much more contact I want with her.

"And I only want the strongest margarita in Texas." An eyebrow arches, her lips a thin line of frustration. "You wouldn't believe the awful day I've had."

"I would," I say, too confident.

She blinks in surprise.

"I'm sorry to hear that," I amend. Putty. I'm like fucking putty in her delicate hands. Standing a little taller, I take a breath. "Try me. I'm a good listener."

Her rosy lips curve into a broad, appreciative smile.

Fuck.

This is not going to be easy. Or worse, it will be too easy, and then what? I'll arrest her for aiding and abetting the Russians, that's what.

"How many?" A perky woman in a black headset looks up from a map of the place, and I memorize it in less than five seconds.

"Four," Pierce pipes up.

"It's a fifty-minute wait for a table, but there's space at the bar."

"Bar sounds perfect," June says.

"Bar will be perfect." I smile.

She squeezes my arm again, and I close my eyes briefly. Then shaking myself mentally, I flash another smile to the hostess, steering June to a four-top table in the bar area.

Pierce and Charlie pull up two empty stools, deep in conversation as June climbs onto a chair. She wrinkles her nose at the sticky spilled drinks coating the surface.

I've been tailing her for ages, and I'm still surprised at all her little quirks. Her purse on her lap, her ankles crossed neatly, the picture of a total prissy princess... yet I can't help but follow the lines of her legs until they disappear under her tight black skirt.

This is wrong. Both my attraction to her, and how she's acting.

It's all sorts of wrong for someone who just went through what she did.

Her behavior—her reactions—don't make sense. The two women are acting like nothing is wrong, and they just ran over a man. A man who pointed a gun at them.

I don't expect Charlie to react, but June? If June is who she claims to be, just a civilian researcher, then she's taking this way too in stride.

There's no way she isn't in bed with the Russians, just like her dad was.

"Everything okay?" June asks. Her forehead is adorably crinkled, and if I didn't know better, I would almost think her concern was real.

"Yeah," I tell her. I make myself smile at her. "I'm gonna go grab us some drinks," I announce, looking around at everyone. "Whaddya want? And uh—"

"I'm Charlie," Charlie unnecessarily announces. Right. Because I'm not supposed to know her. Goddammit, I'm distracted. She wiggles her fingers in greeting, a familiar lopsided grin on her face. "I'll take whatever June's drinking."

"Beer for me, anything on tap," Pierce says, barely taking his eyes off his current target, Charlie Abbot.

Jesus. Apparently, Charlie's just as good at wrapping men around her finger as she is at everything else.

Can't say I regret hiring her... even if her methods are unconventional.

"Something strong," I say, mask firmly in place. "That I can do."

June presses a finger to the sticky spot on the table. Her lip curls up in distaste and she casts a desperate look around.

"I'll see about getting the table cleaned up, too."

She sighs, relaxing back into the chair.

"That would be freaking great." Her eyes dart over the faces in the bar. Like she's keeping an eye out for something. Someone.

I use the mirror behind it to keep an eye on the table. Brightly painted wooden fish hang in schools from the ceiling. The air conditioner sends them swinging on their clear fishing line, slightly impacting my view.

"What'll it be?" the bartender asks.

"Two margaritas, two Shiners, and four shots of tequila, please." It's a bit much, but tequila seems like a good choice. It's strong. Plying June with alcohol for information might feel wrong, but it's a good course of action.

Even though it's exactly what my last girlfriend would do. I frown.

Hell, it's exactly what she did do.

The bartender sets the tab down in front of me, bringing me back to the moment.

"Thanks," I mutter, leaving a few bills behind. "Mind if I get a rag? We've got a few sticky spots on the table."

He nods, producing a somewhat clean cloth, and I make my way back to the table. June watches me carefully as I scrub the thing, and it sets my teeth on edge.

I'm supposed to be watching *her*.

"That's," her voice falters as she speaks. "That's really nice of you. I appreciate you cleaning up."

I grunt, not trusting myself to answer and blow my cover. *You don't have to fake it*, I want to snarl at her. *I know who you are, now tell me where the drug sub is.*

Yeah, that'd go over real fucking well.

"What'd you get for us?" Charlie asks, pushing her blonde hair over one shoulder.

"Something you'll like." Something that'll get June just drunk enough to spill her guts, if I have any luck.

An odd expression flickers across Charlie's face. It disappears as she flutters her eyelashes at Pierce.

"Your friend's a real man of mystery, huh?"

"Dean can be pretty spooky." Pierce laughs at his own joke, a double entendre June hopefully will miss, but my hands flex in irritation. The man grates on my nerves. My hand-picked team would never be so cavalier with the truth, not around a target.

"So, what do you guys do, anyway?" June asks, fidgeting with her purse strap.

"I—" I stop. Clear my throat. I can't bring myself to tell my—our—approved cover story. I shake my head, as if that will help clear the sudden mental fog, and manage to inhale wrong, coughing.

"Dean's a consultant," Pierce supplies smoothly, smacking me on the back. "We work together on international shipping."

Technically… not a lie.

June's eyes narrow. "International shipping, huh? Surprised you two aren't in Houston."

"We work out of there pretty often," I manage to say. "We're, ah, entertaining some clients down here, trying to drum up business. You know how it is."

Stupid, that sounded stupid.

I used to be good at this, at being charming and setting people at ease. Now every lie sounds hollow in my ears.

"Oh, that's cool." Charlie's steely gaze meets me, as if she can see my train of thought. Maybe she can. She certainly seems to be laughing at me.

"Why would I know how it is?" June asks.

Thankfully, the loaded tray of drinks arrives, and I don't have to make up another stupid lie. Fruity green mixer slops over the sides of frosty glasses onto the table as the surfer dude bartender plunks them down in front of us.

"Ladies, I assume the margaritas are yours." Pierce slides their drinks over. "And I think my friend here decided to order—"

June picks up a shot of clear tequila. Her hand shakes as she tosses it back, and Charlie's eyes widen.

"Uh, June, maybe slow down a little—"

But June's already grabbed a second shot, and she tosses it back with a grimace. A moment later, she leans against the back of her seat and presses a hand over her lips.

"This is gonna be easier than I thought," Pierce mutters in my ear.

My frown deepens. Maybe her, uh, *eventful* afternoon had more of an impact than I thought.

"That bad of a day, huh?" My forehead crinkles. An unfamiliar feeling threads through me: doubt.

"Like I said, you have no idea."

If she is involved, then she's green as can be.

She absolutely appears to be involved, and the DEA analysts likewise assessed she is, so this afternoon shouldn't have shaken her.

Not this much, anyway.

My eyes narrow, and I pick at that feeling. I used to be able to trust my gut when it came to people.

Maybe I should try that again.

June coughs, her eyes watering, then picks up the margarita. My eyebrows shoot up. She's clearly not a regular drinker. She takes a long draw from it, her throat bobbing as she drains the frosty glass.

"Brain freeze," she coughs out, pinching the top of her nose.

"June was up for a grant." Charlie's brows knit together, and she shoots me a warning glance. "It didn't go the way she wanted."

I haven't had enough contact with Charlie. I was too worried I'd blow her cover at the school, or worse, let Pierce in on the fact that I had Charlie working this case… without DEA approval.

Too bad I don't trust anyone, it sure as shit would make life easier if I did.

June coughs again, and there's a slightly glazed look in her eyes. At the bar, someone starts chanting to chug, and a group of rowdy college students pick up the cry.

She launches a lopsided grin at me. Guilt slides through me, and I can't help wondering if I haven't pegged her wrong. There's something sweet about June, something naïve, and it doesn't fit at all with the profile.

"Maybe I should grab some chips and salsa," I suggest.

Pierce kicks me under the table, and my smile takes on a hard edge as I slant him a warning look.

I want her tipsy, not incoherent. My foot makes impact with his shin, and Pierce's chair slides back a little.

He glares at me. Serves him right.

"S'fine." June waves a hand, picking up another shot. "I feel better already."

"Uh, I think that's a good idea. I'll go grab some." Pierce is already halfway through the room, maneuvering through the crowd to the self-serve nacho bar.

Charlie gives me a knowing look. "June, you should slow down."

"Don't tell me what to do." She wags a finger at Charlie, leaning so heavily on the table it slightly tilts towards her. I stabilize it, incredulous. "Don't go and try to render aid now. Bit too late to render aid. Render a band-aid. Render-aid band-aid."

Charlie tosses her blonde hair over a shoulder, sighing. "Stop saying render aid."

I'm lost, but June lets out a wild laugh.

"June, you need to slow down. You're going to make yourself sick." Charlie actually sounds concerned, and I glance back at her, confused.

I have never heard Charlie sound like anything but an asshole the entire time we've worked together.

Either she's gotten better at acting... or she actually cares about June.

"Oh, how niiiiiice," June half-sings, half-slurs. "How nice for you to tell me what to do." Even her eyes are half-closed. "I want another margarita. I think I deserve it after what Charlie did. And didn't do. She didn't *render aid,* for example."

June pokes me on the forearm. Goosebumps slide across my skin.

"She did *not* render aid," June repeats, raising one eyebrow, then the other. Her finger points at Charlie, and then she makes finger gun with it. "Bang."

Charlie raises her eyes to the ceiling, avoiding my steady gaze. Then, she slides her margarita toward June before pushing her finger gun down. Charlie slams back a shot.

I bite back a laugh, then try to press my advantage, see if I can get her to start talking. The sooner this charade is over, the better for all of us. Get in, get out, get my company up and running with this op under our belt.

"Oh yeah? What did Charlie do?" I cut my eyes to where Pierce is now at the bar, getting another drink. He's digging into the chips and queso he was supposed to be bringing to June.

Asshole.

"I forced her to come with me here instead of going home to cry into her pillow." Charlie crosses her arms over her chest. "You know, just us girlies doing girly things."

My lips thin at her tone, her eyes narrowing at me. Why the hell is she doing the talking for June? That's not helpful.

June rolls her eyes and sticks her tongue out at Charlie. "Shut up."

Taking another long swig of the margarita, she nearly swallows half before Charlie eases it away from her mouth.

"Hey! That's rude." June turns on Charlie, then hiccups, her eyes going wide at the sound.

Coherent. I need her coherent, dammit.

"I think your friend just wants to make sure you're okay. That's a lot of alcohol." I point at the half-drained glass.

"Who are you to judge, hmm?" June wags a finger. Squinting, she adds another, then laughs at her outstretched fingers. "Peace."

Charlie lifts an eyebrow at me before returning her focus to her own glass.

"June doesn't handle alcohol well," she murmurs, and it's clear it's for my benefit and not the woman in question.

"Not judging." I raise my hands in surrender. "Just suggesting."

What the fuck is wrong with me? I can't even watch a potential asset get drunk without guilt-tripping myself? No wonder I lost all those bids.

Dammit. I need this op to go perfectly.

Need to get my business off the ground.

I need something to look forward to instead of staying stuck in the past.

The air conditioner hums, the frigid air blasting the dangling fish into a frenetic dance, and I take a breath.

Pierce finally returns, the half-eaten chips and queso somehow balanced perfectly with his fresh beer between his hands.

"Mmmm," June lets out a throaty little moan of delight, snagging my full attention, my gaze homing in on her mouth. "I haven't eaten since breakfast. I'm fucking starving. Oh, oops. Sorry," she giggles.

"Sorry? For what?" She hasn't eaten since breakfast? No wonder she's already wasted. That's no way to live. Maybe she's more torn up about her dad than we assessed.

"Shouldn't say fuck. It's not professional." She waves a loaded chip in my face, then moans in distress as a blob of queso splatters against the table.

My muscles lock up at the sound. What that moan did to me isn't professional, either.

"Well, I think you're safe with us," Pierce tells her seriously, all charm.

My hands flex, then ball into fists. It sets my teeth on edge, him talking to her like that.

June's eyes go wide, and her jaw drops, the chip falling from her hand. She grabs Charlie's arm with one hand, her knuckles white.

Her face goes even paler.

"Shit. Charlie, is that the guy?" The question is a breathy whimper of distress.

Before I can react, June's out of her seat, tequila in hand. She lists slightly to the right, all the tequila she threw back making her as unsteady as hell.

Regardless of her wobbly path, there's no doubt she's heading straight for the furious man who just walked into the bar.

CHAPTER
FIVE

JUNE

I SQUINT AT THE MAN. He seems unsteady on his feet, the poor guy. Sure, he had a gun in his hand, but I mean, that's not that unusual. During hunting season. Something about the gun didn't match hunting season, though.

I slam into a dude in a frat shirt.

"Whoops," I tell him. He laughs, catching me around the waist, and I wriggle from his grip. "No, thank you," I say sternly.

The blond man's looking around, still wobbling a little. I bite my lip. Maybe I'm the unsteady one. The shot glass full of shitty tequila sloshes in my hand as I push my way through the celebrating college students to where the man stands.

His mouth is pinched in pain, and guilt stabs me.

Or maybe that's tequila. Can't be too sure of these things.

"Lisen, I am so sorry 'bout what happened. Can I get you a drink—" I start.

"Can you get me a fucking drink?" The man's face turns red, his accent so thick I can barely understand him. Or maaaaaybe my ears have stopped working right. "No, but I'll tell you what you *can* fucking get me."

"There's literally, *lit-er-ally* no reason to yell at me. Maybe a figuraaaative reason, but not a literal one. Wait… did I ge' thooosse missed up? Messed up? Missed up." My lips twist to the side as I tilt my head. What the heck was I talking about? Face tingling, I twitch my nose, trying to recover some semblance of sensation.

"What the hell are you doing?"

My nose twitches again. "You've seen *Bewitched*? You know. That old show?" A sudden laugh surprises me. "Just tell me what it is you want and I'll twitch my nose at it."

Someone laughs at my joke. I blink. Wait, I'm the one laughing.

The man levels a furious look at me, opening his mouth to speak, but my finger goes up to stop him. I blink in confusion when it disappears, a massive hand closing around it.

Dean.

"Hiiiizaiiir." I smile up at him, narrowing my eyes. "Hi. Zair. There." There it is. I got it right.

Dean's other hand presses into my lower back, sending an excited thrill through me, and my eyes squeeze shut.

"She's with me," the Russian says, and I blink my eyes open. His face is still scuffed up, and it looks like it hurts.

"No, I'm not," I tell him. I glance back up at Dean. "I'm not with him, am I?"

I don't think I am.

"I want him to go away," I say plaintively. Dean can't know Charlie ran him over. Even my tipsy—okay, drunk—brain knows that's a bad idea.

"Is there a problem here?" Dean's voice is low, a deep, threatening rasp.

"Is there a *fucking* problem here?" he repeats, his temple throbbing.

"There's no problem, no problem. Seeeeeee." I spread my hands wide. "Charlie kind of had a little accident."

"Charlie, huh? Charlie?" the man nearly shouts, his furious eyes lock on me. "I don't give a fuck about this Charlie."

"You are very rude," I say on a gasp, clutching at my imaginary pearls. My hand misses, though, and I manage to grab my own boob instead. Embarrassed, I immediately drop the boob.

Man-handling myself. Maybe I should have listened to Charlie.

"I want the *fucking* shipment." The man's ranting now, slipping in and out of another language. Russian, my brain reminds me.

"The shipment?" I repeat, slurring. "Poor thing. I bet you have a consuchion. Concunshion. Consuncion. Concushion. Close enough." I sigh.

Dean's knuckles crack.

"Calm down, tiger," I manage.

He gives me a look that's full of reproach.

The Russian grabs at my arm, and I slap his hand.

"Don't touch me," I hiss at him. The effect is slightly minimized by the fact I can't see straight. "You know you're bleeding?" I frown at the offending trickle, closing my right eye, then left, trying to focus on it. "Head wounds bleed a lot. A lot, a lot." I glance back at Dean. "Did you know a lot is two words? A lot of people don't know that. Anyyyywayyyy."

Trying to focus, I look back at the man, swatting away his hands again.

Dean's tucked me up against his chest, and it's nice. Really warm.

"What was I saying? Oh yeah. You realllllly shouln't be out and about. Not like this, anyway, with blood. It's kinda not a good look, you know? Honestly, it's gross. It's reallllllly gross. People are trying to eat. This is a family establishment." I'm not quite sure what I'm talking about. It's getting harder and hard to think straight. It's fine, though. *I have to fix this.* I need to help this poor, grumpy man.

Alcohol!

I know how to fix this. The man reaches for me again, and this time, I let him grab me. Alcohol's a good sanitizer. Everyone knows that.

Dean makes it harder to get to him though, his hand fisting the back of my blouse.

"Heeeere, here, lemme clean it."

The man reaches for something behind his back, and Dean stiffens beside me as I splash a little of my drink onto the man's gashed forehead.

"You dumb *bitch*." He howls, pressing the palms of his hands into his eyes.

"Oh goshdarnit, your eyes, I'm so sooorry, okay, just let me help." I reach for his eyes, splashing the remnants of my drink onto his face.

The world shifts and I'm suddenly airborne, hefted over Dean's shoulder, being rushed out of the bar.

Blowing the hair out of my face, I poke Dean in the side. "I wasn't done with my queso."

"Fuck the queso," Dean growls.

"Why do you hate queso? Are you lactose tolerant? Intolerant. Tolerating lactose badly. Does it make your tummy hurt?"

An alarm blares.

Someone falls into my feet, panicked people fleeing out the front door in a tidal wave of humanity.

"What happened?" I ask, confused. "Where are Pierce and Charlie? Pierson? Person? What was his name?"

Dean just grunts, moving efficiently through the crowd and to the huge Jeep out front.

"Heeeeyyyyy. Wait, where are you taking me?" My head bounces as Dean runs. "Ugh, that makes my stomach hurt."

"Don't puke on me."

I snort. "I'm not going to…"

Well, maybe I am. "Listen, we just met, and this is all moving a lil' bit fast for me."

He's too fast. The palm trees outside blur as my brain pounds against my head.

Oh my god, drunk. So drunk.

Tequila on an empty stomach was a superbly poor choice rounding out a day full of poor choices.

"Queso would have been a great choice," I lament.

My nose scrunches up. Maybe Dean did have a point about the margarita, although he's gone a step too far.

"You owe me another maragrita. Maragarita. Margarita. And queso."

"Hmmph." Dean plops me into the Jeep, reaching over to buckle me in before vaulting over the hood to slide into the driver's side. "You're done with tequila for tonight, babe."

"I'm not your babe," I counter. "Don't call me babe."

"Okay, babe."

Tires squeal as we peel out of the parking lot, his eyes moving from the rearview mirror to me and back. The force squishes me against his shoulder, my internal balance failing miserably as we round the corner onto the highway.

I take a breath, breathing in his rock-hard shoulder. "You smell really good."

"You smell like tequila."

"Well, that's logical, I sppooooose." I close one eye, then the other. *Dang.*

"That was tequila, not water. I threw tequila in his face." I rub my eyes, trying to find some semblance of sobriety. "You know. That guy. Charlie ran him over. That's why he's mad. And consunshed. Conchussed. Concussed? Concussed."

Dean casts a sideways glance at me.

Crap. So much for not telling him that. "I didn't mean to say that."

He grunts, turning back to the road. He doesn't even seem fazed at all by Charlie's, ah, hit-and-run.

"Did you hear what I said?" My head rolls a little, and I press the back of my hand to my forehead, rubbing my numb face. "The man I threw my drink at, at the bar, was bleeding everywhere because Charlie hit him with my truck. He had a gun," I say, smacking my lips. Ugh. I feel like shit. "Why did he have a gun?"

Air whips through the car and I gulp it down, trying again to sober up. Leaning out the open window, my stomach grumbles.

"I need food."

"We need to get somewhere safe," Dean says. "Fuck." He smashes his hand into the steering wheel. The violence acts as a shock to my senses, sobering me up a little.

"Take me home," I manage, stomach churning more now. "I'm safe at home."

Dean shoots a surprised look my way, his eyebrows furrowing together.

"Your face is going to get stuck like that," I say, mirroring my face to his. "I can't feel my face. Ugh." Leaning back out the window, I gulp fresh air. Like that'll help.

"Here." He reaches down, across the center console, his bicep brushing against the top of my thigh, and my lower half tightens. Drunk or sober, I can't say I mind it at all. The feel of his strong—really freaking strong—arm against the bare skin of my leg has me closing my eyes, imaging what else those strong hands can do.

The sound of a water bottle crinkling reaches my ears and I blink, coming back to reality, staring at the open bottle in front of me.

"Drink." He thrusts the bottle into my face, some of the water splashing across my chest, soaking my white shirt.

"Scuse you. This is not a wet t-shirt contest, those are on the Padre Islands, sir."

Dean arches an eyebrow, tugging his eyes from the road to meet mine, then drifts south, to my now clinging, sodden, see-through blouse.

Heat floods me, and I guzzle from the bottle.

I'm never drinking again.

"Don't call me sir."

I want to say it again, just to see what he'll do.

"Here." He tosses a protein bar into my lap, "Eat. Sober up."

I take another drink, hydration being key to any situation, then set the bottle aside. Unwrapping the bar, I grimace at the waxy brown exterior. "This looks gross."

"So does vomit."

I scrunch my nose up and take a bite. "Tastes like chocolate chalk."

"Just eat it." His focus stays on the road, laser tight.

The chalk helps a little, the water and food settling my stomach as I chew. And chew. And chew. Ok, maybe it's more like cement.

Taking another drink, I watch the sun's spectacular orange and hot pink bleed into the purple sky as it sinks below the horizon.

"It's so beautiful out here."

Dean grunts, eyes darting to the rearview mirror and back. His shoulders bunch together, the muscles in his arms twitching as his hands flex, fingers drumming the steering wheel.

A tattoo peeks out from his tight sleeve, and I extend my finger, curiosity getting the better of me. Almost of its own accord, my index finger nudges the sleeve up, revealing more glorious golden skin, and the bottom of…

His hand grips my wrist, not so tight that it hurts, but enough to get my attention. To get me to stop.

"Phew," I exhale. "Okay, okay, I get it."

"Keep your hands to yourself." The words are mean, but his voice is almost gentle.

I should be embarrassed. But I can't help the maniacal giggles threatening to turn into tears at any moment.

Thanks, tequila.

Here I am, in a stranger's car, drunk off my ass, after Charlie hits a guy with *my* truck.

"You need food. Eat." He plucks the protein bar out of my hand, holding it in front of my mouth as he drives.

"*You* need food," I say before taking a reluctant bite. "I need queso."

He chuckles, a low rasp that makes my skin tingle. I grab the nasty bar back from him. At lease I'm regaining feeling in my extremities.

My gaze wanders to *his* extremities, cataloguing their many fine qualities.

"Why can't I look at your tattoo? Do you have more on other body parts?" If I lick my lips, it's because they're dry. No other reason.

A hint of amusement curls his lips.

"You want to look at my tattoos, huh?" His eyes slide from the windshield, taking me in, trailing over my body, leaving more heat in their wake. "I have more than that one."

He raises an eyebrow. Is that an invitation?

"You said not to touch you."

"Now you have permission. I'm ready for it, now."

Ready for it? The thought jogs me further from my drunken state, and I wrinkle my nose. Oh. God. He probably has PTSD. Or something where he doesn't like to be touched. I'm an asshole.

"Sorry I touched you before," I say quietly, slightly stricken. I have a feeling I'd be more stricken were it not for my blood alcohol level. More protein bar it is.

"It's okay. Look if you want to." He glances sidelong at me. "If it will keep you from puking in the Jeep, even better."

I reach out, watching his eyes, but his gaze shifts back to the road. The pad of my finger touches the bottom of the tattoo, the cloth of his black shirt inching up. The muscle tenses as I tug on it. I glance up at his face. His dark eyes stay focused on the road, tight lines forming around his mouth.

He's tense.

"What happened to you?" I murmur, shaking my head.

He doesn't answer, and I look my fill at the ink on his skin.

It's a skull tattoo, a knife in its mouth, a simple grayscale. A flag of text curves around the top of the skull, so I nudge the sleeve higher.

I've seen this before, but my brain can't quite connect it.

"That's enough." Dean shrugs his massive shoulders. Startled, I remove my hand, letting it fall to my lap.

"Sorry."

So, he's taking me home, and he doesn't want me touching him? Maybe he is a gentleman, after all.

Sticking a finger out, my lips screw up as I try to tick off what I know about Dean.

Dean…

"What's your last name anyway?"

"Evans."

"Dean Evans."

Okay. I tap my index finger against my thigh.

One, his name is Dean Evans.

Two—I stare at the number two my fingers make, closing one eye, trying to remember.

Facts.

Facts always ground me. So does food. I force down another bite of the protein bar and refocus.

Two, he's military. Or ex-military. That tattoo is familiar enough. My dad had a similar one, after all. And then there's his massive bulk that seems purely made up of muscles…

Nope.

Thinking about muscles is a bad idea. A real bad one. I stare at my fingers, willing more facts to appear.

Three, he seems, for all intents and purposes, to be a gentleman. Despite the accidental wet t-shirt contest, he isn't giving off any serial killer vibes. In fact, he seems nice.

Well, he's at least not triggering fight or flight. Hopefully the tequila hasn't broken that brain functionality. I table the thought. For now.

Four, he's taking care of me, despite the fact I've been nothing but weird since we met.

"We're nearly there," he interrupts my thoughts and belabored counting.

"What?"

"We're nearly to your house," he repeats. "And I don't think we've been followed."

"Followed?" My mouth twists to the side, and I tear off another chunk of protein bar. "Why would we be followed?"

My paranoia rears its ugly head again, and adrenaline burns off more of the alcohol.

His eyes leave the road, something feral in them, making me sit up straighter.

"You don't have any idea why we might have been followed?"

I shake my head, strands of hair lashing around my face.

"You sure about that?"

"I might be a lot of things, Dean Evans. Like right now, I am a little drunk, and a lot nauseous, and grossed out at this protein bar you had lying around for who knows how long, but I'm not a liar." I glare at him.

He grunts at me.

"Dean, Dean, the ex-Marine, doesn't like to be touched or wear sunscreen."

I cringe at myself. I sound like an idiot. I *hate* sounding like an idiot. Even worse, now I sound like a drunk idiot. Well, embarrassment is a good sign, right? Maybe I'm a little more sober.

"I like wearing sunscreen just fine." He shoots me an amused look, the half-smile curving his lips, making him look younger. That dimple flickering into being, along with the oddest compulsion to reach out and touch it.

"I couldn't think of another rhyme," I babble.

My stomach growls, and my brain finally catches up with what he said.

"Wait, hold on. Why would we be followed?" I guzzle more water, hoping it will wash away the nasty chalky feeling and maybe the drunkenness, too. "You didn't answer me."

"We're here." Dean tugs at the wheel, ignoring my question.

I look out the window, anxiety taking hold as we pull into my driveway.

Fear ripples through me as I reassess the situation.

I'm alone in a Jeep with a man I don't know, a huge, hot man. With no phone. And—

Adrenaline floods my system completely, and my breath starts coming in great big gasps.

I might not be at the top of my intellectual game at the moment, but I know one thing for sure.

I never told him where I live.

CHAPTER
SIX

DEAN

THE ROAR of the Jeep's engine goes quiet and I take the key out.

I count down from ten. Except that little therapy trick doesn't work so well when it comes to a raging libido.

Beside me, June breathes rapidly, her chest rising and falling, the damp material of her shirt clinging like a second skin.

I rub my hand across my forehead, shaking the image of her from my mind. *Concentrate.*

Her breathing's too quick, near hyperventilation.

She's panicking.

"Are you gonna be sick?" I lean in, trying to gauge her expression.

It takes all my control to keep from touching her. I almost lost it when she inspected my tattoo on the drive here. It took everything I had to act like it was no big deal, like her hand whispering against my skin wasn't burning me, wasn't branding me.

I can't question her like this.

I'm too worked up over her, too affected by her proximity, the way her body felt as I carried her away from the Russian hitman.

One thing at a time, I tell myself.

We both need to calm down. She needs food.

"No. The protein bar helped. So did the water." Her voice is a breathy whisper. "I just uh, I want to know why you think someone is following us." The handle clicks as she opens the door, and she slides from the seat.

Well, at least she's recovered most of her motor control. That's a good sign.

The sooner I get this over with and get away from her, the better, because I'm not sure I can tell myself I'm not attracted to her much longer, and that shit will only complicate an already fucked up case.

I tear my eyes away from the soft curve of her ass and swallow, glancing at the rifle case in the back seat.

I shouldn't need it inside. We won't even be inside long enough to need it. I need to get in, get out, and keep this op on track.

June's already halfway up the steps of her small bayside bungalow, perched on stilts like an overgrown bird, before I make it out of the Jeep.

A massive boat is tethered to the dock. Her father's boat, according to the DEA file on him. It's older, but seaworthy and legal, and she inherited it when he died.

I need to look in that boat. It's one of the things Charlie and the DEA flagged as likely having info on the lost drug sub in it, and if June's a dead end, then the boat might not be.

The more I spend time with June, the harder it is to think she has a hand in this.

I don't know if that's wishful thinking or instinct, or both.

Palms and flowering bushes flank the front of the house. Water lapping at the dock, a constant whirl of noise alongside fish splashing in the canal waters. In the dusk, the light blue house fades to charcoal, violet bougainvillea turning black where it climbs against the stairs.

It would be a perfect place to relax.

That is, if I was here for a completely different reason.

My chest tightens. I'm here… with June. The target I've been watching day and night. The key to getting the shipment, to getting respect and getting my goddamn business more work.

Taking the stairs two at a time, I catch up to her as she steps onto the fenced porch, teetering unsteadily. I catch her elbow, and she looks back quickly, the sudden flash of fear in her eyes chased away by a soft word.

"Thanks."

"You okay?" I frown.

In the fading light, the shadows obscure the light in her eyes.

"Dean…" She shakes her head, fishing for her keys, and stops. Her mouth is a pretty 'o' of surprise. "Charlie has my keys. Shoot."

I step closer, hating the look of irritation sweeping across her features, wanting to wipe it away.

Maybe I'm half-drunk from the half-beer.

Maybe it's her.

Leaning down, I lift the 'Hey Y'all' mat from the porch, picking up the extra key.

June stills beside me.

Dammit. I overstepped. I clear my throat, trying to figure out how to smooth this over.

"You should probably find a less obvious place to hide your key," I say quietly, hiding the disgust I have for the blatant lie, but she returns the smile slowly.

She plucks the key from my hand, her eyes still too narrow for my liking.

I push a hand through my hair. God, I'm fucking this up.

Establishing trust is a pretty clear directive when dealing with potential assets, and I'm shit at it. Especially when all I can think about are *her* assets.

She clears her throat, unlocking the door before stepping inside and flicking the switch, illuminating her small house.

I know the layout, but habit makes me assess the exits

anyway. The front door we stepped through. Two windows in the bedroom to my right. The kitchen in front of me, leading out to a back porch and those stairs lead down to the dock and the boat. And another window in the small half-bath directly to my left.

"I'm uh, I'm going to go uh, freshen up. Um, make yourself at home." June fidgets with the top button of her shirt. Causing my eyes to dive to the silky column of her neck, the curve of her collarbone. The lush expanse of breasts.

"Okay if I make you a sandwich? Or something? That protein bar won't be enough." I cross my arms, trying to slow my heartrate. Something about being here, in her house, with her looking like that, with the damp shirt clinging to her curves.

She cocks her head, eyes wide. "Yeah, okay." Her gaze dips to her bedroom, and her smile turns slightly suggestive.

Does she think I want to hook up?

I can play that part. It would be all too easy to play that part.

I school my face, internally shaking the thoughts away, making myself focus. This isn't about the way she looks, the way her house feels less like a front and more like a home.

Shifting on my feet, I take a deep breath and June exhales, sending a wisp of hair flying around her face. It lands on her nose, and it makes her twitch adorably.

Surprising myself, I reach forward, tucking it behind her ear. My hand grazes her cheek, and she shivers the tiniest bit.

Yeah, I can definitely play this part.

I lean in, her focus dropping to my mouth. A pink tongue darts out as she licks her lips. I'm so close now, all I'd have to do is lean down to steal a kiss.

My hand lingers at her neck. I can't do it.

I shouldn't do it.

Thankfully, she ducks away.

At least, I think I'm thankful.

"I'll uh, I'll be right back. There's bread in the pantry. Help yourself to whatever."

Disappointment and relief war in my chest, but I stand taller, rubbing a hand down my face.

She disappears into the bedroom, and I catch a glimpse of white linens and bare floors, clean save for a hot pink bra strewn across the bed.

I turn on my heel as her bedroom door closes with a click and head to the pantry. The kitchen light hums overhead when I flick the light switch. The pantry's full of pristine labeled baskets. Every snack is organized by type and color. My eyebrows lift in surprise.

It appeals to the military part of me that craves order a little too much for my own comfort.

I grab what I need and turn to the fridge, and blink in an effort to take it in.

Nearly every square inch is covered in maps. Old and current calendars and tide timetables compete for space.

I lean in, the sandwiches momentarily forgotten.

Notes scrawl across a page torn from a book, and a portrait of some old guy in a crown stands out in stark relief against the chaos. Exclamation marks, circles. Arrows on maps, Post-its written in some kind of code.

What kind of researcher writes in code then puts it on her fridge for anyone to find? I squint at the papers, suspicion gnawing at me, tightening my ribs.

I trail one finger across a neon orange Post-it.

None of this makes sense. I glance back at the tide charts. They aren't from this year. Or last.

Five hundred years ago?

What kind of woman works with Russian smugglers and uses tide and current maps from four centuries ago?

My gut sinks.

Maybe the DEA analysts were wrong about how much she knows. Maybe I was wrong about her working with the cartel. Maybe this is all a damn waste of time.

I should have made contact with Charlie earlier.

Something about this, about June, is off.

I swipe a spreadsheet and currents map, folding and tucking them into the cargo pocket of my pants. The picture and textbook page come next, along with a list marked 'fishing spots' in an untidy scrawl.

I shift a few things to hide the blank spaces and refocus.

Sandwiches. I'll distract her with food, with questions, with whatever alcohol is lingering in her system.

She'll never notice something's missing.

Digging into the fridge, I locate the deli meat and cheese, along with a half-empty jar of grape jelly. It isn't hard to find, considering the woman seems to live off Goldfish, popcorn, and cheese sticks.

I shut the fridge with a foot and lay out the supplies. Untwisting the bread bag, I line everything up precisely, making two of each sandwich, using up the rest of her food. The bedroom door closes just as I'm about to grab the Goldfish from the pantry.

Looking up, my whole body goes tense with anticipation.

Time for some answers.

June's dressed in a short, flowery dress and sneakers. Her dark hair falls around her shoulders, grazing the tops of her breasts.

And grazing the butt of the black shotgun pressed to one shoulder.

CHAPTER
SEVEN

JUNE

HE KNEW WHERE I LIVE. It's all I can think, the thought a drumbeat in my head, almost as loud as my heart.

"Who are you?" Steadying my aim, I wedge the butt of the gun in my shoulder. Just as my dad taught me. Just as I perfected over the months after the incident.

Dean raises his hands, his narrowed eyes slipping into a relaxed, amused expression.

He thinks I won't do it.

I click the safety off, slightly gratified by the way his throat bobs.

"I said, who are you?" The question goes higher, and I will myself to calm down.

"I am who I said I am. My name is Dean Evans. Like you guessed, I am an ex-Marine. I'm currently working with the DEA. Why don't you put the gun down, babe?" he asks, stepping forward.

I step back, blood pounding through my veins.

Instinct and training tell me letting him get close would be a mistake. That being within reaching distance would be the end of it. He's too big, and my rudimentary self-defense knowledge would be useless against him.

The shotgun is my only real defense.

Too bad I *really* don't want to shoot anyone.

"Stay the fudge back," I yell, hiding a grimace.

Seriously, fudge? Maybe fuck needs to become part of my vocabulary. It seems more appropriate than fudge in these situations.

Not that I would like more of these situations, thank you very much.

A hint of a smile crosses his face as he edges closer, hands still up.

I swallow, fingers tightening around the gun. "Listen, I just redid the damn tile in there, and I really don't want to bleach the grout. You've already ruined laundry night." The knot from the bikini top under my dress digs into my neck, an obnoxious reminder of how badly I needed to do laundry.

"Laundry night sounds like a good time." Dean grins down at me, that cocky dimple flashing.

"Don't talk about my laundry like that." Irritation makes my hands tighten on the gun. Had I *seriously* been about to kiss him?

This night has taken a mother fudging turn.

"The tile looks nice." He glances over his shoulder at it, and a feral noise surges out of my throat. "Your dad teach you how to do that? Did he teach you how to shoot? Ever shoot skeet?" He waggles his eyebrows. "That's a nice gun. Remington Tactical?"

"You sexist jerkface. You think I don't know what you're doing?" My smartwatch dings, and I can't help but glance at it.

It looks like you're doing cardio. Do you want to record a workout?

I grit my teeth, holding back a scream.

No, I do not want to record a *freaking* workout.

Readjusting my hold on the shotgun, I look back at Dean, and he just keeps smiling at me, like being held at gunpoint by a woman who had to put on her bikini because she didn't have enough clean underwear is commonplace for him.

Maybe it is. I don't know what he's into.

"I think you're scared," he says, taking another step closer.

"What gave it away?" I laugh, giving the shotgun a little wiggle, my dizziness coming back. "Was it the shotgun? Was it the fact I'm pointing it at you? Or was it that you knew where I live and where I keep my spare key?"

I make a mental note to take his advice and stop putting the key under my mat.

And with any luck, the last of the ridiculous amount of tequila I ingested is burning off with this new adrenaline surge.

Dean lets out a raspy laugh, lifting an eyebrow. A muscled shoulder shrugs, and I gape at the sheer size of him. Just a little admiration, as a treat.

Good thing shotgun pellets spread wide. Maybe he'll catch 'em all.

"June, we are on the same side." His voice is calm, low, like he's done this a million times. Like my gun aimed at him isn't a threat. "I don't want to hurt you. You don't want to hurt me."

"This is not good. It's worse than not good, because I don't know what you're talking about. On the same side of what? We're not on the same side of the business end of this thing." My throat tightens, knuckles white against the black shotgun. "If you step any closer, I'll shoot you."

Dean freezes at the threat.

Ha! Satisfaction courses through me.

"Explain. Now. Explain how you knew where I live. Where the key was."

"I guessed where the key was." His voice is calm, steady, and it sets my teeth on edge. Even more on edge, that is. "A lot of people keep spare keys under their mats or somewhere within reach. June." He says my name like I'm a feral animal, calm and collected, careful.

It makes me twitch.

"I made us sandwiches." He sweeps a massive arm to where there are, indeed, four sandwiches. "Aren't you hungry?"

"You didn't answer my question," I say, my traitorous stomach growling.

"Put the gun down, and I will." He smiles, like he's won. "Give me the gun, and we can talk. I know you don't want to shoot me. All that pretty tile you put up."

He's crooning to me like I'm a stray dog growling in the gutter.

Worst part is?

He's right.

I don't want to kill him. I haven't ever *actually* shot anything alive. Turns out shooting paper targets and clay pigeons at the sterile environment of a gun range is pretty danged different from shooting a hot stranger in my kitchen.

Especially when I can't quite decide if I want to kiss him or not.

But maiming isn't entirely off the table.

My gaze drops slightly and he inches closer. "Stay the fuck away from me." I sight down the barrel. Though this close, there's no need to bother. Old habits die hard, I guess.

"The *fuck* away, hmm?" Another step. "What happened to fudge?"

I grit my teeth, lowering the gun slightly, swinging down and left. "I'll shoot you in the nuts." My finger lifts off the trigger guard, ready to squeeze.

I let out a little sigh. It would be a real shame to hit him in the nuts.

"I really don't want you to do that."

"I really don't want to mess up my new kitchen either." My mouth twists to the side. Darn it. That's not what I meant to say.

He huffs a laugh, and I'm momentarily distracted by the way his eyes light up. His strong, hard body collides with mine, knocking me to the floor.

The gun fires with a bark, the butt of it slamming hard into my ribs.

CHAPTER
EIGHT

DEAN

GRUNTING, I land, her body beneath me. A quick mental check says she missed. My body is still intact.

Thank fuck.

I really didn't want to deal with shotgun pellets in my nuts.

Plaster falls, dusting a white halo in her hair, and I grip the barrel of the gun. It's hot as hell, but better some burns on my hands than castration by Remington Tactical.

"Fuck." I swear at the heat, then toss it behind me, where it clatters against a cabinet. "Looks like you're going to have to put your handyman skills to the test on your ceiling now, Dr. Legarde."

"I missed?" She blinks, her pupils nearly blown from a heady mix of adrenaline and tequila. She stills beneath me, except for shallow breaths pressing her breasts against my chest. She wiggles, and I nearly groan.

Shit.

Talk about new things to discuss with my shrink. I can just imagine it, me explaining how I nearly got shot, and how I was immediately turned on when I tackled the shooter.

Unpack that.

"Are you… are you going to kidnap me?" She's breathing harder than she should be, her voice edging towards pure panic as her hands scrabble against my chest. "Please, please don't hurt me."

My chest constricts in sympathy.

But I don't get up.

"You fired a shotgun at me, June. I'm not just going to let you go."

Moving my hand over her body, I search for more weapons, and completely ignore her warm skin. I definitely don't notice the soft curve of her hips under the gauzy material of her dress.

I don't notice it one bit.

The sharp inhalation of breath gives her away, and I flinch back right as she attempts a head butt, her forehead connecting with my cheek. Pain sparks behind my eye and I growl.

"I swear to god, if you take me back there, I'll lose it. I will lose my mind. Please don't hurt me. Just tell me what you want." She shakes her head from side to side, tears pooling in her eyes. Her nails dig into my chest.

All I can do is stare at her in confusion as tears roll down her cheeks, leaving clean tracks through the plaster dust on her face.

"Take you back where? I told you, I'm with the DEA. Why would you think I'm going to hurt you? Where do you think I'm taking you?" Something about this is important. My instincts scream at me to figure out what the hell she's talking about.

She stops fighting, her body completely limp. "Prove it."

Like this, I'm even more aware of how well she fits against me, her breathing pushing her breasts against my chest, her eyes so full of emotion and intelligence that all I want to do is prove something else entirely to her.

I lick my lips, forcing control over myself.

"Prove what?" I growl.

"Prove that you're DEA. If you are government, call it in. No. You know what? Give me your phone and let *me* call it in."

"Your dad taught you that too, huh?" Grudging respect for the smuggler starts to form.

Fishing my phone from my pocket, I unlock it, handing it over, trying to ignore what her shallow breaths are doing against my chest. "DEA website," I say, leveling her with a stare. I'm trusting you not to call 911 and fuck this day up any worse."

She glares at me but takes the phone, quickly tapping the screen. "I'm there. What now?"

"Go to the page with the field offices. Houston is overseeing this mission." I smile at her speculative expression, the tightening around her eyes. "Go on. Verify that I'm working with them."

She dials the number, and when she is well past the three digits that would signal she's calling 911, I let out a long breath.

And realize I'm still straddling her.

"Hi, I'm calling to verify a field agent or, er, a contractor? Or something." There is a pause as a tinny voice says something indecipherable on the other end.

"What's your ID number?" June asks, relaxing beneath me somewhat, though her pulse still flutters in her throat.

A lazy grin spreads across my face as I rattle it off, only growing as June repeats it and is given confirmation. Slowly, she ends the call, never taking her eyes off me.

"Dr. Legarde," I say, picking a hunk of ceiling plaster from her hair, flicking it towards the door. "I told you I'm not going to hurt you, and I meant it. I'm not taking you anywhere. At the moment." I tack on the last part, because we do need to get to a safehouse soon.

Her eyes narrow, and she bites her lip.

I should get off her, but my body refuses to move. I don't want to risk her taking a potshot at my crotch, either.

"Okay, so you're with the DEA," she says slowly. She's looking anywhere but at me, her brown eyes wandering around her house. "But what does that have to do with me? How did you know where I live? Why are you stalking me?" The questions fly out of her, rapid-fire.

Somehow, June managed to control her panic.

"You're interrogating me now?"

Surprise and respect mingle with suspicion as I look at her.

"You're the one literally lying on top of me. Least I can do is ask why."

Shaking my head, I resume searching for potential weapons. A quick check of her dress pocket reveals several shotgun shells and what looks like keys to the big boat out back, an orange floatie hanging from the keyring.

I slide them into my own pocket, readjusting my position on top of her. She grunts as my weight shifts, and we both freeze at the noise.

"I'm going to let you go now. We need to talk."

"No kidding," June grinds out.

My mind races.

How much information am I cleared to give her? What can I say that won't make me sound like a stalker? How can I prove that she's not about to fuck me and this op over?

With all the blood rushing to parts that are not my brain, I'm not exactly thinking straight.

"Are you going to run, or can we eat the gourmet meal I made for us like civilized people?" I finally settle on that, and it sounds stupid.

When she lets out a surprised laugh, though, I feel like I've won a fucking prize.

I much prefer her laugh to her tears.

"Gourmet? You made peanut butter and jelly." Her stomach growls again, and I can't help the smile tugging at my lips.

Something moves under me. Is her hand on my leg? My hip?

I shift, frowning, and the slight pressure disappears.

"Are you going to hurt me, DEA Dean?"

"Not unless you're allergic to peanuts." Tilting my head at her, I smile, but she looks away. "Are you going to try to shoot me again?"

"That depends."

"On what?"

She knees me in the groin, my eyebrows rocketing up. "If you stop poking me with *that*."

My smile disappears, embarrassment surging through me. Standing up, I offer her a hand, which she declines.

June crosses her arms, hugging herself, looking up at the ruined ceiling. The t-shirt sliding further off her shoulder, I pull another piece of ceiling from her hair.

"Explain," she orders.

"Eat, and I will."

"Why are you so hellbent on getting me to eat? Are you planning to drug me before carting me off somewhere?" She shakes out her hair, and more plaster dust falls out of it.

"Why are you so hung up on me kidnapping you?"

"You're the one who carried me out of a bar, knew where I live, and made sandwiches in my kitchen, you weirdo."

Exasperation sends my eyes rolling. "I am trying to keep you safe. And even though you seem more sober, a protein bar isn't enough." I point at the hole in the ceiling, unsure if I want to tip my hand to the rest yet. "And, frankly, your drunk decision making doesn't seem to be the greatest. Case in point, you throwing tequila in the eyes of the Russian hitman."

An exasperated sound gusts out of her, and she rolls her eyes before stomping into the kitchen. Where the shotgun lies.

She pauses, looking back at me. Then reaches out and grabs a sandwich.

A little relieved, I slide between her and the gun and take a sandwich for myself.

"Well? Ready to tell me why the DEA sent me a hot stalker?"

I can't help smirking. "You think I'm hot?"

"Shut up." She takes an angry bite of her peanut butter and jelly, and it's adorable.

"You really don't know?" I still can't wrap my head around the idea that June might actually not be involved.

She shakes her head, more white dust falling from the strands.

It takes a herculean effort not to comb it out with my fingers, not to tuck the wild mess behind her ear.

What the fuck is wrong with me?

I settle for shoving the sandwich in my mouth, eating with a methodical quickness born of a lifetime of quick meals made for nutrition, not pleasure. A handful of Goldfish follow.

June chews neatly, precise little bites that have me watching her mouth as she clearly turns theories over in that pretty head of hers.

"Why in the world would the Drug Enforcement Agency be interested in me?"

I swallow, peanut butter sticking in my throat.

"Is the DEA interested in the wreck?" She squares me with a serious look that almost unravels me. "It doesn't fall under their jurisdiction, not in the least," she muses. "State Department, maybe. For repatriating the objects to Mexico or Spain, smoothing out the museum circuit. But not DEA." She licks a bit of peanut butter off her finger and my eyes track the motion. My groin tightens, remembering what those curves felt like beneath me. Wondering what it would be like if she kissed me.

"Repatriating the objects?" I echo, leaving those thoughts behind.

"Yeah? From the *Santu Espiritu*. I still don't get why they wouldn't just approach me normally. Not like this." She gestures to the newly shotgun-shattered ceiling above.

My eyes fly to the fridge. She thinks I'm after a… wreck? A shipwreck.

"For a man who's been stalking me, you don't seem to know a whole lot about what I do. Tell me what the hell is going on, or I'll make you leave." June fidgets, glancing at the gun, still chewing.

"And make me miss this delicious sandwich and your company?" I let loose the lopsided grin that usually gets me what I want. "Nah. I don't think you would. Besides, I'm not interested in some disintegrating shipwreck."

What I'm after is much more modern.

And much more dangerous.

"Why else would you steal my research off my fridge?" She fishes in her back pocket, revealing the folded tidal charts that had been in *mine*.

"You took them?" I rub a hand across my stubble in frustration.

Sneaky little thing.

"You took them first." She jabs my chest, frowning at the folded papers. "Explain." She turns her disappointed expression at me and I decide to fold. Just a little.

Maybe if I give something up, she will too.

"I *am* interested in something in the ocean. Something I think your father told you about." Running a finger over the currents chart, I look back to her. "This ship? The *Santu Espiritu*? The article said it went down with a hurricane in the gulf."

An idea sparks, so I follow my instincts, tugging at the thread.

"Did your father tell you anything about where he thinks it might be lost in the gulf? Leave you anything that might help us, I mean you, find what you need?"

Her lips are a thin line, her eyes narrowing in suspicion. "What does the DEA want with the *Santu Espiritu*? Or my father?" She throws her hands up. "He's dead, though I guess you know that." Her voice sounds rough, her throat bobbing as she swallows. "And no, the only things he was interested in were crabs and tourists willing to spend their money on guided fishing trips on the *Betty*. His boat out back." Her voice wobbles a little. "Looking for the ship was a fun thing we used to do. Then I decided to stake my career on it. Great decision making on my part."

I clear my throat. God. She's either an expert at lying, or she's telling the truth.

Shit. *Shit*.

"Shipment," she says slowly, and her eyes light up. Snapping her fingers, she locks her gaze with mine. "*Shipment*. The man in the bar, the Russian..." Her face blanches. "Hitman, you called him."

I nod when she stares at me.

"He said something about a shipment." Her voice goes slightly squeaky again. "You're DEA... You think my father was involved with drugs? A drug shipment? And you think I know where it is?" She laughs, her hand half-covering her mouth in disbelief.

"I think it's possible," I say, inclining my head.

"You're wrong." She lowers her hand, brushing off some of the crumbs clinging to the countertop. "You're *wrong* about my father. He would never have done anything involved with drugs, not after—he wouldn't have."

I open my mouth, trying to come up with a question for her, with a reason I was cleared to give her, when a sudden flash of light nearly blinds me.

June's mouth opens in surprise, her eyes wide.

The sound of the explosion follows, nearly deafening me.

My ears ring as I see June scream, clapping her hands over her ears in what seems like slow motion.

Out front, the Jeep's a fireball.

They found us.

We overstayed our welcome— her stunt with the goddamn shotgun made things take longer than they should have, and being so close to her... it distracted me. Of fucking course they found us.

My teeth grind together.

"Come on," I yell, but she shakes her head. She can't hear. Tears stream down her face, and in one swift motion, I grab the shotgun off the floor and throw her over my shoulder. Handing her the shotgun as I make a break for the sliding glass doors.

Hoping she'll aim at whoever is about to burst through the front doors and *not* me. Trusting that she *isn't* working with the cartel. Either she's an incredible actress—which isn't impossible, considering my ex—or she *is* a civilian and we're both in deep shit.

Well, either way, we're in deep shit.

My throat tightens, pulse hammering as adrenaline pumps through my body.

"They're trying to kill us," she yells.

"Don't let them."

Blinding light signals she made a shot into the deepening dark of evening, alongside the sharp report of the shotgun. Sliding down my chest, June wraps her strong, bare legs around my torso, the hot barrel of the gun sizzling against my t-shirt, my skin. Her hand dips into the pocket where I stuffed her shotgun shells, expertly reloading the chamber.

The hot barrel torches my shoulder as she uses it to steady the aim of the gun.

Smart.

I dare a glance at her as I run through the sliding doors, grunting as she fires another shot and the barrel sizzles on my skin. I don't dare look back. We have to get to the boat.

Get to open water.

We have to get the hell away from the smugglers, who will sure as shit torture her for information. Or worse.

Fuck.

I shouldn't have left my rifle in the goddamn Jeep.

She fires again, and I sprint. Her legs are locked tight around me, and I use one arm to balance, the other clenched around her waist.

Gulping air, I try to get as much oxygen in my bloodstream as possible.

Speed is our only option at this point.

"Give me the keys!" June shouts, kicking her heels into my lower back. "I only have one round left. You'll have to hold them off."

"Like hell!" The smell of barbecued skin fills my nose, my skin burning against the barrel.

"I have to untie the boat." She kicks me again, and I barely feel it. Adrenaline is a hell of a drug.

"Fuck that."

"Don't talk to me like that." The shotgun barks again, impossibly loud in my ear, and she lets out a surprised, "Oh."

I felt her say it, the way her body collapsed, the air forced out of her lungs, the soft breath against my aching neck.

"Shit." I take the steps down to the dock four at a time. Lungs aching, legs screaming. I ignore it.

But I can't ignore the warm, wet gush of fluid soaking my back.

The dock groans as I pound to the boat, shots pinging around us.

"Hang on, June. Hang in there."

My arm feels limp, but there's no time to think.

Clearing the space between the dock and the boat in one huge leap, I wobble as we land. June clings to me, eyes wide and dark, her face ashen.

"It's gonna be okay, June. We have to get out of here. Hold pressure on it."

She starts thrashing against me, but I don't let her go. The boat is clean, empty save for scuba gear and a few fishing rods on the deck. There's a tackle box near the steering wheel. I jam the keys in the ignition and the boat roars to life.

"We're tethered," June yells, staring at me, a strange expression on her face, pointing to the ropes tied to the wooden dock.

"I don't give a fuck," I yell back over the roar of the engine.

Out of habit, I look back, lowering the motor into the water. Five men race down the stairs from June's bungalow as the triple engines roar, kicking up water and debris.

The men land on the dock and I gun it, shoving the throttle. Diesel fumes fill the air.

The boat gives a mighty heave, straining once, twice, before my stupid plan works. The wood, corroded from the salt air and seawater, rips apart and the dock violently disintegrates. Shots go wide, the Russians firing wildly as they splash down in the canal.

A bullet whizzes by us, embedding itself in the fiberglass seating.

"Guns don't work as well underwater," I snarl.

"You owe me a new dock, ex-Marine Dean." June's arms and legs shake uncontrollably in my arms. "And you better be good to *Betty*." Her teeth are chattering.

She doesn't let go, and neither do I.

"Who were *they*? Are they after the wreck too? What the hell is going on?" Her questions barely make it through the ringing in my ears. And when I look at her, her expression is strained, her face ashen and drawn.

"Smugglers. Russian smugglers. Drugs, weapons, you name it." Pain blossoms across my torso as the speedometer ticks past fifty.

"Russian smugglers," she repeats. Her gaze goes vacant.

Shock. She's going into shock. Gripping her side, I look for the bullet's entry wound.

"This is a no wake zone," she offers with a thin smile.

I follow her gaze to the sign, and the massive wave trailing us in the canal, part of the dock surfing on it. She tips her head back in laughter and I crack a smile, shaking my head in spite of the worry.

"Good thing the Coast Guard isn't around." The words sound muffled in the aftereffects of close-proximity shotgun firing. That, and the Jeep exploding. "They're going to have their hands full with the Russian canal swimming competition, anyway."

Her chest heaves, and her pupils are nearly fully dilated.

"You're in shock," I manage, wincing at the dull pain in my side.

"You've been shot," she whispers.

CHAPTER
NINE

JUNE

BITING MY LIP, I do my best to patch Dean up. Once we hit open water, out of the canal, I set the boat at a good clip and got out of the main waterways. Not fast enough to hit any waves too hard, not slow enough to be caught if we were followed.

Now we're drifting, land a mere spot in the distant.

It doesn't matter that the gulf is calm, glass-smooth, even.

I can't seem to stop shaking. Can't seem to focus. Especially with his shirt off.

"I'm sorry. About what the shotgun did to your hearing. And uh, this burn." The angry red patch is already blistering. "It looks awful. And sorry about the whole being shot thing. And the Jeep."

Oh good. I'm rambling. Great.

Narrowing my eyes, I attempt not to notice anything but the task at hand. Patching Dean up is priority number one. I don't notice his bloody shirt, I don't look at the old scars, and I absolutely do not memorize the ripped body my hands tremble over.

"None of this is your fault. Besides, it's not that bad. His shot went wide. Just a nick is all," he says, as if being shot at is an everyday occurrence. "The burn… it is what it is. You did what you had to do. I'm just glad you keep a stocked first aid kit on here." His breathing steadies, eyes tracking my every movement. "My hearing's already better. I'm fine."

"You're not fine." Blood trickles from the wound, and I suck in a breath. Stretching the gauze across his impressive pecks, winding it around his shoulder and under his armpit, where the bullet grazed him.

Where it narrowly missed me.

My head swims, and I sway with it on my knees, attempting to remain steady. Whether the dizziness is from the lingering effects of too many tequilas or being shot at, or… shooting at—

Strong arms anchor me, keeping me from falling.

"June. June. Look at me."

I can't. My chest heaves as I fight for more air, my breathing impossibly fast. Dean scoots closer, to the edge of the bench seat that hides another gun. Swallowing, I close my eyes.

Can't think about guns.

"Look at me." His thighs press on either side of me, caging me in. A firm hand lifts my chin.

I obey, opening my eyes, looking up at him.

"I'm okay. You're okay, remember?" he says gently.

I nod. "I know."

Dean checks me over, making sure the blood staining my clothes is his, and not mine. His careful hands seek out any injury. He's methodical. Calm.

Eventually my quivering legs still, and he watches me. Seconds stretch into minutes as I breathe, staring into his eyes. Not wanting to say it.

If I don't say it, it's not real.

"How many?" he asks.

Guilt and relief roil in my stomach, and I squeeze my eyes shut so tight rainbow sparks trail across my eyelids.

"How many did you get, June?"

"Get?" I repeat, barking out a harsh laugh and opening my eyes in indignation.

"Talking about it helps," Dean just says.

"Two. Maybe three," I finally admit.

Dean nods once, his gaze firm on me, warming me. His thumb strokes my jawline as his other hand pulls me close. He's so close his breath whispers across my neck.

Collecting myself, I snip the bandage carefully and tuck it into itself. I ignore the warmth rising to my skin.

"June, you had to make a choice." His fingers stroke my back. "It was us or them. You picked us. It's okay."

I tilt my chin up, our lips dangerously close, and his eyes drop to them, but I don't care. I don't want to talk about this. I don't want to think about anything. His hand on my back makes small circles, sending shivers through me that have nothing to do with shock, and I arch into him. His lips part, both hands stroking, one along the side of my neck, the other up my spine. The heat of his bare skin is nearly too much, a contrast to the cold settling over me.

The swell of my breasts meets the hard planes of his chest and he sucks in a breath, his eyes heavy. His grip on my waist and the column of my neck tightening.

Leaning closer, I wait for him to close the gap between us. For our lips to touch.

A half-second passes, breathing the same air.

His eyes meet mine as he moves in, and my heart races.

A horrible screech fills the air, the sound of metal on metal jerking me back to reality.

"Shit." I scramble off the deck, stomach sinking, and head to the steering wheel. The screeching dies away as I shift the wheel left. "We scraped a buoy. Can you hold the wheel straight while I check the damage?"

Dean winces, unsteady on his feet, but nods.

"You need water."

Keeping my eyes on the dark sea, I rummage around one of

the under-seat storage bins. Sure enough, the heavy flashlight's there, along with two gallons of water. My emergency stash.

If there's ever been an emergency to use the stash up, this is it.

Dean grabs a gallon with his left hand, and I put the seat back in place.

"*You* need water," Dean says, holding the jug out to me.

"Take the aspirin from the med kit." I ignore the water, picking up the flashlight instead.

"I'm fine." He unscrews the cap, tipping water into his mouth.

"You want to be in pain? Whatever. Stupid Marines," I mutter, sure he won't be able to hear.

He chokes on the water, patting his chest. "I'm not a…" Shaking his head, he lets out a heavy sigh. "It's ex-Marine."

I shake my head. Apparently, he can hear just fine.

"Once a Marine, always a Marine. My dad didn't believe in pain killers either." I squint, trying to make out his face. It's unreadable in the settling dark.

"Check the boat." He nods to the water. "Don't have the light on longer than necessary."

"I'm not an idiot," I snap, suddenly beyond annoyed. "You think I want them to catch us?"

I'm furious with this stupid ex-Marine, who is the reason my house is torn apart, my dock in pieces. I'm furious with myself for almost kissing him. For even *wanting* to kiss him. The only thing I truly know for certain about him is that he looks hot as hell with his dumb shirt off.

Well, and that he's working for the DEA in some capacity.

Anchoring myself on the side of the boat, I lean over the metal railing. Saltwater sprays, coating my face and body in a fine mist. I turn the flashlight on, quickly whipping it up and down the side of the *Betty*, assessing the damage.

"Fudging fudgesicles." The bilge pump.

Teeth bared, I flip the flashlight off and push myself back into the boat.

Of course, it had to be the bilge pump.

Resting my forehead in my hands, I curse myself for never getting around to fixing the faulty automatic sensor. Worried I'd need to replace the whole dang thing, I set up a manual switch instead. And now we're on the freaking water with a bilge pump that needs to be manually activated every six hours or so, if we want to keep the boat from sinking. Which we do. Especially since we're on it.

Casting my gaze skyward, stars begin to wink into view. Shining in the velvet sky, illuminating it and us.

Carefully, I find the janky manual switch on the control panel and flip it. The noise of water ejecting from the pump starts, and I sag against the captain's chair.

At least the manual switch hasn't failed. At least the battery's new enough that it can power it.

The watch screen on my wrist lights up, the haptics buzzing against my wrist.

Standing up for one minute can help keep you on track to your goal!

"I am standing up, you jerk," I mutter. Why do I let this stupid thing boss me around? Tapping the screen, I set a six-hour timer to check the bilge pump again. "How you like that? You work for *me*."

"Did you say something?" Dean's gravelly voice surprises me, and I clutch at my chest. God, I'm so jumpy.

"No." My eyes stray to Dean, and I carefully guide the boat between the faintly glowing buoys. Red for port, green for starboard. Drifting in the gulf in a boat this size, the chances of us hitting a salt flat and tangling the propellors in sea grass aren't slim. It would be a pain to get free of them, so the deeper we can get, the further out we go, the better.

"How bad is the damage?" he asks, glancing back at me.

"It looks worse than it is. It'll cost a fortune to fix it, but if I don't get it fixed, it'll weaken the hull. We're fine for now, though."

I don't mention the bilge pump. That problem's taken care of, too. For now.

If my dad was around, he would do it himself. Would teach me how to do it. A sharp ache sears my chest.

But he isn't around.

He would be teasing me as he sanded it down, telling me about elbow grease and hard work.

"That's good." Dean nods.

Carefully, I step over to the empty live well where my hand-gun's taped inside, safe in a waterproof Ziploc. Ammo taped next to it. Not that the Glock would make him tell the truth. In our close quarters, there's no guarantee I'd be able to fire off a shot before he tackled me again.

I shouldn't think like that, though. I think… if Dean were out to hurt me, he'd already have done so.

He's certainly had every opportunity to do something.

His heavy hand settles on my shoulder, spinning me around.

"You ready to have that talk?"

"About how you've put me in danger since you ran over my phone in the bar parking lot?" It comes out rude, and I don't care. Rude is better than noticing his smooth skin, his rippling abs.

Moonlight dances across the water, the light brighter as the moon rises, and I'm grateful for the fact we at least have good weather.

"What do you know about what your father did for a living?" Dean cocks his head, an eyebrow raised. I expect anger when I look into his eyes, expect judgment. He isn't angry, though.

His eyes are sad. Understanding, even.

"He's gone now. He's dead." My throat closes, the familiar panic building until my chest aches.

I doubt swallowing grief ever gets easier.

Dean just waits for me to truly answer, his soft brown eyes never leaving my face.

The bilge pump shuts off, the gurgle of water and whine of the bilge motor dying replaced by the steady lapping of water at the hull.

"He was retired," I finally say. "Like I told you, ex-Marine. You know something about that. He made investments, played the stock market. Worked as a fishing guide and was great at it." I gesture around the boat, resigned. "Obviously. Now tell me what you've gotten me into, or I'll…"

"You'll what?" Finally, a smile dawns across his face.

I can't help sighing in irritation. "You've got me there. There isn't much I can do." But I don't feel unsafe with him. I'm irritated. On edge. Overwhelmed by what just happened, definitely.

But… he doesn't make me feel like I'm in danger.

No, Dean Evans makes me feel safe.

"Fine." He sighs, then winces and touches the bandage on his side. "Let's start over. I'm Dean Evans. Marine." He points to his tattoo. "And now a contractor for the DEA. Which brings us to the smugglers," he pauses, his eyes tracking over me. "And to your involvement with them."

He holds out a hand, but I don't shake it, and he finally drops it, a hint of amusement causing that dimple to peek out.

"And why, Dean Evans, does the DEA suspect me? Why are Russian smugglers trying to kill us?" My stomach clenches, and I bring a hand to it. A nasty suspicion rockets through me, but I clamp down on it. Refusing to let that voice have a place in my head.

"You're a person of interest in an ongoing investigation." He frowns, his hands clenching at his sides. "I'm not sure how much information I'm cleared to give you."

"Uh-huh. That sounds convenient." I raise my hand to flip the hair off my shoulder, but he catches my wrist.

I lock eyes with him, his fingers gentle on my skin.

A frisson of heat passes through me before I wrench out of his grip.

"Dr. Legarde, do I look like I'm lying to you?"

"It's dark. Hard to tell what anything looks like right now."

He snorts a laugh. "Fine. Do I sound like I am?"

"I don't know you." Still, I relax slightly, sinking down onto a pleather chair. I put my head in my hands, trying not to cry as the adrenaline finally abates, leaving me exhausted and hollow.

And scared.

"None of this makes sense," I mutter. Part of me doesn't want to know. My stomach sinks. I don't want the answer. I've spent a lifetime suppressing the mere idea of it.

I glance up to find him studying me. His eyes drift to my lips, only noticeable because of the bright moonlight, before he finally shakes his head.

"Fine. The smugglers are after a missing shipment, and they think you're involved, too. Because of your father." His voice is low. Gentle.

"My father?" Anger and suspicion curdle my stomach.

"You handled them just fine, though, even the guy you blinded at the bar. You know, after your friend Charlie ran him over." He lets out a low chuckle and I take a deep breath, wrapping my hands around my chest so he won't see them tremble. Dean settles next to me, the boat rocking as the ocean swells beneath us. "Is that what they mean when they say, 'Don't mess with Texas'?"

"No, that was an anti-littering campaign."

"June," he hesitates, "there's no easy way to say this. Your dad ran drugs for them. For about ten years, maybe more. They think *you* have them. Or that your dad told you where to find them."

CHAPTER
TEN

DEAN

A JAGGED PULSE rockets through my body, the ache in my chest intensifying as my heart rate goes up. June's skin pales under her tan, the wan light from the sliver of the moon turning her ghostly.

The boat's drifting in the gulf, saltwater-soaked air turning chilly without the sun to warm it. It's not a safehouse, but we're likely as safe here for the night as we would be anywhere else.

"That can't be true." She clutches her stomach, staring at the navy expanse of water and sky.

I swallow, my throat dry. "It is."

Goddamn, I'm no good at this.

"What proof do you have?" Her hands curl into fists on either side of her torso, then relax. Before clenching again.

"Dr. Legarde, all I can give you at the moment is my word." An uncomfortable emotion ripples through me.

Guilt. But I need to press her, get more information, despite her apparent ignorance.

It could be an act.

June doesn't strike me as a liar. For one, she is wildly different from my ex. My therapist would be proud of me, realizing not all women are like her, would probably call it a breakthrough and have me do a positive affirmation.

I cough to hide a chuckle at the thought.

"Why?" she asks.

"Why what?" For a second, I wonder if I've said a positive affirmation out loud.

"No way would he work with them," she scoffs. "Not after everything that happened to me. Why would he..." She trails off, her face inscrutable under the heavy veil of night. "It's not important." She straightens her back, becoming little taller, like she's ready to face the facts.

I've seen that look on fellow Marines before.

She sucks in a breath.

"What is important is that you think he did these things, and that there are," she pauses, pressing her hand to her stomach, "*bad dudes* after us."

"Bad dudes," I repeat. I choke back a laugh as her watch buzzes, the light from it briefly illuminating the scowl on her face.

"What is it?" I ask, concerned by her reaction. "Do you have service out here?"

"It's telling me I need to move around, as though I haven't been hunted down and chased or shooting and fighting. I swear on all that is holy I hate this mother fudging thing."

"Mother fudging," I echo, a real laugh finally bursting out. It seems like the wrong emotion at this moment. I rub the back of my neck, then wince as the bandage pulls at the wound.

"Dr. Legarde, I hate to ask you this..." I pause, realizing I don't want to delve into her obvious grief. Wanting to keep her ranting about her watch. There is something so normal and sweet about it, about *her*. "Do you have any idea where your father might have hidden the shipment?"

"Are you being serious?" She wheels on me, even the darkness unable to hide the fury blazing across her face. "You come into my life, whisk me off like a hostage on my own gosh-darned boat, drop this… this *bombshell* on me and then expect me to know where a boatload of drugs are?" Her voice cracks, sadness seeping through her fury.

"Probably a sub full of drugs, actually," I correct.

She makes a feral noise of frustration, her feet slapping against the fiberglass floor.

"Anything could be helpful," I add.

She steps closer and I hold up my hands, trying to look as non-threatening as possible.

"Just think about it. Maybe he hinted at something. Or there is a place, some location, where he traveled often." It sounds cold, but I don't know what else to say to her. "Anything you can tell me about your father could help." It sounds cold, but I don't know what else to say to her.

I'm not good at warm and cuddly.

I doubt I ever will be.

She taps her foot against the deck, starlight reflecting in her eyes as she considers me. "The only thing my dad did was take tourists fishing and diving, and look for the wreck with me."

I still. The wreck.

Is it as easy as that?

"What? Why is your face like that?" She leans down to me, her nose crinkling as she stares.

"The wreck? You really think this is about *that*?" Clearing my throat, I run my good hand through my hair. It's hard to think straight with her close enough to wrap my arms around.

"So you're telling me you know where I live, but you didn't bother to look up all my research?" She sighs, then looks to the sky. "Will anyone ever read my research?"

I laugh in spite of myself, and her gaze finds mine, a slight smile on her lips. "Your father was looking for the wreck with you, right?"

"Yeah, and if I had gotten that grant today, I could've found it. I know I could have. I would have earned tenure, made a mark for myself in academia. Heck, I would have *written* the history book. But nooooo, nope. Charlie had to run over a guy with a gun, and then I went and threw tequila in his eyes, and now drug smugglers and the government think I know where a bunch of crap I have nothing to do with is!"

A lead weight settles in my stomach. "Did your father go out a lot to look for it without you? How often do you think he looked for it?"

It would be a good cover, and I silently berate myself for not considering it before.

"Sometimes. Especially when I taught evening classes. You don't think he was looking for the wreck." Her voice is thick with disbelief. "You're saying when he was out there… when he was supposed to be looking for the wreck, he… he was running drugs. Or whatever. Working with them. The smugglers."

"'Whatever' is doing a lot of work there," I say slowly.

"It's not funny," she says. A hand scrubs down her face.

"He could've been." I stand.

Our bodies press together in the small space, but she doesn't step back, doesn't make any moves to distance herself from me.

I clear my throat, ignoring the dull throb of pain on my side. "Any chance he dropped any coordinates to, ah, the wreck? Or maybe something else?"

Smooth as fucking sandpaper. I wince at myself.

"No." The word is flat, final. She moves away, bracing herself against the metal deck railing.

"What was he like in the weeks leading up to his death?"

"Sure, why not interrogate me about that?" she says, throwing her arms up. "Let's just make this day as crappy as possible. Maybe I'll cry! Would you like that?"

"I would not like it if you cried. Not at all."

She seems startled by that, freezing in place.

I blow out a slow breath. "Were there any changes to his routine?"

She pauses, searching the starry night sky as though it holds the answers. "He was crabbing more. Brought me blue crab every night. But they're in season, that's not out of the ordinary… Well, not by much."

I step closer, her eyes now wider as though she, too, has the same thought.

"How many traps does he have out?"

"About thirty."

"That's a lot of crab."

"He has… he *had* a commercial license." The words turn thick. "It was a hobby. With crab as the result." She levels me with a glare.

"Did he leave you anything, any letters, anything at all, when he was killed?" I ask it gently as I can manage.

"He was killed? I thought…" Her face crumples.

"Most likely." No reason to lie to her. "June, I don't know how to break this to you easier. I don't know about you, but I want to make it out of this alive, and with any luck, find the lost sub before the smugglers do. We want it in the right hands, and not with them."

She nods once. Twice.

I inhale deeply, breathing in rhythm with her.

"The crab traps." She lifts her chin, her pretty brown eyes finding mine, wide with surprise.

"What about them?" I'm suddenly afraid to ask too much, afraid to ruin this momentary peace between us.

"For the record," she holds up a finger, "I am not sure I buy what you're saying about my dad willingly working with the smugglers." She spits out the last word. "But what if he *was* using the crab traps to leave me a message? About the wreck?" Her lips purse. "He did seem more invested in talking to me about them than he usually was."

"Then we'd have to find them."

I don't like that she doesn't believe me about her dad, but denial is a helluva drug, and I'm the last one to judge her on that.

Regardless, she's loyal. That means something to me. Always has.

"He might have left me coordinates for the traps. On his fishing spots list." Her hands shake as she pulls the wad of papers out of her dress pocket. "I guess it's a good thing you tried to steal it."

"Crab traps." Why not? It's a better lead than anything else I have.

"He loved puzzles. Loved this kind of thing. It would be like him…" She's talking to herself, riffling through the papers I tried to swipe off her fridge. "It would be like him to leave me clues and let me work it out for myself."

"Okay." I nod. "Then we need some sleep."

"Huh?" She tilts her head.

"Gotta be well-rested if we're gonna haul up traps all day tomorrow."

"We should go now," she says, her face pinching in irritation.

"Right. Because we want to pull crab traps into the boat in the dead of the night. That seem safe to you?"

She juts her chin up, then her gaze flicks to the bandage on my torso. "Fine. You probably do need your beauty sleep."

"You sure as hell don't," I blurt out. "Couldn't get any prettier."

Her jaw drops, and she stares at me. "What?"

"What?"

"Are you trying to hit on me?"

"Babe, if I was hitting on you, you'd know it." I am an idiot. Idiot.

"Right." She scoffs, and I'm glad the moon isn't any brighter, or she might be able to tell I'm flushing in embarrassment.

"I'll sleep up here. You can have the cabin," I offer.

"No." Her face pales against the dark fall of her hair.

"What?"

"No. I'll sleep up here."

"It will be more comfortable inside the cabin. There's no need to be polite."

"I'm not being *polite*. I'm telling you no." She crosses her arms over her chest.

"If you sleep down there, I'll be the first line of defense."

"If they get close enough to the boat to where you have to protect me, you'll be the last line of defense, not the first. Besides, I can protect myself. I don't need protection."

"Uh, yeah, you do." I roll my eyes, exasperation and exhaustion making my tone sharp.

She takes four steps, and hinges squeak as she lifts up one of the boat's banquette seats. The sound of plastic wrinkling is barely audible over the noise of the waves, followed by the unmistakable click of a magazine being loaded in a gun.

"Not this again." I can't help but laugh at her sheer audacity. "Listen, I've already been shot once today. That's my quota."

"I'm not sleeping down there," she says, taking a step toward me.

"You don't have to point a gun at me to get me to agree."

"Sure seems like it."

"Fine. You can sleep up here. With me," my lips say, with no regard for my brain or self-preservation.

"I'm not sleeping with you! You… you donkey." She gapes at me, but lowers the gun.

I bite my cheeks to keep from laughing. "That's not what I meant."

Though my heart races inside my chest at the sudden image of us together, her hair tickling my neck, my mouth trailing kisses across her jawline.

"We both sleep on deck. You can keep your gun. On one condition." And there go my lips, saying whatever the fuck they want again.

"What?" She tilts her head, the dim moonlight caressing her features.

"You tell me why you won't sleep down there."

A choked noise erupts from her mouth.

Shit. I made her cry after all.

CHAPTER
ELEVEN

JUNE

"I'M CLAUSTROPHOBIC."

I never explain why, and I'm not about to start now. It's been years, but I still sleep with the blinds open and the window cracked.

I still can't stand to shower.

Or walk too far into the closet. I took the door off the hinges as soon as I moved in.

My breathing shallows, chest rising and falling too fast. Silence stretches, heavy with the need to explain. The memories surface, bubbling up, waiting to explode off my tongue.

The heat of the closet. The shadow of the fan making the light flicker until I thought I'd go crazy. The ropes digging into my wrists.

The burns lasting for weeks, though the fear's lasted much longer.

The worst part was not knowing. Wondering if this would be the day they finally killed me. If I would ever be rescued. If anyone even cared I was gone.

If my father even knew I was missing.

It felt like months.

It was only six days.

Placing a hand on my side, Dean eases me onto the boat's seat and I sink onto it, clutching his forearm for balance. A cold sweat breaks over my skin, despite the heat of the night.

Dean's gone from my side, and I try to breathe normally, try to exist in this moment. I'm not trapped. I tip my chin up, looking at the stars in the clear night sky.

The engine dies before a splash signals Dean casting the anchor overboard. The boat lurches delicately as the anchor catches the murky bottom.

His eyes meet mine, dark and full of understanding.

Without a word, he hands a fresh water bottle to me.

I take it, tipping it and savoring the cool, clean water on my tongue, like it can wash away the bad memories.

Only then do I register that Dean's brought the cushions from the cuddy cabin, spreading them across the deck in a snug, makeshift pallet. I settle myself down on one, giving up.

He tosses the lone blanket over me. It's somewhat musty but soft, and his hand brushes my side as he tucks it around me.

The cushions squeak slightly as he lies down next to me.

The sound of him counting down from one hundred quietly, over and over, soothes me. Settles me. Until exhaustion claims me.

I wake at some point, as fingers of early morning pink across the horizon. I re-adjust, slinging the blanket aside, too warm.

A little too late, it hits me. The warmth curling through me isn't thanks to the barely rising sun.

It's thanks to Dean.

His strong, warm body cocoons mine. A muscled arm's tossed over my torso, his fingertips lightly grazing my wrist.

I can't quite bring myself to move away.

Eventually, the rhythm of his breathing and the sound of water against the hull lulls me back to sleep.

―――――

The sun sears across the horizon as I attempt to scramble up from the deck. The light fleece blanket tangles around my ankles, and I struggle for a moment before sinking against the rails.

I passed the heck out. My head throbs, and I wince as I remember the tequila.

The tequila definitely remembers me.

The rest of last night crashes over me and I sag, tired all over again.

"You're up." The deep pitch of Dean's voice rolls across the boat, and I spin on my heel, ignoring the heat spreading through my stomach.

"Did we cuddle?" I blurt out.

He cocks his head, white, even teeth glowing against dark stubble as he throws a half-smile at me. "If we did, it was probably just for warmth."

"Right," I echo.

It's already hot, and it takes a lot of energy not to smile at his easy joke, but I manage it.

Don't want him to get the wrong idea and think I liked cuddling him, or let him know I slept better with him around me than I have in a long time.

"Good morning," he says, and dang if that stubble doesn't make him look even more delicious.

"Hi." My voice is husky. Huskier than it should be.

Dean's eyes crinkle at the corners, his grin growing.

"How you feeling?" he asks, tilting his head.

"Fine. Wonderful. Never been better in my life. Love spilling all my trauma to a stranger after having my house blown up."

He arches an eyebrow, one hand gripping the hardtop roof of the cuddy cabin, the other arm cradling something against his chest. His bare chest.

Unf.

My throat bobs. A dull ache pounds against the back of my eyes. I close them briefly, pressing my palms against my eyelids.

"You sure? You don't look so good." The arm holding the roof flexes, and I try not to notice.

"A little hungover." I shrug. "Tired. Just girlie things girlies do after a normal night out."

"Girlie things," he repeats with a snort.

I grunt. I can't decide if I am mad at him or myself or maybe even at my dad.

I immediately bury the thought in guilt.

"I found rations." His eyes, despite the rising sun pinkening the sky all around them, remain fixed on me. Hungry. "There were some tiny toothbrushes in there, too."

"Oh?"

"Food should help. I bet you have a killer headache today." The distance between us shrinks, and Dean hands me a wrapped granola bar and a warm Gatorade. "Do you want to talk about it?"

Eyeing the makeshift pallet still on the cockpit deck, heat and embarrassment rush through me.

"About how I slept better than ever with you wrapped around me?" I ask awkwardly. Does he really want to talk about that? Why?

"Uh, I actually meant about your dad. Or the claustrophobia thing." Dean shifts, distinctly uncomfortable.

"I, uh," I fumble with the Gatorade until he takes it, easily twisting the cap off, stepping even closer. Close enough I can feel the heat from his skin. "I didn't need help with that."

"Uh-huh." He squints down, his eyes assessing. "Just thought I'd be nice," he says, holding the bottle out like a peace offering.

"Oh."

No doubt my brain is short-circuiting from the amount of gorgeous man flesh right in front of me. Golden skin, rippling six-pack, a light sheen of sweat only serving to further highlight a deep vee of muscles that are probably illegal somewhere.

I will not look lower than his face, I will not look lower than his face.

I am a paragon of hungover virtue.

I mentally pat myself on the back.

"Drink up. You look a little intense." He grins, and I manage not to choke on the Gatorade.

Last night's adrenaline must still be making me loopy. Is adrenaline also a sex hormone? Does it make people horny?

Sounds plausible.

I drink. And drink. In fact, I finish the bottle. Dean picks up the cushions one by one, securing them under his arm before putting each back with fastidious care.

He's taking care of me.

Feeding me, calming me down last night, being a gentleman.

Certainly a better partner than most of the men I've woken up to.

My lips twist to the side as I consider it. Sure, he wasn't really able to get up and just leave my bed... seeing as how we're on a boat in the middle of the Gulf of Mexico.

Still. Gratitude wells, a deep-seated wave of emotion nearly overwhelming me.

The bar must be in hell. I snort.

When he bends over, though, showing off his spectacular government-issue butt, I decide the bar has been decidedly raised.

I refocus all my attention on keeping the granola bar from disintegrating before I can eat it.

Not nearly as fun, but definitely safer.

"June, if you want to talk about it..." The cushions click back into place on the bench seat.

"It meant nothing, probably just an involuntary reaction," I snap, then wince, not meaning it to come out so rudely. Especially when he has been nothing but nice this morning. There's not a snowball's chance in hell I'm going to talk about how we may or may not have been cuddling.

For warmth!

"Your panic attack seemed pretty serious. But yeah. I guess that's normal for a civilian after what we went through last night." He scratches his stubble with a free hand before ducking back into the cuddy cabin with the rest of the cushions and blanket.

Okayyyy.

He didn't want to talk about how we woke up entwined, or that I was staring at his half-naked body like he was a piece of meat and I was a starving dinosaur.

"I'm going to brush my teeth." I start to stamp around him, but he performs some kind of magic trick and the tiny toothpaste and travel brush appear in his hand. Scowling, I grab it from him.

"Thanks." I bite the word off, and he snorts in amusement.

"There was a tiny bottle of shaving cream and a razor too, but I wasn't sure if you wanted to shave your beard or talk about last night."

I scoff at him. "Rude."

It's easier to call him rude than admit what it is we're dancing around.

Talk about it? Talk about that I wanted to make out with him last night until I lost all self-control? Or about the fact that he even might just be a nice guy when I sort-of want to hate him for calling my father a criminal?

I give my teeth the most aggressive teeth brushing they've ever hand, delicately taking the proffered water bottle from Dean to swish and spit.

"Don't look at me," I tell him, then spit overboard.

"I wouldn't dream of it, princess," he drawls back.

Sure enough, a quick glance tells me he's turned his back to me. He *is* nice.

I should be nice back. I set the toiletries down on top of the control panel and stare at his broad back, before finally making up my mind to call a truce.

"How's your shoulder?" I look down to where he's still putting things away in the cabin.

His fingers tentatively touch the bandaged wound. "I'm sore, but not bad. You did a good job patching it up."

"Oh. That's good."

"Why? You worried about me, Legarde?"

"Dr. Legarde. And no. Maybe… Professional curiosity."

"I didn't realize PhDs had professional medical curiosity."

"Okay fine, I was a little worried," I grumble, out of sorts. Why is he so good at getting under my skin?

He grins over his shoulder at me.

I scrub a hand over my face, forgetting about the granola wrapper still in my hand. Dumping crumbs down my shirt.

Incredibly rude of him to be gorgeous *and* nice.

Selfish.

Simply thinking about it made my head hurt worse. The start of a killer hangover, thanks to Charlie's margarita obsession—

Holy hell. Charlie.

"Do you think Charlie is okay?" I blurt out, too loud. "They wouldn't have gone after her, would they?"

"She's fine," Dean says, sounding completely sure of himself.

"How do you know?" I squint at him.

A beat of silence passes, and a muscle in his temple twitches. "Pierce would have made sure of it."

Something about his tone bothers me.

A sudden vibration distracts me, and I blink a few times before my eyes dart to my watch.

"The bilge pump." I scramble to the driver's seat, flipping the bilge switch. Fresh relief courses through me at the whine of the mechanism starting up. Thank goodness the boat's battery hasn't died, otherwise we'd be floundering in deep water.

Under the sea.

Flounder.

And we're about to be searching for crab. Might even encounter a seagull. All I need now is red hair and a seashell bra.

"Mermaid tails and coconut shells." I slap my hand over my mouth as a hysterical high-pitched laugh trickles out of my mouth.

Breathing slowly, I finally regain control of myself, and the gravity of the situation truly hits me.

This is so bad.

Endless water sparkles around the boat, equally endless blue sky stretches overhead. And it's just the two of us, on this very old boat, hunted by Russian smugglers.

All of this is so very bad.

"What is with that?" Dean re-appears, the cabin door slamming shut behind him.

"With what? Like you don't laugh hysterically at sudden vivid visions of yourself as a princess thanks to stress and a slight hangover? Sure, sure."

"No." He raises his eyebrows. "Why don't you cuss? Though I'm open to discuss your imaginary roleplay."

"Oh. That."

"Yes, that, though discussing roleplay isn't off the table, is it?"

"I'm going to choose to ignore that," I tell him.

"If that's what you want, princess."

I start to tell him to not call me that, but it's better than babe, so I switch tracks at the last minute.

"Cursing is unprofessional." I stand up taller, trying to command professionalism, as though I can manually override my now dirty off-the-shoulder dress, and beneath it, a very professional bikini doubling as underwear.

Multi-functional.

"I don't know about that," he grins at me. "I've heard some pretty creative ones in my line of work."

He nods at the captain's chair, and I toss the empty granola wrapper in a small bucket and sit down. "Where are the crab traps?"

"Where's my gun? I noticed it was missing this morning."

"Back under the seat. Why, you think you need it? Still don't trust me, princess?"

There's a witty retort on the tip of my tongue, but I really look at him, taking my time. His face is handsome enough to set off alarms, his body a weapon in its own right, a fact I know all too well after holding it close as we ran from…

My mind struggles, the previous day's events crashing over me.

If he is telling the truth, my father was involved with the smugglers.

My heart hurts at the logical possibility that he might be right. That my father worked for the Russians.

I closed my eyes.

So the question remains, can I trust Dean?

Can I afford not to?

"We need to get the anchor up." It wasn't an answer, but it would have to be enough.

"Aye-aye, princess." He winks, a slow grin spreading across his face. That treacherous dimple appears again.

Climbing up and over the bow, his broad back bunches as he wrenches the anchor free from the sea floor. Mud and muck drips off it, and he dips it in the water until it comes back clean, carefully stowing it back in the compartment.

Water droplets cling to his skin, and the whole show probably burns off the rest of my hangover.

Watching Dean Evans competently work around the boat is better than any espresso I've ever had, and I am fully awake now.

Yikes.

I am also in so much fudging trouble.

CHAPTER
TWELVE

DEAN

CLENCHING MY JAW, I swirl the remnants of the blue Gatorade in my hand. Sweat rolling between my shoulders, as the latest crab trap buoy bobs on the surface.

Three down.

We found the first three traps handily, right on the coordinates June's dad left her three weeks ago. Nothing in them but blue crab. Crab we now have in spades, crab we'll have to toss back or find a half dozen other people to share with.

Luckily, I know just who to call.

Shaking my head, I put down the Gatorade, ready to haul up more crab. The late morning sun beats down on us, and it's hotter than hell. Unzipping the bottom half of my pants, creating shorts, I wad the pieces up and toss them into the cabin. Then inspect the scrape on my chest. It's healing nicely, already scabbed over.

Damn, we've been lucky.

"Those have to be the most ridiculous shorts I've ever seen." Her small laugh accompanies the criticism, a slight smile spreading on her face.

"They're practical."

"They're absurd."

"Says the woman wearing a bikini and a dress while being hunted down by so-called bad dudes." My mind snags on the memory of searching her yesterday, of trying not to be an asshole while trying to make sure she didn't fulfill her promise of shooting me in the nuts.

"They fit enough ammo yesterday, didn't they?" She tilts her head. "And don't even get me started on the travesty of women's pockets."

"Fair point." I shrug, gaze wandering over her backside as she steers, slowing as we reach the crab trap.

June eases the big boat close enough for me to easily reach out and hook it. She cuts the engine and flips the bilge switch again. Smiling to herself, she launches herself up the bow, dropping the anchor. Despite the fact she's barely spoken to me, she seems happy.

Hell, I'd be happy too if I had someone to do the backbreaking work for me. Hauling these crab pots is hard, dirty work.

I drag my eyes away from her legs and focus on the trap.

Seagulls swoop above the boat and several pelicans drift in the water alongside us, long beaks ready at a moment's notice in hopes of a free meal.

With a grunt, I grab the barnacle-crusted rope, hauling the trap up hand over hand. Without gloves, my hands are worse for wear, but it is what it is.

Behind me, several mesh sacks writhe as dozens of crabs from our previous catches struggle to get free.

June's eyes misted when I suggested dumping the crabs back in.

That was all it took for me to agree to keep part of our haul. A now much larger haul. My shoulders burn, this pot fuller than the last ones.

"Sure you don't want me to do it?" June twirls the end of her hair, nibbling her bottom lip.

"No," I manage, kicking the spare rope out of the way. "I'm

fine." My wound seers from the strain, but pain is nothing new. "Can't have the princess getting tired."

She makes a strangled noise of frustration at that, and I grin.

I like getting under her skin.

I probably like it a little too much.

I'd like to touch that skin again, and every passing minute with her on this boat has me considering what it would be like.

The top of the trap breaks the surface, and several gulls dive-bomb, splashing saltwater across my face. I grunt again, heaving the trap up the side of the boat. The wire frame scrapes against the fiberglass hull. The trap contents come into view, and I raise a brow.

It's full enough—a dozen or so adult crabs bubbling as they hit the air, a stunned catfish flopping around—but it feels heavier than the other traps.

"Huh," June says, close enough now that when the gulf breeze catches the ends of her ponytail, the bright scent of her lemony shampoo teases me.

"There," I say pointing to the middle of the trap. Surrounded by bad-tempered crabs, the bait pot holds something new. "Look."

"It's a dry box for diving." June's voice comes out strangled, and I cut my gaze to her. She looks stunned… stunned and sad. "Waterproof, so you can store stuff in it. Sorry, you probably know that. Oh my god. He really found the ship." She takes a sharp breath, her excitement chasing away the storm clouds of her grief.

"It might not be the wreck, princess," I say quietly.

"Why didn't he just tell me he found it?" she asks at the same time, and I briefly wonder how someone so intelligent can be so deep in denial.

"I say we find out what he has in here." I squat over the crab trap, my pulse accelerating. So close now, so close to finding this thing and getting my reputation back, getting my business off the ground.

"Let's do it." She nods at me, opening a mesh sack.

In one smooth motion, I unhinge the top and dump the crabs in.

"You're getting good at that." Her voice is slightly choked, and when I glance up at her in confusion, her eyes are wide, pupils slightly dilated.

The fish flops onto the deck. Its gills work overtime, trying to suck in water that isn't there.

I grab for him, trying to get him back in the water.

"Don't—" June exclaims, her palm squeezing my bicep. God, her hand feels good.

"Worried about me, princess?" I croon, then throw the fish overboard. Stunned, it floats for a second before swimming into the dark green waters below. "I know what I'm doing."

"Catfish have poisonous barbs, I just didn't want you to—"

"Didn't want me to what?" I pause, watching the way the climbing sun shines against the dark fall of her hair, new freckles sprinkled like stars across her nose.

The way her chest rises and falls as she takes hectic breaths.

Either she doesn't want me to know what's in the crab trap, or *she* doesn't want to know what's in it. Especially considering how firmly she's stuck to the idea that her dad was innocent in all of this, like he didn't bring the smugglers down on her head.

"Are you worried about me, princess?" I raise one eyebrow, giving her my best sexy grin.

Because I know being annoyed with me will distract her from whatever's going on in that brilliant, pretty head of hers.

Sure enough, her expression goes flat with annoyance, and I chuckle at it.

"Want to open it?" I gesture to the dive box in the bait pot.

June fidgets.

"Fine." She cringes though, biting her lip. "I don't know if I want to know." The words are bleak, and there's a sudden breakable quality about the woman that makes me want to draw her into my arms, to keep her safe.

I don't want her to cry.

"Princess, if you want me to handle your box, I am all too happy to oblige."

That fragile quality turns to outrage as she processes what I've just said.

"You're out of control."

"Just trying to keep you on your toes," I tell her honestly. "You okay?"

"No." She shakes her head, then fixes me with a steely gaze. "I'm not. If what you're accusing my father of is true, then I'm about to find out, and I'm not sure what to do with that. Now get the goddamn box out or I'll do it myself." She rounds on me, the panic bleeding out of her features, replaced by steel and anger.

"Goddamn, is it?" I blow out a breath, suppressing a smile. "Well, I had no idea you felt so strongly about it, *princess*."

"You really are a donkey sometimes, Evans." Her nose scrunches up.

"Just sometimes?" I smirk, flipping the trap over and unlatching the bait pot, indulging the impulse to keep ribbing her. "Or is it just that you like my assets so much you're afraid to use that word?" I tease.

"There's nothing special about your butt. Not that I've looked at it."

"Mm-hmm. Sure."

June's delicate features are set, her eyes tight and focused. If not a bit angry at me. *Good.* I need her angry. It will be easier to keep her at arm's length if she stays annoyed with me.

I need to keep her there.

She's too nice to keep any closer.

The remains of whatever godawful mixture her father baited the pot with spill out on the white decking, the violently yellow dry box following.

June reaches for it, but I'm faster.

With one last look at her fuming face, I unscrew the cap. It opens easily, the suction that kept the inside dry popping as the seal gives way.

"What the fuck?" I shake my head in frustration.

I dump the open dry box into June's waiting hand. She stares into the cylinder with furrowed brows, then pours the sea glass onto her other hand.

Smooth green pebbles glitter gently in her palm.

Eyes watery, she stares at them a full minute before turning her attention to the horizon, resolve etching her features.

I was right.

She does know something.

June Legarde is the key to the whole damn thing.

I thought I'd be happier about my hunch being right.

Instead, I feel like shit. June knows just enough to be dangerous to herself, knows enough that I need to keep her with me instead of keeping her safe.

"What does it mean to you?" I keep my voice low, gentle. Calming.

"It means he found something. It means he wants me to go somewhere." Her dark laugh stills the air. "Although I guess I should use past tense. He doesn't want anything now, does he?"

"June, I…"

"You can tell me whatever you want about him, you know that? You can tell me he was a bad man. That he hurt people trafficking with the Russians." She shifts her focus back to me. "But he was my father, Dean. He was *my* father. And he took care of me when no one else could. I loved him." She looks tired, drawn. "He might have made some mistakes, but you can*not* take him away from me." Her knuckles are white on the yellow box.

I move toward her, drawn by the fury, the angst in her eyes.

I want to soothe her pain.

"I'm not trying to take him away from you." My fingers feather over her wrist. "I am here for a job. This," I point to the sea glass, "is the best lead I have. I feel lucky that the lead is… you, June."

Her eyes widen as I say her name. Not babe, not Dr. Legarde, and not princess.

"June." I repeat.

Her breath catches. For a second, my brain short-circuits, the need to kiss her, to taste her lips overriding any sort of sense I have left.

She buries her head in my chest, her ponytail tickling against my skin, chest heaving as she lets out one sob. Two.

Hot tears mingle with my sweat.

I hold her close, burying my nose in her citrus-scented hair, breathing her in.

We stand like that, holding each other, until she stops crying. Her breath slows, gentle and warm against the bare skin of my chest.

I wonder if she can hear how loud my heart's beating against my ribs.

Kissing her would be so easy. A small tilt of her face is all it would take.

The dull roar of an outboard motor fills the air and June freezes, then pulls back, every line of her face etched in fear.

"Get into the cabin and stay there." The words clip out of my mouth. The authority I tuck away around Pierce and the DEA stream from me like this is another Marine op.

To her credit, June doesn't argue.

She doesn't obey, either.

My jaw drops as she tugs her dress over her head, revealing tanned, smooth skin and a barely-there purple bikini.

I can hardly think straight at the sight of her.

"What are you doing?" I finally manage.

The boat's definitely coming closer.

"Sunbathing. Seems like a good time for a distraction. You know, if it's the bad guys?"

"Did you hit your head last night? Get in the cabin, princess."

June stabs a finger in my chest, exactly where she was snuggled up just seconds ago.

I lick my lips, unable to look away from her. The way her body moves with the rolling of the boat is incredibly distracting.

"Listen, buddy, you said you need me. That means you don't get to boss me around and tell me to get in the mother-loving cabin. My boat, my rules. I'm no use if I have a panic attack."

Her tears are gone, eyes now blazing.

"My op, my rules." It sounds stupid, repeating her words like we're having some kindergarten spat on the playground.

"Oh, are you paying me? I'm part of the 'op' now? Do I get some kind of finder's fee if we find your stupid drugs? And what if you turn out to be wrong, huh? What if this is about the *Santu Espiritu*?"

"It's not about the fucking wreck, princess." I shake my head, the noise of the outboard motor intensifying. "Either way, I don't want you to get shot."

"I don't want that either." She frowns.

"Then get in the damned cabin."

But June winks at me as she heaves herself onto the catwalk, walking the narrow strip to the bow, then unrolls a towel I'd somehow been too distracted to notice. In one smooth motion, she sinks onto the towel, rolling over onto her stomach, looking for all the world like she's been there all day.

The glint of the shotgun shines from under the towel.

Clever girl.

CHAPTER
THIRTEEN

JUNE

SECONDS TICK by and the boat approaches, bigger than the *Betty*, from the looks of it. Definitely nicer and newer, not that that's hard to accomplish. My breath comes in short bursts, my pulse somewhere around a hummingbird's.

I keep one hand on the shotgun under the towel, the other under my chin.

That's me, yep. Not a care in the world. Except, you know, the whole being hunted by drug smugglers thing.

The boat rocks. A shadow passes over me.

Dean's stalking toward me, murder in his eyes.

"What are you doing?" I hiss.

"Adapting to the plan."

"You don't have a plan. This was *my* plan." A good one, too.

He shakes his head. "Fine, princess. Have it your way. I'm adapting to *your* plan."

"I only have one towel."

"So? Way I see it, that makes it even easier to sell."

The incoming boat motor roars loud enough now to drown out the squawking gulls overhead.

With any luck, Dean will slip and fall overboard.

"It's hot as heck on the deck. Not my problem if you want to burn your abs, though."

"No, it's hot as hell. And besides, I thought we could share." His grin is slow, sexy, and all too tempting. "That is, if you have room on there for all the abs you've noticed." He trails one hand over his stomach, and I look away quickly as he goes lower, to the band of his shorts.

"Excuse me?" I splutter.

Smooth, June, real smooth.

"You said distraction. Let's give them one, you know, make it believable."

My eyes narrow, but I don't have time to react.

Dean's body covers mine, blocking the heat of the sun... but replacing it with an entirely different kind of heat. I watch with rounded eyes as he holds himself up in a plank position perfect enough to make any Pilates devotee jealous. His arm snakes around my waist, and before I can throw it off, he's flipped me onto my back. His other cradles the back of my head, tangling in my hair.

Ooohhhh.

This is nice.

I melt into him, living for the way he makes me feel safe and protected.

Desirable.

I can't look away, can't even think about the sound of the boat drawing closer. The half-smile on his lips, his intense focus on me, makes the world fall away. My breasts graze his bare chest, his knees on either side of me.

It isn't until my hands are tangled around his neck that I realize he now has the shotgun. The whole thing a ruse, designed to get the gun from me. Again.

"Ugh, you mother—" I start to yell, completely annoyed.

"Shhh," he tells me, and when his lips faintly brush against mine, I can't help but comply.

Out of shock. That's all.

The sound of the approaching motor dies, replaced by Jimmy Buffett crooning about fins on the other boat's speakers.

Even the incongruous sound of Jimmy Buffett can't stop the desire pooling deep inside. Dean flashes a full smile at me, triumph in his eyes at having the literal upper hand. Unwilling to be outdone, to lose this little battle, I make a split-second decision.

Tugging his head down, I feel a flash of victory as his breath ghosts across my lips, shock clear on his face. Closing my eyes, I press my mouth against his, nibbling his lower lip, throwing a leg over his waist.

His mouth opens slightly, and I moan against him.

It unleashes something in him, and he lowers himself further onto me.

Oooh boy. I'm in trouble now.

The pressure from his big body is delicious against mine, and I writhe, trying to escape the ache screaming for more.

"I don't know, man, it doesn't look like he needs help," a southern voice drawls. "Evans, you need a hand?"

What. The. Fudge. I push him away, staring at him with pure hatred in my eyes. He knows them?

"You *donkey*," I mutter, furious. Mostly at myself, because damn, that was a good kiss.

"You liked it. I liked that little noise you made," Dean tells me, not even bothering to look up at the men calling to him from the other boat.

Well, I won the battle, but at what price?

"Hell, I'd give her a hand," a second speaker says before a chorus of laughter.

The price of absolute, utter embarrassment.

Dean practically vaults from the bow, the searing heat of his body replaced with the cold slap of instant regret.

"Shut up, Thompson," Dean barks, and the laughter dies. "How did you guys get here so fast?"

Propping myself up on an elbow, I shield my eyes, attempting to see just *who* is on the other boat. To see who knows Dean enough to make fun of him for kissing me.

Oh god, the kissing. Unf.

Dean stands at my side, a grim expression on his face as I take in the other boat. Their fancy double decker cabin cruiser pulls alongside the *Betty*, giving me the perfect view of the hulking bodies still smirking at us, all built similar to Dean. Like they've spent years of their lives packing on muscle.

He's glaring at them. He looks pissed.

Huh. Not entirely happy to see them, then, is he?

It shouldn't make my stomach flutter with butterflies.

Reaching back lazily, my hand lands on the barrel of the shotgun. In one smooth motion, just like my father taught me, I'm sitting up, the butt of the gun resting in the hollow of my shoulder.

"Woah, woah, woah. Uh, Evans, your girl is loaded for bear." The man with the Southern accent, reflective aviators showing just how good a shot I have, tilts his head to where I sit. He raises his hands, his eyebrows joining them.

"I'm not his girl," I grind out. I nudge the gun sideways until the other man on the boat raises his hands as well. "And who the heck are you?"

Dean gives an exasperated sigh that I promptly ignore.

"We're the heckin' cavalry, darlin'." The one who said he'd give me a hand smiles. I move the gun to him, and his eyes widen slightly, darting nervously between me and Dean.

"The cavalry better keep their hands to themselves." I shoot a look up at Dean, who appears to be suppressing a laugh.

That is about enough of that and his stupid dimple.

"Is something funny about this, Dean?" I aim a kick at the back of his knee, but he dodges before it lands. "Who are they, and how the hell did they know where to find the *Betty*?"

"Don't be pissed, June. I radioed them while you were asleep with our coordinates. The one in the glasses is Thorne. Thompson's the jerk."

His little wave doesn't stop me from keeping the gun leveled at him. I grin at him, but it's not a very nice one.

He pales a little.

Ha.

"They're part of my team. They're assisting on this. Trust me, we'll want the help."

That's the problem, though. Trusting him.

If I do, it means admitting he might be right about my father—about his involvement with the Russian smugglers.

My throat tightens, the ache in my chest returning full force.

"Men, this is Dr. Legarde."

"Oh, so not princess, now, huh?" I mutter, low enough so that only he can hear me.

"You're not princess to them," he says roughly.

The other men dip their heads, their eyes never leaving my face, telegraphing the possibility of violence you wouldn't see coming until it was too late.

"They're not DEA." They look like a CrossFit gym and Dwayne Johnson had babies. Nothing like Pierce.

Why didn't he radio his partner? Where the hell is Charlie?

Unease nestles inside me.

"No, we're not DEA," Thorne offers, his bright blue aviators glinting in the sun. "I see you've got a bushel of blue crab back there. Looks like y'all have had quite a morning. Sorry if we spooked you, ma'am, but would you mind lowering the gun?"

Ma'am. Definitely military. Or at least used to be… maybe even ex-Marines. My mouth twists to the side.

"Where's his partner? Where's Charlie, huh?"

"Evans trusts us. Charlie's fine. I'm sure he'll be in touch with his DEA *handler* as soon as he's sure you're both safe." Thompson spits the word out, his mouth curling with something like disgust.

Handler?

"How do you know Charlie is fine?"

"She's with Pierce, isn't she?" Dean answers. "She's safe, princess."

Thompson's eyes tighten slightly at his response.

I dare a glance at Dean. A quick confirmation nod from him, and I automatically lower the barrel.

It's like my body knows I should trust him even when my head's fighting it.

My hands shake from clutching the gun tight, but I hide it. Pretending I'm fine. The men loose a collective sigh of relief before tethering the boats together and making small talk, as though I hadn't been about to shoot each of them.

"That's a good haul of crab, y'all thinkin' bout sharing, or what?" Thompson asks. "Be a shame to waste it."

"If you play your cards right." Dean hops off the catwalk and into the cockpit and I stand stiffly, the shotgun still at my side. I wrap the towel around me, all too aware of the bare expanse of skin still electrified from Dean's attention.

Beneath the men's gentle ribbing and catching up, there is an undercurrent of unease. They're ready to descend into violence at the drop of a hat.

They're built for it.

Carefully, I balance the towel and gun, stepping down from the boat's catwalk and into the cockpit. Bending, I retrieve my hastily abandoned dress. Conversation slows to a stop as I unwrap the towel to throw the dress back on.

Ugh.

Distraction from the bad guys in theory is one thing. Being the center of attention of all the men now idly chatting is another. Men who've seen me kissing Dean Evans, resident donkey, is yet another.

Heat spreads across my face, moving down my chest and neck. Dean snaps the towel up, blocking my body from view. Conversation restarts, and I dare a look up at Dean, grateful for the assist.

He's glowering at them.

I've read the word before, of course, but seeing Dean perform it, all hard lines and flinty stare, it's now indelibly attached to the syllables. My own personal Dean Pictionary.

My stomach clenches.

No, not my own personal anything.

I can't risk catching feelings for a man like this. In a situation like this, where we're literally running from smugglers.

My chest heaves.

Dean's eyebrow rises, a muscle twitching in his temple. "You okay?"

"I'll pretend."

Dean freezes, his gaze going glacial before reverting his attention back to the newcomers.

Glower.

"Well, you gonna tell her why we're here? What's the play, Evans?" Thompson's arms flex as he crosses them over his chest.

I tug the hem of the dress down and plop into the captain's chair, stretching my legs up onto the console, shotgun across my lap. Waiting.

"They're here for backup." Dean says, throwing the towel on the bench.

"Pierce isn't enough?"

They all avoid looking at me.

"Did Pierce seem like enough after what happened yesterday?" Dean asks, no gentleness in his tone, all firm.

I shiver, remembering the sound of the explosion, the feeling of firing the shotgun at actual human beings. The way they fell when the pellets tore into their bodies.

"No, but you said Cha—"

"I'm sure Charlie is fine." Dean sounds sure, but I squint up at him. "We'll rendezvous with them later."

"Fine." As though I have a choice. Still, his confidence that Charlie is okay, that my friend is safe, soothes me, just a little. "So I guess you brought the entire squadron of Mattel Military Ken Dolls in because you don't trust him."

Thompson chuckles. "Does that make you Barbie? Thought

she was a blonde. Besides, we're all GI Joes over here," he says, puffing his chest out like some deranged peacock.

The twitching muscle near Dean's eye goes into overdrive.

"Why don't you tell us about what that sea glass in the dry box meant?" Dean's voice is slow, a deliberate rasp. Like he's trying to maintain control but losing the battle.

"Yeah right, so you can leave me behind and take your band of merry military spec ops men to find my wreck? Or drugs, or whatever." I level him with a stare. "Either way—" My voice breaks, because I've just admitted it out loud.

That my dad must have been involved in this crap.

"Either way," I continue, "the *Santu Espiritu* will be *my* find. I've spent a decade looking for that treasure and I'm not about to give it up to some bossy know-it-all."

I don't exactly trust Dean, but I'm not about to be left out.

Besides, he said I was the key.

I'll be my own leverage. I lift my chin, waiting for him to tell me no. Expecting it.

"If this has something to do with your ship, and not the *shipment* we're after, then by all means, take the credit. We're not interested in the wreck." Dean glares at me. And dang, even like that, he looks hot.

"Stop glowering at me."

"Glowering? What?" He shakes his head. "Don't try to distract me, princess. You don't know enough about this world and what you're asking to walk into."

"You don't get to boss me around. I already told you, my boat, my rules."

The men on the other boat still. As though I've crossed a major line.

I seize on the idea. I can use this.

"These clowns are used to taking orders from you. They don't like that I'm not falling in line." I tilt my head, considering. "Lemme guess, you all served together, and you were in charge.

They come when you call, so you're all still working together, likely all at the same firm."

Thorne looks surprised, but Thompson wears a huge grin.

Dean says nothing. Just glares. *Glowers.*

"Tell me I'm wrong." I can't seem to stop pushing.

No one answers, but Thorne shifts from foot to foot.

"What do I hear?" I ask, cupping a hand around my ear. "Oh, that's right. Plausible deniability. My father taught me more than how to shoot a gun." It's my turn to glare at Dean. "Besides, not one of you knows these waters better than I do. I've built a career out of researching the reefs and sandbars the wreck could be at. All that's been stopping me is money and manpower." I give Dean a smug look. "Now… well, now? It looks like I have both."

"Woman's got a point, boss," Thompson drawls.

"It's Dr. Legarde to you," Dean snaps.

"I'm coming, whether you like it or not." I look up at Dean, taking in the tendons tight in his neck, and I stand. "And I'm an asset."

"You're a liability, princess." The boat rocks, punctuating his words.

"I can handle myself," I say, raising the barrel of the gun. Just enough so he knows I'm serious.

He turns on me, gently pushing the shotgun barrel down, and I let him. A little frisson of excitement passes through me.

"Fine. But when I tell you to jump, you ask how high." Dean draws himself up to his full height. Which is really very tall.

"Why would I need to jump?" I shouldn't bait him.

I can't seem to help it.

"And when I tell you to hide, you hide."

"Hide? What, you didn't like our distraction?" I bat my eyelashes.

He grunts. Thompson lets out a low laugh, even taciturn Thorne chuckling.

"Those are my conditions," Dean finally manages.

Gotcha.

Lifting a finger, I give him a lazy salute.

"Now, what the hell does the sea glass mean?"

I swallow my first reply, words passing the lump in my throat. "June?"

"It means we're going to a beach and having ourselves a crab boil," I say, handing him the shotgun.

He immediately takes the shell out of the chamber.

"I'm guessing you aren't going to tell me what beach ahead of time?" Dean's eyes narrow.

"You're catching on," I say in a sing-song voice. "But I'll tell you where you and your band of merry military men can pick up a propane tank and the rest of the boil supplies. Ever heard of Wal-Mart?"

Thompson guffaws. "I like you, Dr. Legarde." He rubs his hands together and claps a hand on Thorne's shoulder. "Alright, doc, you make the list, we'll do the shopping. But when I get back, I wanna hear all about this treasure ship you're huntin' for. Deal?"

"Deal." They'll regret asking, probably fall asleep as I drone on and on. My students certainly do from time to time. "And you don't need a list. All we have is crabs. Get everything else." I shrug.

"You got it. Until then, you two lovebirds can work out your issues." Thompson grins.

Lovebirds.

The word sends a little thrill through me until I catch Dean's glacial stare. That muscle in his forehead working overtime.

That kiss? Had to be pure acting.

A distraction.

A long sigh pulls from my chest, and I roll my eyes skyward.

No more kissing.

CHAPTER
FOURTEEN

DEAN

"LOVEBIRDS? IN HIS DREAMS," she retorts.

June throws my men a self-satisfied smile, like a cat who's gotten the cream and the canary. But a blush blooms on her cheeks, and I bite back a grin of my own.

Thorne and Thompson laugh quietly, sharing an amused glance. I still can't quite bring myself to believe how quickly June managed to turn the tables on me.

"She's sure got your number, Evans. We'll rendezvous with supplies at the drop point." Thorne pauses, eyebrows rising. "Once you find out what that is, of course. Here's your sat phone, try not to blow it up this time." He lobs the black satellite phone, and I catch it one handed before clipping it onto a beltloop.

June grins, her eyelashes batting, a mischievous glint in her eyes.

"Oof, Evans, I can stay here if you'd rather go into port." Thompson claps his hands over his chest, as though he's been struck.

My chest tightens, and I swallow against the sudden envy, counting down from ten on reflex.

"Easy, boss. We'll be back. Just send us the coordinates." Thorne shifts, taking up the wheel, shooting me a warning look. I must look as pissed as I feel.

Thompson, however, grins like a shark, unwrapping the ties from the boat cleats and shoving off.

Employees, she pegged that one right.

Insubordinate employees.

She's even smarter than I imagined, much quicker on the uptake than the DEA analysts gave her credit for in the sparse bio. A bio I must've done a shit job reading, considering her shipwreck hunt—no, obsession—hadn't even registered.

But how did she miss her dad's involvement with the smugglers?

"Hmmph." The innocuous noise speaks volumes.

Smugness rolls from her skin.

I don't need to look down to see June's self-satisfied expression.

She might've won this battle, but she won't win the war.

The thought tugs at me. Everything with my ex—with Fiona— was a constant battle. Especially when I found out she was under deep cover. Nothing more than a honey trap. A high-value target, that's what the government pulling her strings told her I was, and she played her part well.

My stomach turns, and I close my eyes.

Nothing was real with her, our instant chemistry, the way she said my name... even her own name. All just some minor battle in an information war that cost me my military credibility and confidence. My heart races, the memories needling me, and I flex my hands, looking at the water. Foam forms on the crests of rolling waves, and I take a deep breath.

June is not Fiona. June is not out to get me, out to use me in any way. I know that. No matter how much my learned distrust nags at me—it lies.

I trust June.

Mostly.

Not that it matters, since I'm not in a relationship with her.

Haha. I can almost hear my therapist telling me to celebrate the small victory. *Score one for team trust*. The small progress surprises me.

That June Legarde, PhD and princess, is the one to elicit such a feeling—*that* surprises me more.

"You okay?" June looks up at me, her full lips quirking in a smile as she tosses her ponytail over a shoulder.

I exhale, counting down. "Yeah, I think I am."

"Ready to go to the beach?"

"Let's do it." A corner of my mouth kicks up.

The props of the other boat spin to life, sending a white capped wake behind it as they maneuver back towards mainland Texas.

"Well?" She pokes me in the chest, challenge in her gaze. "You just going to stare at me all day, or are we going to get moving?"

Grunting noncommittally, a bizarre, unwelcome emotion courses through me. *Off-kilter*. Having my men around should make me feel *better*. But the way they looked at June, especially Thompson with his wolfish grin, irritated me. Made me... jealous.

"What's the name of your little man-squad? Where're your female employees?" Her finger taps against my pec again. I really shouldn't like it so much—shouldn't want her to keep touching me.

"They're not a man-squad," I say. I catch her hand, and her eyes widen. "And there are female employees."

I just don't want to tell her who, exactly.

June's eyes narrow, and she tugs her hand from mine.

My fingers flex as if searching for her again.

"What, you don't trust a woman to get the job done? Is that why she's not here? Is that why you gave me your little 'jump when I say jump' macho-man bull?" Her voice drops an octave, and she holds her arms out at her sides like a monkey. "And the 'hide when I say hide' speech? Gotta have man parts to hang tough?" A wave splashes against the side of the boat, and her lips press together.

"No." My voice is short, the syllable clipped.

"Well, what's the company name?"

"That's not what I look like. Where is this coming from?"

No way am I going to fess up to my trust issues with women. Fiona is off the table.

"Man parts?" I repeat, my brain catching up. "Princess, what the hell are you talking about? You're thinking about my man parts?"

I grin at her, full of mischief.

Her eyes go wide, and then narrow. "How dare you."

"You brought it up. And you kissed me, too."

"It was a diversionary tactic," she barks.

A laugh hurtles out of me, and she just glares. It's not tough, though. No, she looks fucking adorable. Delicious.

"Lemme guess, your company name is probably something really toxic and masculine." She purses her lips, tapping the same finger that was just on my bare skin against her chin. "Guns and Money, Inc."

I press my lips together.

"Is that a no? How about Hired Muscle, LLC, is that it?" She wears a mock serious expression, but her eyes glitter with humor.

At my expense.

I love it.

"Bodyguards R Us?"

"That's the one."

"You want me to trust you, but you won't even tell me the name of your company?" She makes a noise of mock distress, shaking her head.

"You're having such a good time making fun of me, I didn't want to ruin it for you." Overhead, a seagull squawks before winging low over the water.

"Well?"

I grunt.

"Alright, wouldn't have guessed that, but I can see the appeal. Grunts For Hire. Got it." She winks and tilts her head, her long ponytail sliding over a shoulder, and I want to catch it. Wrap my fingers in the silky strands. Pull her head back, press against her hot body and—

"Can you focus?" It comes out feral, nearly a growl. So much for my anger management. "Where is the beach?"

And just like that, the hint of humor in her expression disappears. "You don't have to be such a jerk. I was just teasing. Who hurt you?"

Fiona. With her petite curves, her easy smiles, the way she seemed to know just what to say and do to soften me up. To get me to relax. And when I found out who she was, who she worked for—

"Dean…" Soft fingers press against my arm. "Dean, are you okay?"

I shake myself, clearing my head. "Let's go." The words bark out, an order.

June holds her hands up, backing away from me. "Sorry. I shouldn't have pried."

I close my eyes. This infatuation with June will pass. It has to.

Over the swell of water on fiberglass, I register the squeak of skin on vinyl, a switch being flipped, and the sound of the boat revving to life.

I count again, backwards from ten, though maybe I should start at a hundred around June. The metal railing is hot under my hand, and I grip it tight as the boat roars to life. Ignoring the burn, welcoming the distraction.

June's back is ramrod straight, her hair whipping behind her like a banner.

She doesn't deserve me yelling at her.

Disappointment wells in me, fierce and furious. Why can't I just be normal around her? Being so careful, so on guard all the time—it's exhausting.

The boat slams into a wave and I jerk my head up. June glances over her shoulder at me, a wicked smile curving her face.

"You still hanging on back there?" She shouts to be heard over the noise of the motors and the wind roaring across the deck.

I grit my teeth as the boat slams across the waves. A few crabs bounce out of the mesh bag, claws pinching at nothing. Slowly, I avoid them, making my way to the captain's chair, where June wears an all-out grin.

"Sorry," I manage, holding onto the back of the chair as the boat slams over another wave.

"What's that?" June cups an ear. "I can't hear you."

"I said, I'm sorry," I yell.

"You should be," she shouts, then pulls back on the throttle, slowing the boat.

It takes everything I have not to sigh in relief.

"I shouldn't have taken my frustration out on you."

"You shouldn't have," she agrees. The boat hits another wave. "Why did you?"

"Stress." It's not quite a lie.

"Mmhmm," is all she says, and I can tell she's not fully buying it. Of course she isn't.

"How far is it?"

"We need gas first."

"Shit." I ignore the pain as the burn on my shoulder pulls. "I don't want you to be seen."

She looks up at me. "Okay."

"What?" My eyes narrow in suspicion. "That was too easy."

"Listen, if you wanna pay to gas dear, sweet *Betty* up," she pats the console affectionately, "I'm not going to stop you."

"Fair enough, princess." I roll my eyes, though, and laughter peals out of June like a bell.

Something tight in my chest loosens, just a bit.

CHAPTER
FIFTEEN

JUNE

"WHAT ALL DID YOU GET?" I frown at the three brown paper bags from the marina. "That's a lot of bags."

"Water. Sports drinks. Nothing too exciting. No one saw you, right?"

"For the last time, no one saw me. I stayed in the cabin. Which, for the record, was awful. Now tell me what you got?"

The incorrigible man just pulls out a water bottle. "Drink up, princess."

While I chug it, because he's right, I need to hydrate, he makes a quick call on the satellite phone to his HQ, muffling his voice as he talks to his chain of command. He rattles off the coordinates of my beach, with instructions for Pierce to meet us there.

My stomach twists at that.

GPS coordinates are numbers, tidy and neat. They don't convey the enormity of what it means to let other people in on where we're headed.

I swallow, watching the blue-on-blue horizon line fly by. It was my dad's and my secret. Just our place, though other people knew about it, and sometimes we even saw other people on that stretch of lonesome beach.

But giving it to the government, so Pierce can meet us there? It feels *wrong*.

It feels like fully admitting that my dad was a criminal, and it hurts.

It's silly, illogical, but that's the truth.

"We're here." I focus on the jetty looming on the port side of the boat. Massive blocks of rough black granite mark the edge of the channel. White water froths along the manmade rocks, waves crashing onto the barrier as the tide rushes out.

"So this is it, huh?"

There's no judgment in Dean's voice, but the question rankles.

Words stick in my throat, so I nod, silent.

Past the jetty, the remote beach, the very tip of South Padre Island, clean sand stretches as far as I can see. Patches of dark brown line the edge of the surf, seaweed left glistening on the shore as the waters recede. Sea glass hides among the tendrils of washed-up vegetation; at least, it used to.

My father always loved pointing it out. He'd signed me up for jewelry making classes, brought me supplies and endless sea glass when I was in middle school and fascinated by the stuff.

We spent countless mornings searching for it, washed ashore after stormy nights, too many lazy afternoons spent picnicking on this very beach to count.

"This is it, huh?"

"Yeah, it is. What about it?" I ask softly, waiting for him to call me on the way I've been happy to bury my head in the sand all these years.

He peers at me, his gaze softening. "It's beautiful."

His eyes never leave my face.

I take a deep breath, slowing the boat even more as we approach the shallow sandbar.

"Grab the anchor for me?" I turn it into a question at the last minute. My fingers rapping against the wheel. "We don't want to risk running aground. We'll anchor here and to swim in."

He doesn't respond, and for a moment, I wonder if he has it in him to obey. Finally, he nods. A strange look passes over his face, like he wants to say something, and then he simply climbs up to the front of the boat and opens the hatch where the anchor lies coiled and waiting.

"I'm going to cut the engine and angle onto the sandbar," I yell up to him. "Hang on."

He nods once, squatting low.

I promptly forget what I'm supposed to be doing.

His thick legs are a sculptor's dream, or a personal trainer's, likely rock-hard like the rest of him.

My lips part on an exhale, my fingers grip the wheel more tightly.

Get it together, Horny McHornster. One wrong move and the strong riptide along the jetty could push the boat too far off...

I cut power to the engines, pushing another button to raise the dual propellers. The mechanical whine of the bilge pump replaces the sound of the diesel engine.

Thank god that's still working.

Checking the depth finder, I allow the boat to continue cruising forward on momentum alone. Fifteen feet, now eight, five, and—

"Throw it now," I bark out.

Dean reacts in an instant, tossing the anchor with skill that only comes from years of practice.

That might be one of the hottest things I've ever seen.

The rope uncurls near his feet, and he keeps one hand on it as it sinks into the water. Snapping taut after a few seconds, he ties it off on a bracket.

I am a sucker for a competent man, and Dean is about as competent as they get.

He grins back at me, and I realize I've been staring. The cocky wink that follows makes my heart race in a way that has nothing to do with adrenaline.

A wave, stronger now that we're in shallower water, breaks on the sandbar, rocking the boat, and I force my gaze away from him.

"We need to get the crabs back in the water. If they die on the hot deck, our dreams of a crab feast go with them." My voice comes out slightly strangled.

"Got it." He heaves the sack over the side, like he's done it all his life. His forearms flex as he ties the rope off to the boat with ease.

Competent, caring, and cool as a cucumber under pressure? The dash of cockiness doesn't exactly hurt, either.

I sit, open-mouthed, slightly dumbfounded, as it hits me.

Okay, extremely dumfounded.

I am attracted to him.

I admire him, even. After years alone, too focused on work, on finding the *Santu Espiritu* to make room for a man. *Of course* I was going to like him. Dean's the first man I've allowed in my orbit since college, and I couldn't have picked out a better match from a mail-order boyfriend catalogue. Not that they make those. Not that I've looked.

Under all his sharp edges and stubble, under all that bravado hides a secret soft interior.

Now he's taking orders from me.

A little too easily.

My eyes narrow.

"Why aren't you arguing with me?" I strip off my dress. No reason to get it all salty.

"Why would I?" He puts his hand over his eyes, shading them from the brutal sun. "You know what you're doing."

"You didn't seem to think that," I check my watch, which has a dangerously low battery, "about an hour ago."

"Dr. Legarde, you made your point. I'm choosing to trust you." The words strike a chord, and I look up at him. He pauses, his golden-brown eyes unflinching from my face, and I tug at the bikini string around my neck. "Why don't you grab two of the bags and hand them down?" With that, he lets the ladder down from the side of the boat and hops into the water frothing over the sandbar.

Wordless, I duck into the small cabin, ignoring the walls pressing around me. Breathing deep, I haul all three up with a watertight bag, then load the brown bags into the watertight one. Dean takes it easily, tossing the strap around his chest.

"What about the crabs?" He points to the rope hanging off the side.

"They'll be better in the water till we're ready for them." I check to make sure everything is secure before turning back to Dean. "That is, unless one of the locals gets hungry and decides they're easy taking."

"Locals?" Confusion wrinkles his brow.

"Sharks," I clarify.

"Sharks," he repeats.

"This is their home," I tell him, gesturing to the ocean all around.

"Well, we better hope they aren't hungry. He offers me his free hand, that elusive dimple making an appearance as his abs ripple.

I clear my throat, unsure where it's safe to look.

Not his broad chest, white scars standing out against otherwise tanned skin.

Not the dips between his hips, the tease of dark hair on his lower abdomen.

His smile it is. All white teeth and dimples, promising danger and something much, much, sweeter.

"Don't worry, I'll catch you if you fall."

I scoff. "I'm not going to fall."

I reach for his hand. Cool water licks my skin, and I shiver as goosebumps pebble my flesh, holding his steady hand even harder.

Water pulls against us, and my eyes lock on his.

"Wave," I warn.

"Tide's going out," he says at the same time, grinning down at me. "We need to make it fast."

"I know."

"Race ya?" Dean's eyes flick over my body. "Winner take all."

I narrow my eyes. "You're on." I've never been able to resist a challenge, and I'm certainly not going to start now.

Without another glance, I dive into the water, slicing through the waves with sure strokes born of years of practice. Maybe my watch will even deign to consider this my exercise for the day. *Unlikely.* As I break the surface for air, angling my head from the surf, I waste a split second looking for my competition.

Dean is in line with me. He barely seems to notice the water-proof bag he's towing behind him. He's matching me stroke for stroke, massive arms and shoulders working like he'd been born to swim. Of course he's a good swimmer, he's a Marine.

Losing to him suddenly doesn't seem so bad.

CHAPTER
SIXTEEN

DEAN

THE BEACH, strewn with seaweed and crushed shells provides a less than comfortable landing spot. But I sprawl across the sand, dropping the bag next to me, before propping up on my elbows, feet still submerged below the foamy water. June stayed right beside me, matching my pace until we hit the shallower water. For a second, I worried she would beat me, but I won. And I can't wait to collect on our bet.

She emerges from the ocean, her ponytail lost to the saltwater waves. Water trickles from the ends, running in tantalizing rivulets down the curves of her body.

I get it now, the myths about mermaids and sirens, because I would let this woman do about anything to me.

She flashes a hint of a smile in response to my steady gaze. Heat rises deep in me, desire making me fist my hands.

It's a struggle to look away.

All she has to do is smile, and I turn to mush. Well, not mush. Something much harder than mush.

"You lost." I smile.

"So it seems." A quick nod, and she settles next to me. Her chest rising and falling.

"Winner take all." I shouldn't push her, but I can't seem to stop.

"What do you mean by that, exactly?" She pushes one palm against the sand, leaning back and inspecting her other hand.

"What's wrong?"

June leans forward, her wet hair hanging in a sheet against her cheekbone, examining her palm. "Nothing. A cut."

Before I can stop myself, I grip her hand, inspecting it. "It's not bad."

"It's nothing," she agrees.

When I run a finger along her palm, though, she shivers.

"Are you cold?"

"A little."

The sun on the sand is anything but cold.

Her chest rises and falls with her quick breaths. She tilts her head, and my gaze drifts from her hand to her face. To her lips, parted slightly, to the way the water slicks across the angles of her cheekbones.

"What does 'winner take all' mean, anyway?" Her voice is breathy.

All I know is that I can't pretend anymore. I want her.

Still, I take my time answering. I rub a thumb across the back of her hand, marveling that she's letting me hold it, that she hasn't reclaimed it.

"I could show you what I mean."

"Show me," she whispers, her dark brown eyes large, doe-like.

Moving slowly, I press a kiss to the small cut on the palm of her hand, and she gasps a little.

Would she sound like that if I kissed her again? Really kissed her, and meant it?

I trace the line of her jaw. I revel in the soft skin, memorizing the way her eyes half-close. My hands almost move on their own accord, dragging down the smooth column of her throat, the hard ridge of her collarbone.

I brush my lips there, and the light caress makes her shift toward me.

I breathe her in, dragging her onto my lap, then pause, waiting. Her eyes flutter fully open.

"Are you okay?" I ask quietly. As much as I want this, I want her to want it too.

She nods fervently, her fingers scraping across my torso. "Yes."

My lips are so close to hers I can imagine what they taste like: salt brine from the sea, sweet when she parts them.

I cup her cheeks, pulling her face to mine, my mouth meeting hers in earnest.

Perfect.

She rolls her hips slightly, and I groan as my cock immediately gets hard. She tastes like summer and sunshine, and she feels even better.

It's just like before, when she wanted to fake it, as some kind of half-baked diversion plan.

Fake it.

The surf chases up to my knees, the cool kiss of water slamming sense back into me, and I pull away from her.

This is a bad idea. No matter how good it feels, how right.

June blinks up at me, her eyes wide with confusion. I close mine so I don't have to see her disappointment turn to hurt.

"I didn't see any sea glass on the beach." I hear her sharp intake of breath, and in the next second she's off my lap.

I open my eyes, and her lips are pursed, her gaze shuttered. She's looking down the beach, her arms crossed.

It was the right thing to do.

"It doesn't wash up all the time." She won't look at me. "Just after big storms. The last one we had was about a month ago. There's probably some buried under the sand, if you want to dig."

I brush my palms off, sand trickling back to the beach as a I stand.

"Why would your father have brought you out here? To the beach?" I sneak a peek at her.

She's upset.

I fucked up.

"Hey—"

"Is this some kind of game to you? Am I some kind of game?" Her watch buzzes against her wrist, and she spares it a single angry look before turning her face back to me.

"No, listen, I don't—"

"You don't get to just… use me like some kind of tool on your weird man-squad operation to save the world. Or finish the 'op.' Or whatever it is you tell yourself. Whatever you think is happening between us, it isn't real. This," she gestures to the space between us, "is the product of hormones and adrenaline. It's not real. I don't have energy for your games."

A single tear tracks down her cheek, and she locks eyes with me briefly before storming off towards the jetty.

"Princess, wait," I call out.

I can't help but notice her ass looks really good storming off.

Still, I have no business thinking that.

Across the beach, June walks slowly in the surf playing around her ankles.

She's right. That's the worst part. I just treated her like a means to an end.

Exactly like Fiona treated me.

If I'm going to explore the chemistry between June and me, then I'm going to do it right.

If she even still wants me at all.

CHAPTER
SEVENTEEN

JUNE

MY HANDS FIST at my sides. The sand is making stomping difficult, but I'll manage it. Can do attitude for days. Just like my last performance review at the university said. Why in the world I want to help his stupid ass is beyond me, but here I am. Almost kissing him. Like an idiot.

And why? Because Dean Evans is hot? And right there?

Yeah. Those are good reasons.

I scowl at the ocean, like it's responsible.

Oh, and obviously because of the massive load of adrenaline. It's just like one of those old action movies said, relationships form faster based on shared terrible experiences. Or was it an old *Oprah* episode? Ah, the lazy afternoons of a misspent youth.

I scowl, shaking my hair out, water droplets peppering the sand.

Waves crash into the dark gray granite jetties ahead, sending sprays of seafoam arcing over the cubed stones. If my father left me a message, it would be there. I pause, staring at the circling gulls.

Should I share it with Dean?

Would he rip it out of my hands and take all the glory of finding the *Santu Espiritu* for himself? I suck in a breath.

Worse, it might prove the worst of his accusations about my father to be true.

I turn around, already in motion to run back to him, to try and put this off.

Momentum sends me crashing against his bare chest, the sensation of his hard body fraying my resolve. His hands catch my waist before I go ass backward into the sand.

"Princess." He tilts my chin up, forcing me to look into his darkening eyes. "It's not a game to me. You're not a game. This isn't a game."

Desire curls in me, hot and traitorous. Delicious.

He must have seen it, because he leans closer.

It takes no effort at all to capture his mouth, the tentativeness of our earlier embrace disappearing into heat. My lips part on an exhale.

He seizes on it, dragging me closer, until my nails curve into his shoulders and I can hardly breathe for wanting him. His tongue slides against my lower lip, and everything in me goes tight and loose all at once.

We're skin on skin, the thin material of my bikini not enough and too much all at once.

He lifts me up, my butt in his hands, and I wrap myself around him just like I did last night, except this time?

This time, I'm exactly where I want to be. I nibble on his lower lip, and his sharp inhalation feels like a prize. More. I want more.

"June," he murmurs. My name, my real name, coming out of his mouth, ragged and desperate, is nearly enough to send me over the edge.

I draw back slightly, letting out a small whimper.

His eyes devour me.

"What do you want?" he asks, his fingers kneading my lower back, the curve of my butt. "What do you want from me?"

I lean my forehead against his, trying to calm my racing heart, trying to sort out the tangled knot of my emotions.

"I don't know. I don't know, Dean." I shake my head and his grip loosens, my legs unwinding.

The sand's hot on my bare feet.

"Do you know? What you want?" I ask him, biting my lower lip. He lets out a groan, gaze dipping to my mouth, and my core tightens.

"I know I want you." It sounds desperate, wild almost, like he wishes it wasn't the case.

But no matter how much I want him—

"I *need* to know the truth," I finally answer.

I stare up at him, challenging him to deny me or kiss me again, I don't know. I might be fine with either.

The waves pounding against the beach amplify the roaring in my ears.

Dean steps towards me, and I stand my ground.

A sea breeze catches my hair, sending a damp lock curling across my face. Dean steps closer, and I narrow my eyes at him. His strong hand pushes the hair out of my face, tucking it behind an ear, but he doesn't let it go.

"I'm not perfect. I'm not… I'm not good at being *with* some-one," he finally says. "I think, though, I think we might have something here." He shakes his head. "I don't know what."

"Not exactly a rousing endorsement of your, ahem, abilities." I let my gaze track down his torso meaningfully, then pause as I fail to ignore the evidence of my effect on him. His hand tightens against my loose hair until I look back up at his face.

"That's not what I meant." The words are a low growl.

"Good." *Good?* My voice sounds breathless, and I close my eyes. Trying to find my bearings.

"I'm great at that." His thumb strokes against my throat, and I can't help leaning into his touch.

"Then what?" I make myself ask.

"You… you deserve someone you can trust. Someone who isn't carrying around a decade's worth of baggage."

"Baggage?" The problem is, maybe I do trust him. I do, in fact, feel safe with him. Around him. In his arms.

"Therapy talk. Must be rubbing off." His lips screw to the side before melting into a half smile.

That dang dimple is going to be my undoing. Not to mention his possessive grasp on my hair, the way his thumb strokes up and down, so sure.

What else can that thumb do? I wouldn't mind finding out.

"Therapy," I echo.

"You don't want to hear about it."

"I think therapy is great. Important. I think it's great you're in therapy." I twist my lips to the side, his words finally hitting home. "Don't tell me what I want."

His smile deepens, something dark flashing in his eyes. "I think you'd like it if I told you what you wanted, princess."

"Oh." It comes out a squeak, and his dimple deepens, drawing my eyes back to his mouth.

"But what do you want, June?"

The way he enunciates my name, the teasing lilt of his mouth, the promise of what else he can do with it…

Too much. This is a bad idea. He is too much, too fast, and too good.

I will not be undone by Marine Ken Doll Dean Evans.

Not right now, at least, not with the sea glass message so close hand.

"I want to find my ship." My heart slams against my chest, so rapid there is no way Dean can't feel it. His hand slips from my neck, grazing my collarbone. "That's what I want now."

"Then let's find your ship."

"I thought you said this was about drugs." I squint at him, shielding my eyes from the Texas sun.

He gives a small shrug. His shrugs should be illegal. Public indecency. My gaze sweeps over the empty stretch of shore. Whatever. It's public enough.

"Why can't it be about both?"

"Both?"

It can't be both. Because that would mean my father *was* a drug runner. The man who kept me safe since… since the unspeakable happened.

Something I keep deep inside—bottled up safe and tight, so secure I refuse to even think about it—leaks through to the conscious part of my brain.

My throat goes dry, my skin somehow too tight.

I don't want to believe it.

Anything to keep you safe. I can almost hear his voice, the way he looked at me when he rushed me to the hospital after he collected me.

Collected me from the Russian smugglers, the year I turned thirteen.

CHAPTER
EIGHTEEN

DEAN

JUNE'S FACE pales under her tan. Her perfect mouth is round with surprise as I move closer, gripping her slack arm.

"Breathe, June. Breathe." I've seen this too many times.

Pure fear.

Her eyes are dilated, remembering something. Whatever it is, it terrifies her. My heart stutters.

"I'm going to count to ten. You're going to breathe in deeply the whole time," I say before counting. "Now out. Breathe out. Again."

Slowly, so slowly, June regains some of her color. Her eyes welling with tears, for the second time today.

At least this time, it isn't all my fault. *I hope.*

"It can't be. My father couldn't have done this. He couldn't have worked with the smugglers. I don't want to believe it." She swallows, blinking back the tears before covering her eyes with her hands.

I stay silent, not wanting to press her for more.

A moment slips by, minutes ticking, evidenced only by the

water rushing from the shore and the insistent passing of time on her watch.

I just wait. I'm good at waiting.

Slowly, June collects herself. Her toes uncurl in the sand, the hard muscle in her calves relaxing, the rise and fall of her chest slowing. Her color returns to normal, her breathing turning even and deep.

I would wait for her all day.

Finally, June peels her hands off her eyes, squaring her shoulders. "There's only one way to find out."

Her voice no longer shakes.

This woman is strong as hell. She's seen something— I triggered some memory, and she beat it back. Moved on.

"Let's find whatever message my father left."

With that, she turns on her heel, heading for the mass of rocks that make up the jetty, nearly jogging. I follow quickly, sand sifting underfoot.

June stops, crouching down. Her finger jabbing against blocks, counting. Up, and then to the right, away from the beach.

"He used to leave things for me here." Her voice doesn't break, though there is a heaviness to it. "When I was little, we'd come out here and picnic, fish and swim. He'd leave gifts or shells or some silly thing he thought I might like. Right here."

She scrunches up her nose, looking into a hole, and I step closer.

"Are you sure it's safe? Sticking your hand into a dark hole is asking for trouble."

"Mostly." Her elegant hand disappears into the gap. "Oh. Oh."

Her eyes go huge, her mouth dropping open in surprise—or is it pain?

"Princess?"

She screams.

I grab her wrist, my heart beating faster. "What is—"

"Gotcha." Her shoulders shake with slightly hysterical laughter, and she retracts her hand. "I'm fine. Sorry. My dad always…"

Her voice trails off, leaving the sound of seabirds and surf filling in the silence.

"Here," she says quietly, holding up a bag she's retrieved from the hiding place in the jetty.

My chest tightens. She's hurting. Hurting badly, and here I am, digging into her fresh wound. "He sounds like he was really good to you."

"What does that matter if he was a smuggler? Hurting other people?"

I fucking hate the smugglers. Hate the people who spread crime and drugs across the country.

Still, I can't shut her down again.

I don't want to, either.

"People aren't just good or bad. Life's not…" I struggle, trying to find the right words. "Life's not a superhero movie where everyone is a bad guy or a good guy. People are complex. Your father was no different."

"I know that," she says, but her fingers smooth across the bag she pulled out, seeming to consider my words.

Words I actually believe. Words I need to be true. I'd done shit in the Marines, followed orders, been called a patriot. But there's right and wrong, and as complex as I know people are, I also know the difference between the two.

I have to believe it's true.

My gaze dips to the bag in her hand.

"What's in it?" My therapist would call that deflection.

She opens her palm, upending the small, waxy bag, letting the contents fall into her hand. Bright metal glints in the sun, garish sprays of lime green glittering next to it. Two massive hooks protruding from the end and center.

"A fishing lure?"

"Looks like it," she says. The lure glitters, the hooks sharp against the soft skin of her palm.

"Any chance you're going to tell me what that means to you? Or are you going to keep that to yourself?"

She frowns, her forehead creasing. White teeth gnaw her lower lip, and when she looks up at me, my breath catches.

"I don't know what it means. Fishing was his thing. I just went along for the ride and his company."

My fingers brush her skin as I pick up the lure. The South Texas sun glints across the metal.

"Did he have any spots he took you to fish when you were little?" I lower my voice. "You know, since this beach was special to you both?" Carefully, I slip the lure back in the bag.

"Not that I remember. This—" She gestures around at the beach, the salt grass waving in the dunes behind us. "This was our special spot. We both knew I didn't care about fishing. I always wanted to be under the water with them, not reeling them into the boat. That's how I got into scuba and later, marine archae-ology." She smiles at the memory, and while there's pain in it, in her eyes, there's happiness too. "He always helped me work towards my dreams. Except, according to you, he was running drugs to make it happen." Her humorless laugh echoes off the granite jetty.

"It doesn't mean he was a bad father."

"What?"

My sudden shift in subject must have caught her off guard, and I rock on my heels. "So he wasn't perfect. He still loved you."

Her eyes go watery, and she looks past my shoulder towards the ocean.

"Perfect?" That same brusque laugh sounds again. "Running drugs isn't the same as not coming to my school play or staying late at work or something. Even if he was doing it for me—which he wasn't." She stops, clamming up. "It doesn't matter. What I believe doesn't matter. At this point, we just keep following the clues."

My brows knit. An iridescent oyster shell catches my attention and I lean over, picking it up.

Running drugs for her? My brain snags on the phrase.

"Wait. What do you mean, for you?"

Her gaze slips back to mine.

She sighs, her eyes narrowing at something behind me.

"Say you're right. Say he did this thing. Worked with the smugglers." Her face screws up like the words hurt as they came out. "School is expensive. A PhD? Even with fellowships, still expensive. He sent me to archaeology camps in the summers, then scuba camps, and all the gear, you know."

I turn that over in my head. It sounds true. She chews the inside of her cheek, the sun playing off the sharp curve of her cheekbone.

But it's a lie. Every instinct says so.

"Okay." My eyes never leave her face.

"Okay?"

"Yeah. Okay. You can tell me what you really meant when you're ready."

She turns the full force of her attention on me, and for a second, I'm awestruck by everything I see in her. The perfection of her lashes against the tawny brown of her eyes, her full mouth. Intelligence working overtime. The way she matches me, would complement me. The way we would fit together like puzzle pieces.

In every sense of the word.

It takes everything in me not to steal another kiss, to see how hot I can stoke the barely banked fire in her eyes.

"Your little man-squad is back from their retail mission." She tosses her hair, sending rivulets of water cascading down her collarbone. The oyster shell in my hand falls to the sand and I take a step closer, a moth to flame.

Sure enough, the noise of a motor roars into earshot behind me, the unmistakable strains of Jimmy Buffett still blaring from the speakers.

"Are you avoiding answering?" I shouldn't press her—I should know to back off. I can't resist.

I want to know exactly what's going on in her head. I want to know more.

I want to know everything.

Her mouth parts in surprise, though. "I'll tell you when I'm ready."

I expected a witty comeback. A smart remark, a sassy look. Not her reaching up on her tiptoes and pressing a quick, searing kiss against my mouth. One that's over before I can even process it.

"We'll finish this later." She ducks around me, racing into the surf, waving her arms, shouting at the boys to anchor at the sandbar, the lure glittering in her grasp.

Leaving me on the beach, wondering just what, exactly, she'll let me finish later.

CHAPTER
NINETEEN

JUNE

THE BLACK AND silver inflatable dinghy the guys brought to ferry supplies skids across the shoreline, the surf rushing and foaming alongside it. Tugging the ropes, I help haul it onto the sand. Though, with the three-massively-muscled-man squad, I'm not sure I'm actually helping at all. My hair, mussed from salt and sand, sticks to my eyelashes, and for the fifteenth time, I wish I had an extra hair tie.

"Back again, huh?" I say, twisting my hair into a low knot. There. Maybe it will stay put.

Thompson grins. "You're stuck with the two of us." He dips his chin at Dean. "Three, if you count him."

I flick my gaze to Dean, who, alongside Thorne, is stacking supplies on a massive beach blanket. His muscles ripple in the late afternoon sun, and my throat goes dry. The sticky, wet sand underfoot gives way as I dig a little pit in it with my toes.

I shouldn't have kissed him.

It might have been the best kiss of my life, but everything is mixed up and harder than it needs to be. He's barely looked at me since his team got here.

"You guys thought of everything, huh?" I nod at the loaded Zodiac raft. "Smart to grab the inflatable, too."

"Well, we tried to, at least." Thompson points at the supplies already offloaded. "Propane tank, fire starter, cooler with ice and drinks for tonight, some groceries to go with the crab…" He pokes around the raft, snagging three overflowing plastic grocery bags. "Here. Some shampoo and soap, clean clothes for you, and…" he clears his throat, "some unmentionables."

I peer at him. "Unmentionables?"

"Stuff to wear, you know? Just take it, will you? We even brought Sir Shirtless over there something clean to wear." He thrusts the bags at me. "Have Evans set you up a makeshift shower when you're ready."

Peeking into the bags, I see a bright blue loofah, some herbal shampoo, soap, and as promised, new underwear and clothes.

A shower sounds incredible.

"This was really—" I cough as my throat closes up. "Really thoughtful. Thank you, thank you so much."

On an impulse, I throw my arms around his neck, his wet t-shirt clinging to my skin. Sniffling, feeling gratified that they thought of my comfort, that I'd at least sleep clean tonight.

"Thompson, did you want to help? Or were you two going to stand around all day?" Dean's voice sounds from directly behind me.

Thompson pushes me away and I realize, with a start, I'd clung to him. The hole I dug with my feet is half full of water now, my chipped pink nail polish barely visible under the sand.

"Honey, we better get to work." Thompson gives an exaggerated wink before brushing past Dean.

"What's in the bags?" Dean's voice is causal, nonchalant, and I turn, confusion settling in.

"They brought us some clothes to change into and some soap to wash up with."

"Good." His throat bobs, his mouth a thin slash across his face. "That's good."

He says good, but he looks pissed. I frown, wondering what the heck changed.

"Don't get too close to those two," Dean says, and my eyes go wide as he stares daggers at Thompson's back and I realize what's wrong.

Thompson, himbo crew member, who I just hugged.

"Are you jealous?" I tilt my head, incredulous.

"That you get to shower?" One side of his mouth turns up. "No, I'm glad." He raises an eyebrow and looks meaningfully at my armpit.

"Shut up." I push the bags at him, laughing, and he catches my forearm, pulling me close. The sand and water suctioning around my feet.

"I was *maybe* a little jealous," he admits. "It looked like a nice hug."

"Well…" I trail off, flustered. "Jealousy isn't a desirable trait in a partner, just so you know."

"Is that so?" His hands grasp my elbows now, and he steps closer. "You trying to say you want to be my partner, princess?"

"I just mean, ah, we're working together. As partners. Part-ners." I shove at his shoulder a little, making a finger gun, the bags falling to the crook of my elbow. "Pardner. Like a cowboy, howdy pardner."

Dean steps even closer, close enough for me to see the sweat beading across the dip between his collarbones.

"I knew you were into roleplay," he says roughly.

"Am not," I tell him, shooting one more finger gun for good measure.

He laughs, and before I can do anything about it, he presses a gentle kiss to my forehead.

"Cut it out, you two," Thorne yells. "We've got shit to get done if you wanna eat anytime soon."

"Get a room," Thompson adds from where he is sorting supplies into four identical backpacks.

"Speaking of rooms." Dean's eyes shift from my face to the sky and back again. "They bought two tents. They each sleep two."

A wave crashes against the shoreline, seafoam chasing up to us. The two boats, anchored to the sandbar, bobbing on the horizon.

Dean is silent. Waiting.

"Oh. They sleep two," I finally repeat, cottoning on.

He nods, the smile gone. "I know you're claustrophobic—"

"Tents don't bother me." The words slip out in a rush. "They breathe."

"They breathe," he echoes, hooking a hand on his hip. And I try not to get distracted by the muscle packed against the tips of his fingers. *Focus.* "I can sleep under the stars, if you want privacy. Or to be alone."

Oh. *Oh.*

"Are you trying to ask me if I'll share a tent with you, Dean Evans?" A smile curls around my mouth.

He refuses to meet my eyes, instead watching a sandpiper's progress across the bank of rust-red seaweed. Biting the insides of my cheeks, I stall. I don't want to say no. Or do I?

Dean Evans is an unknown, and despite my rising suspicion that he hides surprising vulnerability behind his cocky edges, I have no doubt getting more tangled with him would only lead to heartache.

I follow his gaze. The pale little bird nibbles at something in the seaweed, then gobbles it down without a second thought.

"I understand if you say no, but I want you to know, what happened earlier." He coughs. "It won't happen again. If that's what you want, I mean. I respect you. I wouldn't want you to feel pressured or unsafe or anything like that. So, if—"

"Dean."

He looks at me, and there's hope and something else in his expression.

"You can share my tent."

"Roger that." With a soft smile, he steps back, walking away to where Thompson and Thorne manhandle supplies.

The sandpiper, unperturbed by the fact that my chest is suddenly hollow, flits off to the safety of the grassy dune behind me.

But I can't. A swell of emotions has me grounded in my little hole. Incredibly perturbed. Irritated. Raw.

The *Betty* rises on a swell, the men's boat keeping it company. What would my father think of this? Me, working alongside three former Marines, on a hunt for the storied buried treasure he brought me up searching for?

What would he think of Dean Evans?

It doesn't matter what he would think, not really.

The wind whips my salt-dried waves across my face, and I peel my hair from my lips, braiding it back as my mind swirls.

Dean Evans is not a long-term relationship guy. If, and this is a big if, we manage to find his precious shipment, he'll go back to wherever he came from. Or on to the next contract, somewhere no doubt more dangerous than the abandoned stretch of South Texas beach my feet dig into. My chest tightens, and I press my palm to the exposed skin above my heart.

Totally exposed. That's how I feel.

Like Dean sees every inch of me, and not just because of my bikini. Like he sees who I am, deep down, and after one kiss, said he wanted more.

"Dr. Legarde, we could use some help getting set up for the night and getting veg chopped," Thorne calls out, his voice the very picture of politeness.

Squaring my shoulders, I turn.

"Point me to the tents. I'm no good at cooking." Sleeping on solid ground, even in a tent, is better than the boat. An instant later, worry thrums through me. "I mean, y'all are sure it's safe? To camp here? With—" I wave a hand around, incapable of forming the words that fear pushes to the forefront of my mind.

The men wait for me to finish my thought, and I find myself at the receiving end of three steely stares. I swallow.

"With the smugglers still after us—after me?"

"The only people who know where we are are on this beach already," Thorne says gently.

My pulse picks up.

"No, that's not true. Dean called it in to his boss at the DEA. So the person who took the call knows," I tick off a finger, "the person who relayed the message knows," another finger, "and Pierce, who you all are acting really sketchy about, by the way, also knows. Not to mention whoever sold y'all all this stuff knows you plan to camp somewhere." I blow out a shaky breath, familiar fear wending through me.

"Princess," Dean says carefully, "my people are the best in the business. You are safe with us. They took necessary precautions when purchasing supplies, didn't you, Thompson?"

Thorne and Thompson nod, their eyes glued on my face, which feels oddly bloodless. Pressing my fingers against a cheek, I will myself to calm. Fear is a funny thing. It sharpens and sharpens and sharpens, until I'm as brittle as can be, always in danger of breaking.

"And you trust Pierce? You trust everyone at the DEA?"

"I trust my crew and myself." Dean steps closer, into my personal space. "You are safe with us. I promise."

His men share a look, then nod in wordless agreement.

Realizing I'll either have to trust them or spend the night a hair's breadth away from a panic attack, I nod. "Well, I can't cook. So tents it is."

"That's okay." Thompson grins, pushing back his sandy blond hair. "Dean's the best cook out of the three of us. He'll handle the food."

My gaze sweeps back to Dean, but he doesn't look at me, just grunts.

Agreeing, I guess.

He strides off towards the groceries, turning his entire focus to sorting them.

That's fine. I don't want to talk either. Knotted like an abandoned fishing net, my emotions need time and space to breathe.

Moving to the supplies, I reach for the first tent and still.

He never said if he trusted Pierce or not.

————

After some trudging around, Thorne and I find a relatively level location to set up the tents. It doesn't take long at all to get them together after that. As for Thorne, he's content to work in peace, offering up words only when completely necessary. Strong and silent, he makes good company for the mood I'm in.

"It'll do," I say, dusting sand from my thighs. Sweat trickles down my neck.

On the main stretch of beach, Dean and Thompson have the propane tank fired up. Citrus and the unmistakable scent of spiced crab boil waft through the air. Gulls flock overhead, drawn to our dinner in the hope they'll be able to share in the scraps.

I inhale deeply, hair falling over one shoulder. Seriously. I can't believe I didn't remember to ask for a hair tie.

"He's a good man, you know."

"What?" I scrunch my nose in confusion.

"Evans. I saw the way you two looked at each other."

I sputter in surprise.

Thorne waves a big hand, a serious expression on his face, eyes crinkling as he studies me. "I know he comes off hard sometimes. He had a rough time of it with another woman."

I step closer, curious despite myself.

"I'm not responsible for what anyone else has done to him." My voice is soft, so quiet I almost don't hear myself over the waves on the beach. Embarrassed, I look down at the sand still sticking to my hands.

"It's his story to tell. But he's a good man. He'd treat you right if you let him. And he didn't lie to you on the beach. You are safe with us."

Some of the tension leaves my body at his words, and I wait for more—for an explanation. For any hint of what Dean is going through, of why Thorne is so convinced of his leader's intentions with me, of his ability to protect me.

Thorne just smiles at me.

"Thank you," I finally say.

It's true, though, what Thorne said.

Dean is a good man.

The kind of man I could see myself falling hard for. Every moment with him is a revelation, the discovery of new facets of his personality as addictive as his mouth's proven to be: his protectiveness, his loyalty, his competence and kindness.

Thorne nods at me once before making his way carefully down the dune to the beach.

My gaze darts to the massive bonfire Dean and Thompson built. A thrill goes through me as Dean glances up to where I stand on the dune, his face contemplative, his body still.

I'm anything *but* still.

In fact, my entire body seems to tingle.

I don't think it's just adrenaline, not anymore.

CHAPTER
TWENTY

DEAN

I DID my best to tamp down the jealousy that rose when June took off with Thorne to scout a good location for the tents.

As if I could control my unreasonable emotions through sheer force of will. Cutting up oranges and prepping the boil helped. That kind of monotonous work always does, giving me something else to focus on.

Except, now my focus is broken, my attention returning to her again and again.

On the grass-speckled sand dune, her hair slips loose of the tight braid she managed, whipping around her face in a riot of waves.

"Stop it," Thompson drawls, opening a cooler.

I just grunt.

"Yep, that's what I thought. You got it bad for her." Thompson sits a six-pack of Gatorade on top of the lid, pulling one off for himself.

"I don't know what you're talking about."

"Don't act like that. You two need to get it out of your system. Whatever it is."

"Don't even think about her system." It was low, a warning. The driftwood fire crackles, accentuating my unspoken threat.

"I wasn't. Jesus, Dean, I'm your friend. Stop acting like an asshole. Talk to the woman. If you want to be with her and she wants to be with you, you'll make it happen. And if not, I'm more than happy to talk to her."

"This is just a job," I say. "It's part of the op."

"If that's what you need to tell yourself to sleep at night."

I swallow thickly. I won't be sleeping tonight, not with June curled up next to me again, my emotions a tangled knot of distrust and need. And bitter, bitter hope.

"Just a job, my left ass cheek," Thompson continues, clearly not caring about my discomfort.

"Drop it." It comes out colder than I intended.

"Yessir."

Fuck.

A moment passes, Thompson swigging the drink, checking on the status of the crabs.

"James." I clear my throat. "I shouldn't have lost my temper."

Thompson turns back, an eyebrow lifted in surprise.

"I'm sorry."

He claps a hand on my shoulder. "No worries, man. I know that whole clusterfuck with Fiona messed you up. I shouldn't have pushed."

Fiona. The mere mention of her name typically sends me spiraling into anxiety and regret and I wait for the feeling to come, the sensation of drowning on dry land. The regret is still there, the hurt, a small, coiled thing in my chest. I suck in a breath, the drowning never coming. Fiona is gone, the relationship over as dramatically as it started.

Therapy might be working.

Who knew?

Besides everyone.

"No, you were right to push." I rub my jawline. The massive pot we hauled to the beach boils furiously, lemons and oranges bobbing next to huge spice packs, and my stomach rumbles. "You might be onto something."

"That's good, boss." Thompson grins, taking a swig from a water bottle. "By the way, I told her you'd help her shower."

"You did *what*?"

He gives me a shit-eating grin.

"He did say that." Her clear voice rings out from behind me, and my whole body reacts. "But I don't need help *washing*. I just need someone to hold a towel up for some privacy."

June stands off to the side of the fire, flushed from the heat and sun. Her lips twist to the side, eyebrows raised slightly, as if she fully expects me to say no.

"I can squat behind the tent and wash off, but..." Her voice trails off, the hope in her eyes dying. "I'd rather not. I'm gross after being on the boat."

The woman wants a shower. I can at least be a gentleman about it. I won't dwell on how she'll look with water slicking over the curves of her body, soap lathering the soft skin I have no business thinking about.

"Of course, princess." I dip in a bow, and I catch a hint of a grin on her face.

Her eyes drop to the boiling pot. "It smells so freaking good."

"Are you ready to shower now?" My heart thumps in my chest, and I force myself to take a long breath in.

"I would love to get clean before dinner so I can crash afterwards." She coughs delicately, arching an eyebrow at me. "If it's not too much trouble."

"You heard her." Thompson shoves me a little, and Thorne, who I hadn't even realized was sitting behind him, lets out a snort.

"Alright, lemme grab the jug of water. Thompson, Thorne, don't overcook the crab."

"Sir, yessir," they intone in unison, and I roll my eyes.

June's lips curve in a small smile, catching her lower lip between her teeth as she wanders off, collecting the bag of toiletries I asked Thompson and Thorne to pick up for her. To make her more comfortable.

Because she is an asset. A happy asset is an asset who is more likely to help.

Or, as Thompson so delicately suggested, because I care about her.

I grind my teeth, and I find I can't deny it.

I do care about her, and it's time to stop telling myself she's a means to an end.

She's more than that already, so much more.

Her hips swish as she walks further down the beach, and I track the movement like my life depends on it. A jug of clean water under one arm, a clean towel under the other, I set off behind her. The sand is soft, leaving graceful footprints behind her, and I step next to them, loath to erase them with my own. Finally, she stops walking and looks around.

The stretch of beach is clear of seaweed, and she inches up toward the dune, light beige sand coating her feet.

"Here okay?" she asks.

"If it works for you, it works for me." I unfold the towel.

We must've walked further than I realized, or I'm hungry, because my knees are a little weak. Carefully, to avoid catching sand on it, I raise the towel up as high as my arms will reach, effectively blocking her from view.

"Wait." Her voice is soft. "I don't know if I can pour the water out of that thing." She points to the five-gallon jug. "I really would like to wash my hair. I'm sorry, I should've thought to bring a cup or something."

"What do you want me to do?" Almost kissing her was one thing. The peck on my lips, that was another. This, her asking for help, her asking me for help with *this*, choosing to trust me—is something else entirely.

"Could you," her throat bobs. "Pour the water on my hair? I'll wait to take off my—" Her voice falters. "Um, I mean, then you could put the towel back up."

Not trusting myself to speak, I secure the towel around my neck and nod once. Then bend to pull off the plastic cap.

Carefully, I lift the jug, and her back tenses as she braces herself.

"It might be a little cold." Water trickles out of the jug, turning her dark brown hair inky, goosebumps shivering across her skin.

"That feels nice." Eyes closed, a stream of water slides down her face and neck. Underneath her bikini top, her nipples pebble.

It takes everything I have to avert my gaze.

"Is that enough?"

"Mmhmm." A small noise of satisfaction. and I wish I was wholly responsible for it. "Can you put the towel back up?"

I glance back at her, and her eyes flutter open. I can't help but wonder if what I want to see in them is really there. My own desire, reflecting back.

I snap the towel open, holding it high enough that the top of her head disappears, as much for her sake as mine. Temptation is a dangerous thing, and I won't give in to it. Unfortunately, holding the beach towel that high means it stops right below her knees.

Pink bikini bottoms fall to the sand, followed by the triangle top.

I bite back a groan. I should look away—but I can't bring myself to. Behind the towel, I hear her lathering her hair, the swish of soap and water across skin. I imagine it running between the luscious curves of her breasts, her pink mouth parted, eyes closed.

My fingers tingle, aching to touch something infinitely softer than the terry-cloth towel. To see if what my brain supplies matches reality. Or if reality is better. My mouth waters as the scent of coconut wraps itself around me, my body stiffening.

Closing my eyes for a beat, I attempt to regain control. She makes a small noise of contentment, and I open them, zeroing in on a clump of soapy bubbles sliding down the muscled length of her calf.

"Okay, I think I can lift it now that you poured some out." June's arm reappears as she wrestles the jug behind the towel. The sound of water running has never been this arousing. Running all over June's body, in all the secret places I wish to explore.

Thompson was right. I want June like I haven't wanted someone in a very, very long time. Resolve stiffens my shoulders, and I shift my weight, a bit concerned with other stiff parts.

I'm not going to give up a chance with her without a fight.

"Okay. I think I'm clean." She tugs on the towel and I let it go, then she wraps it around herself.

The soap bubbles she missed slide further down her calf and, without thinking, I slowly bend, wiping the excess from her skin. My thumb skates over the curve of her ankle, pulling a sharp inhalation from her.

Straightening, a sense of purpose now to my thoughtless movement, I enter the battlefield.

I will win her over.

A wicked smile curves my lips. "You missed a spot, princess."

"Oh." Her eyes are huge, her wet hair glued to her shoulders. "Thank you," her voice is a little breathless.

Breathless is a good sign. My smile deepens.

I still got it.

"Why don't you dry off, and then I can hold the towel back up while you get dressed?"

"No peeking." Her answering smile is tentative.

I wink, and a rosy blush brings out the color in her sun-tinged cheeks. Carefully, she peels the towel from her torso and I hold it out lengthwise, then close my eyes.

An eternity seems to pass.

"Tada," she sings out. I open my eyes to find June in a loose t-shirt. On it, a striped cat wears American flag sunglasses. Long shorts complete the look.

"Walk, walk, fashion baby." June saunters towards me. "Cat-walk, get it?" She plucks at the shirt and lets out a snort. Her amusement is infectious.

"Stylish." Not that I care about the clothes. Not when my brain has more than adequately imagined what is beneath them. "How do you feel?"

"Much better."

"Good." I smile at her. "Glad to hear that the princess is pleased."

She tugs the towel from me, then flips her hair into it, twisting it up like a turban on top of her head. "There. Now I'm all done. And starving. And so freaking sleepy."

I resist the urge to tuck her into my side, to hold her close as we walk back to the campsite, worried it will scare her off. The last thing I want to do is break whatever fragile thing is building between us.

Instead, I settle for hauling the mostly empty water jug over my shoulder and carrying the odds and ends of her toiletries back.

"Can I ask you something?"

"Anything." The force with which I say it surprises me. The fact that I mean it, even more so.

"Tonight, when we sleep together—"

I whip my gaze to her.

She tugs at the turban, now lopsided, as we walk. "I mean, when we share the tent, can we be careful not to track sand in? I hate sleeping with dirty feet. And you know sand. It's coarse and gets everywhere."

I narrow my eyes, lips curving up into a smile. Is she quoting what I think she is?

"Yeah. I'll put the rest of the jug outside and we can rinse before zipping up." I adjust my grip on the water bottle and her eyes narrow, seemingly waiting for something.

"Not a *Star Wars* fan then, huh?" she finally asks.

"Not of *those* movies," I answer emphatically, a huff of laughter escaping my lips.

She beams up at me, and I wonder if this is what it feels like to win the lottery.

"Me neither. And that would really be nice. About the water, I mean."

Warmth floods me.

Nice.

She makes a simple word sound sweeter than anything I've heard.

CHAPTER
TWENTY-ONE

DEAN

THE ONCE-EMPTY ICE chest teems with the red shells of boiled crab, steam curling into the spice-soaked air. Smiling, I shut the lid, satisfied with a job well done.

"Your *partner's* here." Thorne nods at the end of the jetty, a rental cruiser rounding it, coming in hot. A massive wake ripples across the boulders, sending salt spray well over the rocks, and I shake my head in disgust.

Cutting it that close and fast to the jetty is asking for trouble.

"He's gonna bottom out on the sandbar," Thorne observes in a non-committal voice.

"Nah, he'll be fine." Thompson squints at the boat. "Who's that with him?"

"Charlie." June gnaws her lower lip, fiddling with her hands.

"I talked to Pierce on the sat phone earlier," I say, casting her a concerned look.

"You're sure she's okay?" She inhales deeply, worry creasing her brow. "Why would he bring her out here? I don't want her to get involved... well, any more than she already is."

"Pierce thinks the Russian smugglers might latch onto her, use her as leverage."

I'd like to see them try.

"Keeping her with him was the best solution he could think of in the short term," I finish.

"Or so he says," Thompson interjects.

Toting a civilian along on an active mission is a fool's errand, and there is no way Charlie would have let on she was anything but that.

"You think they would do that?" Guilt colors June's words.

It's an emotion I know all too well.

"Do I think they would use a friend as leverage to get to you? Yeah, I do, princess. How well do you know Charlie?" There's a hint of judgment in the question, but I make my tone as neutral as can be. This woman has a blind spot where friends and family are concerned.

June's face pales under her mild sunburn. "I've been wondering the same thing." Her forehead wrinkles, her frown deepens, and the wild urge to wipe it away grips me.

The boat pulls up short, and Charlie's unmistakable white-blonde hair bounces around her as she throws the anchor out on the sandbar.

"Think they need help?" Thorne doesn't seem able to tear his eyes away from the tall woman.

Pierce appears, waves a few times, and drops the ladder off the side. Helping Charlie splash down the ladder, their laughter carries on the sea breeze.

This doesn't feel right.

Sure, Charlie's safe, and Pierce is the DEA-sanctioned head of this op, but... I can't put my finger on what feels wrong, exactly.

I tear my eyes away from the two of them.

"Nah. No way does Charlie want help." Thompson picks up a paper plate and piles it with crab, then grabs an entire package of salad.

"June, wanna share this bag of salad with me?"

"Sure." She grabs her own plate of crabs and a plastic fork and plops on a towel in the sand next to Thompson. Frowning, she looks at the steaming crabs. "Are there crab crackers? You know, to get the meat out?"

"Nope." Thompson fishes a water bottle out and hands it to her. "We forgot those. But your body comes with these little things called hands? I don't know if you've heard of them."

An ember of frustration ignites in my chest as June stares, crestfallen, at her plate.

She's not used to the usual teasing of my crew, and I give him a reproachful glare.

In half a second, I'm at her side, thigh brushing against hers, her plate in my lap, cracking open her crab for her, throwing the discards into the crackling fire. White meat piles high on her plate.

Without a word, I hand her plate back.

Her eyes are round, and wishful thinking tells me that's not just sunburn that's pinking her cheeks.

"Thanks," she says around a mouthful.

I drag my gaze away from her long enough to see Thorne and Thompson grin at each other over their own plates before they notice me looking.

Am I that predictable?

Maybe I am.

Standing, I force myself to pile my own share of blue crab on a plate, adding a second plate full of hot boiled potatoes to share with June.

The sand crunches underfoot as I sit down awkwardly, balancing two sagging plates. "Here. Saw you didn't get any potatoes or corn." Her meat is nearly gone, so I crack open another crab, spearing the meat with my clean fork and putting it on her plate.

"Well, isn't this cozy?" Pierce's voice rings out over the waves.

Pierce and Charlie walk down the beach, hand in hand. Charlie glances at him from time to time with an expression so clearly vapid that I can't help frowning.

"Pierce, glad you could join us." I tip my chin up. "What's she doing here?"

"Oh, I wouldn't miss a crab boil, right, June?" Charlie smiles. "When Pierce told me you were having one, I begged to come along."

June shifts uneasily next to me. Her knee rubs against my thigh as she repositions, sitting cross-legged on the sand.

She doesn't like this either.

You learn a lot about a person after surviving with them.

June has good instincts.

"Well, help yourselves, folks. There's plenty, thanks to these two." Thompson points at the cooler full of steaming crab. "I'm Thompson, and that's Thorne. You must be Pierce, but I reckon I don't know your name." He grins at Charlie, and she grins right back, not giving anything away.

Pierce's body tightens as though Thompson has said something completely inappropriate.

"Didn't think you were cleared to get more manpower on this, Dean," he says, radiating a sort of killer calm that makes me sit up straighter.

"I thought we could use all the help we could get after how it shook out last night," I tell him honestly.

If I trusted him, I might tell him that they've been privy to the unclassified basics from the start.

But I don't.

I can practically feel the tension radiating from June, as if she also sees the barely contained violence that sweeps through Pierce. It's there and gone so quick I can almost convince myself I imagined it.

I didn't imagine it.

Pierce telegraphs instability, from the way he holds himself to the odd glint in his eyes. Thompson and Thorne both go fully relaxed, smiling at him in a way that doesn't fool me at all.

They see it too.

Thorne steps closer to Pierce. "Are you here to eat?" he asks, his tone casual. His fists, however, are clenched at his sides.

He's ready to fight if it comes to it.

"Of course we are," Charlie says, her gaze tracking up to Thorne's face. "Why else would we have come all the way out here? Right, Pierce?"

He laughs, and some of the tension dissipates from his body. "Right."

June sags with an audible sigh of relief. I scooch my hand closer behind her, in case she needs a place to lean. In case she needs my support.

Or maybe I just want to touch her.

Thompson lets out an easy chuckle, and some of the crackling tension diffuses.

"Then grab a plate and load it up. Princess here was just about to tell us the story of her shipwreck before we go hunting for it tomorrow."

"We're coming along to help too, June," Charlie's eyes gleam in the firelight. "Pierce thought we could make a date out of it." She bats her eyelashes up at him, and Thorne and I exchange a look.

June's lower back meets the waiting support of my forearm, and she glances up at me. She's worried for her friend, I can tell in the way she's looking at me with her heart in her eyes.

That makes me feel like shit, because of all of us, Charlie is the least likely to need anyone's help.

"Are you sure that's a good idea, Pierce?" I ask, teeth bared in a smile. To Pierce, Charlie is a civilian.

And he would just drag her into this mess?

"Of course it is. A brilliant mind like Charlie's will be a huge asset, don't you think?" Charlie's ice-blue eyes blaze as Pierce sinks a world of meaning into the word 'asset.'

"Gross." June's barely audible, but I hear her, squeezing my hand around her hip.

I keep my expression as blank as possible.

Either Pierce knows something about Charlie, or he is trying to get in her pants. Maybe both. My lip curls in disgust. I wouldn't put it past him.

Worst part is, I can't even disagree with him, can't push back. Pierce is in charge. Technically, the one who selected me for this mission. Even if I did plus up our numbers without running it by the powers that be.

Fuck.

"Well, I guess that's settled then. Welcome to the team, Charlie." Thompson claps her on the shoulder with an easy friendliness.

Charlie grins back at him, tight-lipped.

"Oh, I see you all brought tents. That was smart. This is all so exciting." Charlie settles across from June, the fire between them. Pierce sits next to her, feeding her bits of food off his fork while she giggles outrageously.

June stares at her in disbelief.

"There's only two," I say loudly, trying to divert attention from the fact June's about to realize that she doesn't really know Charlie at all. "We can sleep four total."

I am not about to send Thompson and Thorne off. I promised June safety, and the three of us are it.

Pierce better not pull rank and order my men to clear off, either.

"That's perfect," Pierce looks up from Charlie, that all-American grin plastered across his face. "We can go back to the boat, right? Sleep there?" He raises a suggestive eyebrow at Charlie, who lets out another giggle.

I resist the urge to roll my eyes at her obvious obliviousness. She's laying it on thick.

"Oh, you're so bad." She takes another bite off his fork. Regardless of what I think, Pierce seems to be eating it up.

June says nothing, spearing a boiled potato with unnecessary force.

"Soooooooooo," Thompson drags the 'o' sound out for an

outrageously long time. Charlie looks up from Pierce, giving Thompson a withering stare.

"Dr. Legarde, why don't you fill us in on your shipwreck?" Thompson finally asks.

"If she's done eating," I grind out, then immediately regret it. She can speak for herself. "Are you done, princess?"

She smiles at me, a slow, lazy grin, like a cat who's gotten the cream, and nods once.

"I'd love to tell you about it."

Pierce pulls Charlie into his lap, who sits stiffly for a beat before nuzzling into his neck. Thompson and Thorne are quiet until Thorne's huge hands snap a crab in half.

June glances around with a deep breath, clearly gathering steam to tell her story.

I lean forward, curious as to what exactly it is about this shipwreck that's so fully captivated her.

"The *Santu Espiritu* was the flagship of a flotilla of four, all traveling from New Spain, now Mexico, to Cuba. The original colonists were sent to the New World," June puts up air quotes around the name, "to pillage, to steal, and to claim the land for God and country. All under the auspices of spreading Christianity to the peoples who already lived here. What they actually spread was disease, violence, and hatred. The colonists took root here and in Mexico, collapsed a society, a virus in every sense of the word."

Her voice has the natural rise and fall of a storyteller, the cadence soothing and sure.

"The *Santu Espiritu* set sail in early June, according to some reports, to avoid the danger of hurricanes that spin up in the later summer months. The other three ships were laden with gold and precious gems as well, but the *Santu Espiritu* was the best among them. Her figurehead inspired poetry, a beautiful woman with flowing hair and blazing eyes, supposedly a likeness of the artist's beloved. Her holds were full of gold bullion and chests with rubies and emeralds, according to legend, the lost treasure of Cibolo, the city of gold."

Waves pound against the shoreline, providing a dramatic soundtrack to her tale. The light fades, the sky blazing gold and pink and red. June holds up two fingers, her face alive with the story.

"Two months later, in August, two of the four ships landed in Cuba. Two months. It should have taken weeks, not months. A third foundered in the Caribbean, blown off course. The treasure ship, the Santu Espiritu, loaded with the ill-begotten goods of colonial greed, was never seen again. Lost, according to the sailors' accounts, in a surprise storm."

She smashes her hands together for impact, and Thompson makes a low noise of assent in response.

Charlie catches my eye across the fire and I bite back a laugh at the familiar annoyance in her expression.

"Some say she was struck by lightning, a sign of God's wrath at the greed of the Spaniards, sinking in a blaze of fire and fury, flames licking like hair across the face of the beautiful figurehead. Others say the treasure of Cibolo was cursed, and any who searched for it, much less took it out of greed, would find a watery grave."

We're all silent, save for the fire popping and waves breaking on the beach behind us.

Charlie coughs delicately, breaking the spell. "Tell them why you think you know where she is now."

June's face becomes more animated, and she leans forward.

She's entirely captivating.

"I found a journal in an archive of a man set to become captain of the ship. He took ill, as did most of the crew, and the *Santu Espiritu's* trip was delayed. She didn't set off with the rest of the flotilla in June, but a month later, in July. She slammed into the famed hurricane of 1554, which took out several coastal villages, and sank somewhere near here, not far off the shore of the Padre Islands."

"Then why hasn't anyone found the rotting thing yet?" Pierce snorts in disbelief, voice brimming with sarcasm. "There are countless oil rigs around here."

"The gulf is huge," June tells him, eyes narrowed.

"Man, what a load of liberal garbage," he mutters under his breath, but not quiet enough that we don't all hear him.

Anger flares.

"1554 was a banner year for storms." June tilts her head, considering, and a lock of hair slips over her face.

I catch the scent of the shampoo and inhale deeply, relaxing into the flow of her voice.

"I think between the storms and coastal erosion over the last few centuries, she's been covered up. Besides, no one has charted the entire seafloor of the Gulf of Mexico. The only reason to spend the money doing that is for oil, and there's no oil around where I think the *Santu Espiritu*'s buried, so no one would have disturbed it. But we had a huge storm a few months ago, and…" She trails off, raising her hands in a shrug. "Based on current maps and where the tropical storm is, it's likely the seabed shifted enough that she could be uncovered again."

"I see why you didn't manage to get your grant," Pierce says with a derisive laugh.

My hands curl into fists.

"Believe it or not, Pierce, what I told you sitting around a campfire isn't the same thing I presented for my grant. I had to take into account my audience's own shortcomings." June's grin turns sharp. "I'd be happy to lecture you on tracking coastal erosion and the science of bathymetry, as well as all of the gruesome firsthand details of the captain's illness, even the local myths and the historiography of this area. That is, if you think you can keep up."

Pride swells in me, and I let out a laugh. Something dark passes across Pierce's face, illuminated by the crackling fire.

"You know what the most interesting part of this is?" June continues, blatantly ignoring him. "The colonial history. Colonialism, especially American colonialism, didn't stop centuries ago. It just kept going. And going. Most of the instability in Latin America can be traced to American imperialism, interference, and destabilization." Her dark eyes are intense, her chin lifted as she stares defiantly at Pierce, whose mouth twists to the side.

Charlie stills in his arms.

"June's right," she finally says.

Pierce's jaw twitches, an ugly expression marring his pretty-boy features.

"S'mores?" Thorne stands, throwing his soggy paper plate into the fire. The quiet man glares at Pierce, daring him to say shit.

"Dessert." I nod, less at the idea of sugar than at the fact Thorne sensed something ugly in Pierce, too.

Fuck.

I hate wading in distrust. And yet, as I size up the man and woman sitting across the fire, that's about all I can manage.

CHAPTER
TWENTY-TWO

JUNE

STARS, brighter here than they have any right to be, twinkle overhead, the moon low and heavy against the light-studded sea.

I inhale deeply, sleepy and stuffed to the gills from the huge dinner. Empty paper plates crackle in the bonfire, and chocolate oozes from the half-eaten s'more on my lap.

Pierce and Charlie retreated back to their boat not long after dessert, borrowing the inflatable dinghy to get off the beach. Pierce barely spoke to me since I called him out at the bonfire.

A real loss. Not.

"I can see why you didn't get the grant."

The words left an ugly smear in my mind, and I wish I could put my finger on what else it is about Dean's partner that irritates me so much.

I have no idea what the heck Charlie sees in him.

Or maybe, just maybe, I really don't know Charlie as well as I think I do. Maybe I read her wrong from the start, ignored any red flags in favor of having a friend.

Behind me, metal and plastic clink as Thorne and Thompson

sort a ridiculous amount of weaponry and food into backpacks with price tags still on them. Guns, knives, and something that looks frightfully like a hand grenade.

It's not like they sell *those* at Wal-Mart. And why the heck do they think we each need a survival bag? I'm not entirely sure I want to voice that question.

Ignorance is bliss and I sure as heck could use a blissful night of sleep.

Dean says I'm safe with them. If that means a backpack full of weapons and protein bars, then I trust his judgment. Which, I do. I do trust his judgment.

I've gone from panicked to soothed all because these men, especially Dean, make me feel safe. Cared for. His men trust him implicitly, are loyal to him. Protective of him. He inspires them, a natural leader. Heck, he inspires me.

And despite our conflicting beliefs about what my father was leading me toward, Dean never makes me feel stupid for hoping. He's been accommodating and kind and careful.

Affection swells in me.

I like him.

I like how he makes me feel. His men are right; Dean *is* a good man.

As long as I don't think too hard about why they want to keep me safe, I'm… content.

Biting my lower lip, I push clean hair out of my eyes. The fire dances against the dark night sky, brilliant oranges and reds. Thorne is deep in conversation with Thompson as they continue sorting supplies.

Sneaking a peak, I look at the man settled next to me on the sand, swigging from a Gatorade, a sleeping bag rolled up under his arm.

"Hey."

"Hi." It should sound silly, greeting each other after all the time we've spent together today. But the deep rasp of his voice, the simple word, and the weight of his presence by my side is a comfort.

I turn the fishing lure we found over in my hand, firelight dancing off the metal.

"Still no idea what that means, huh?"

Gently, he takes it from me, dangling it so the poison-green strips float behind it.

Thompson walks over.

"Think fast." He tosses me a protein bar, and I catch it easily. "Good reflexes."

"I'm full. I couldn't possible eat any more."

"Keep it. You might wake up hungry." He winks, and Dean throws him a murderous look. "Going fishin' for amberjack, boss?" He stuffs his hands in his pocket.

"Amberjack?" It comes out a whisper, barely audible over the crackling fire. I smack a palm against my forehead. Of course.

"What?" Dean asks.

Even Thompson wanders over, and the three men stare at me. Waiting.

"Amberjack. It's a fish." I gesture at the lure. The puzzle pieces start to click together in my head.

The gigantic patriotic cat t-shirt slips off one shoulder as my mind races.

What did my dad tell me about amberjack? I know, I know he mentioned it. I'm sure of it.

Dean reaches over, heat rising in his eyes, to slide the shirt back up my shoulder, but doesn't move away.

"It is a fish. A damn big fish, too. We used to call them the money fish where I grew up. Hard to find, harder to land," Thompson supplies. Thorne shoots him a silencing look.

Dean's knee nudges against me, leaving it there, and I lean into him. "You said your dad used to take you fishing, that he was a fishing guide."

"And you said my dad was a drug runner."

Thompson shifts from foot to foot, and Thorne settles in the sand next to us.

"Why would he have left an amberjack lure for you?" Dean's voice is soft, low. Gentle.

Closing my eyes, I pull my legs in tight to my chest. As though my knees might stave off the deep hurt in my chest. A hurt that only seems to get worse the more I learn about my father's past.

Our past.

I suck in a shaky breath. How much of it is real? My father loved me, I know that. Could feel it, see it in the way he'd look at me. It was as quick and sure as breathing. But did I really know him? Can a child ever truly know their parent?

"June?" Strong arms wrap around me and I look up, squinting at the stars spangling the surface of the water, breaking and foaming in front of our makeshift camp. Thompson and Thorne wander off, talking in low tones next to the cooler of supplies.

"Listen. I know this must be hard for you. I don't know what you're going through. Not exactly. But," Dean pauses, then scoots so close I can smell the pine-scented soap he washed up with. "But I'm happy to listen, if that's what you need."

"If he did this... it was my fault." I choke on the words, hot tears flooding down my face, eyes never leaving the horizon. Unable to look at him.

"No, no, princess." Dean pulls me onto his lap, and I bite my lip. He strokes my back through the thick blanket as Thompson and Thorne start walking down the beach. "It wasn't your fault."

"They took me. The Russians. Right before high school."

Dean stiffens underneath me, then resumes stroking.

"I thought... I thought it was a boy from school I had a crush on texting me to meet him at the mall. That's all it took." I need to get it out before it swallows me whole. "To get me out there, for them to grab me. They put a bag over my head." I bury my face in his neck.

It's been years since I let myself think about it. Sure, I took some self-defense, know how to handle a gun, a knife, but it takes more than physical competence to erase the scars.

I don't think they'll ever really be gone.

Dean tightens his grip, his fingers ghosting along the back of my neck.

"You're safe. I've got you."

"Dean, he paid the ransom. But that must not have been all they wanted. I'm not an idiot, but I've been so stupid. I should have seen it. They must have forced him to do it. Right? That must have been the payment they wanted."

"Could be." I expect him to be patronizing, but he genuinely sounds like he is chewing it over, analyzing everything. "Doesn't change anything."

"No, no." I bite off a harsh laugh. "Doesn't change anything, does it?"

Dean places his hands on either side of my face, forcing me to look at him, to really look.

"That's not what I meant. I meant it doesn't change the fact that your father loved you. Look at you, princess. You're one of the most intelligent, capable people I've met. Beautiful. Smart. Infuriating." His low chuckle sets butterflies off in my stomach. "Deadly shot. Fearless."

I try to shake my head, but his hands make it nearly impossible. He's the incredible one. His thumbs sweep over my cheeks, wiping away the salty tracks of my tears. His eyes glitter with refracted starlight. His lips so close we must be breathing the same air.

"I'm not fearless. I'm so afraid."

"That's good." He grins, that damned tempting dimple blooming in his cheek. "Fear makes you quick. Keeps you alive." His lips brush against my temple. "So, what are you afraid of, professor?"

His thumb continues swiping across my cheek, though my tears have dried. I swallow as he massages the back of my head with his fingertips. Finally relaxing, the tension slowly ebbing from me.

"I'm afraid they're going to catch me again. I'm afraid there is no wreck, only the smuggling. I'm afraid I've made a fool of myself for a long time."

"What else?" His clever fingers work a small knot in my neck and I sigh, closing my eyes.

"I'm afraid you're going to hurt me."

His hands stop moving, and I open my eyes.

"June." The way he says my name, like it's a promise, makes me weak in the knees—it constricts my heart.

I press a finger to his lips, not wanting him to lie. Whatever happens next won't end with us together. Our lives are too different. *We* are too different.

But I don't care. Not right now.

His gaze encourages me, the heat I saw earlier blazing to life. I look around, but Thompson and Thorne made themselves scarce.

"Kiss me." I reach up, fingers feather-light against his skin.

Dean leans forward, repositioning me so I straddle his hips, and I let out a small moan as he places a gentle, searching kiss against the side of my neck. My jaw. His fingers press into my backside, still massaging, sending heat spiraling through me.

His eyes lock with mine, then fall to my mouth. *God, I want him to kiss me.* Need it. And finally, he does.

So gentle at first, as though I am some fragile thing. Wiggling closer, feeling the hard evidence of his desire between us, I can't take it anymore. I run my hands up under the shirt he tossed on after he showered, reveling in the dips of his muscles, the way he groans as I rock against him. The way his mouth opens, his tongue sliding into my mouth.

Promising pleasure.

Breaking the kiss, my hands fist against his chest, my head following, resting against his collarbone. "I think I should get some sleep."

"I'll come with you." The intensity in his voice sends a shiver through me.

I peel my forehead from him, memorizing the lines of his face in the moonlight.

"Okay." It's hesitant. I'm still afraid.

Dean's expression smooths out, banked desire in his eyes. "We can sleep. I'm tired too, you know, recovering from a bullet wound and all that."

A smug half-smile triggers the dimple's appearance, and I reach for it before I can stop myself, tracing where it appears in his cheek. His stubble has grown out, making him look rougher. More dangerous.

He catches my hand, pressing a kiss to my palm, and I let out a surprised gasp, lust threatening to overwhelm me. He tugs me up with him. Unsteady on my feet, he wraps the blanket around my shoulders.

"I put your swimsuit in your pack." He nods at the backpacks lined up in the sand before snagging two of them.

My head spins from the sudden change of conversation. Exhaustion tugging at me, I lean on Dean, wrapping my arm around his waist.

We walk across the dune in silence, our new flip-flops crunching against bleached out shells.

"They really thought of everything, didn't they?"

"I trained them to," Dean answers simply, his fingers hitching on the waistband of the decidedly unsexy shorts they bought me. The way he says it, all casual confidence, matter of fact—whew. It does something to me.

Dean is ridiculously competent. Smart. Brave. But the kindness under his cocky exterior? That's what's going to do me in.

Unsexy shorts or not, patriotic cat shirt or not, I have never been more ready to climb a man in my life. My good judgment's slipped away with my energy.

Outside the tent, the water jug glints in the moonlight.

Dean unzips the flap. "Ladies first."

I crouch, setting my butt inside first. Dean tosses the sleeping bag onto the floor of the tent while I remove my flip-flops. Kneeling next to me, he unscrews the cap of the water jug, then carefully puts my feet on his knees. Cold water sloshes over them and he rubs at them, careful to remove the sand from between my toes.

He remembered.

He tucks my feet inside the tent, careful to keep more sand from getting on them. Grabbing my hands, he flips them over, scrubbing at a smear of roasted marshmallow on the back of one.

Dean kissing me was incredibly, searingly hot. But being cared for? Cleaned off? This is better, way better. The flare of desire I attempted to bank is replaced by a hollow ache, a desire for something more than his body.

Once he is satisfied that my hands are clean, he places them gently in my lap. His eyes meet mine, and I can't look away.

"That was really nice of you." Nice doesn't even begin to cover it.

"Can't have you pulling an Anakin in the middle of the night, what with all the sand around."

I tip back my head, laughing, and when I look back, he wears a self-satisfied grin, his eyes intent.

"I'm going to wash my feet off, too. Why don't you unzip the sleeping bag and make a pallet? It's too hot to sleep in it."

I try to speak, try to say thank you or sure, but all I can manage is a nod. His eyes slip to my lips, and I force myself back into the tent. If he kisses me now, I will pull him into this tent, and then there will be sand everywhere.

Not like he has a condom on him anyway. Not that we would have sex, but in case—I shake my head.

"Are you okay?" He leans back in. "You have a funny look on your face."

"Just tired," I lie. *And ready to jump your bones.*

"Then go to sleep." He grins at me. "Easy as that."

"Easy as that," I repeat, grumbling. "Go to sleep, June, it's so easy to sleep."

"Nah, I'd say, 'Go to sleep, princess, I'll watch your back so you don't have to worry.'"

He lets out a laugh as the sound of water splashes.

I grunt in annoyance at his tone, but secretly, I'm pleased.

When he curls up next to me, one arm thrown over my waist, I snuggle close to him, enjoying the cuddle.

And promptly fall asleep.

CHAPTER
TWENTY-THREE

JUNE

I SIT STRAIGHT UP, panic in my throat, gasping for air. The heavy night presses around me and I rub my eyes, trying to dispel it. Confusion clouds my awareness as I take in my surroundings. Dean lies next to me, shirtless, wearing the same tactical pants he unzipped into shorts. The unmistakable scent of Irish Spring rolls off him as he sleeps, his chest moving with deep breaths.

"Dean!" Thompson's voice sounds a long way off. "Dean, June, we gotta go or we gotta make a stand. Get a gun and a pack and get on a boat!"

"Shit, Dean, wake up." I shake his shoulder and he blinks up at me twice before his eyes snap open.

"Get up, everybody up and to the boats!" Thompson's shout is louder now, and Dean sits bolt upright. My heart pounds against my chest, adrenaline shaking off any lingering sleepiness.

"Fuck." Dean crouches, the blanket dragging into the sand as he throws open the tent flap. "Get your shoes on. We need to get to the boat. We need to get out of here."

"What about Pierce and Charlie?"

"Fucking Pierce. Their boat left hours ago, right after you

crashed." Dean throws on his t-shirt, a twin one to my patriotic cat.

Under normal circumstances it would've made me laugh.

These are anything but normal circumstances.

"They left," I echo.

A box of ammo peeks out from a zippered pocket of the backpack Dean slides into. He straps a rifle to himself. The glass scope glints in the moonlight.

"We have to worry about ourselves right now. We can't help anyone if we get mowed down in a firefight."

Dropping my corner of the blanket, I grab a second backpack, following Dean's lead.

Sure enough, the low rumble of ATV engines follows Thompson's cries to get to the boats.

Heart in my throat, pulse racing, I open up the black backpack. Ammo, a pistol, more shotgun shells. A grenade? I tilt my head, considering it. Maybe the overprepared Ken Dolls are onto something.

It sure seems like they had the right idea with being overprepared.

"How long?" Dean asks.

"We've got three minutes or less." Thorne bites off the words, emerging from the neighboring tent, shouldering a pack of his own.

I look around, somehow dazed, fear so tight and high that I can't quite process what is happening.

Food, check, water, check. Soap.

We need the soap. Just in case. Can I fit the blanket in my backpack?

"June, let's go. Come on, princess, we don't have time to waste."

The rumble of the ATVs grow louder and my stomach knots, Dean's words forgotten.

"We gotta go, Dean." Thorne slips down the sand bank, catching himself as he runs towards the shore, backpack clipped across his chest. A wave catches him at the hips, and he dives into the surf like a dolphin. Or a Marine, more likely an ex-Marine.

I laugh, a choked, high sound.

"Princess, breathe."

This is it. This is it. They'll take me again, they'll put me in a musty closet. Shut me up in it and I'll never see the sun again.

"Dr. June Legarde." Dean's hand fits around my wrist, forcing my arms through the straps of the backpack. "Snap out of it."

He clicks the strap across my chest and I suck in a breath as though he slapped me.

"Okay."

"Okay." He bends his head down, assessing my face. "Okay."

He tugs at my wrist and I follow behind him, sliding down the sandy dune. He hauls me past the embers of the fire, still glowing. It couldn't have been more than a few hours since I fell asleep.

My eyes snag on the propane tank next to the fire, Dean continuing to propel me to the water. Ahead of us, Thompson and Thorne are already to their boat, Thorne pulling up the anchor as Thompson clears the ladder.

The ATVs roar now, the first coming into view on the clear, starlit night. Two hundred yards away. A hundred and fifty. Shit. We'll never make it.

"We have to go." Dean pulls me hard, and the salty surf kisses my bare feet. My flip-flops must have come off at some point.

"June?" Dean tugs me towards the shoreline, and I half jog after him. My hands shake on a rifle I don't remember grabbing. By the fire, the amberjack lure sparkles prettily where we left it.

"Get to the boat," Thompson roars from the sandbar, his pack slung across his back, a rifle in his hands. A wave slaps into his hips, and I've never wished more that this stretch of beach was easier to park a damned boat on.

I glance back at the lure, and it hits me.

"I know where the wreck is," I whisper, my eyes wide.

"I know you do." It's full of his signature cockiness. That's how sure he is of me.

We walk into the water, bathwater warm and pitch black. I've done plenty of night dives, but I don't love the idea of stepping on a pissed off sting ray at the moment.

Or getting shot.

Neither seem like a great plan.

Deeper now, Dean keeps a hand on my backpack, half towing me along in his wake as he powers through the water.

Thorne or Thompson open fire from their boat, and everything dissolves into chaos.

The unmistakable sound of bullets rip through the night, shouts of "Don't shoot the woman!" follow, along with Russian that bounces right off me.

A fleeting moment of gratitude passes through me for the foresight of buying black backpacks. Hopefully we'll be harder to aim at, impossible to see in the pitch dark.

Aim at.

That's it.

My mind flashes back to the shore, to the embers of the fire. The meal cooked on the propane burner.

"I have an idea," I gasp out, rewarded with a mouthful of saltwater.

Dean is silent, an underwater missile. He'd put Michael Phelps to shame. But Michael Phelps has never been under the gun quite like this.

I choke out a little laugh, gasping for air, and kick out, finally urged into a maximum effort swim. The current tugs at the rifle strap along my back, and this is not my idea of a fun workout.

If only my stupid watch had battery to see me now, it would probably be shocked by my cardio output.

My lungs burn, crying out for air, and I swing my head to the side, spending a precious second to look over my shoulder. The men are on the beach now, four ATVs parked around the dying campfire, flanking the white propane tank. A group peels off shirts and boots and swim after us.

Not great.

I kick harder, my quads and shoulders burning with the extended effort. Swimming with a pack in the dark with this current is absolute insanity.

I am not going to die. I will not let them take me.

Not again, not now. Not ever.

My knees hit the sandbar. Salt stings my eyes and I stand, the laden, soaked backpack and rifle threatening to topple me over backwards.

"Fuck."

The men in the water are closing in. Panic grips me.

These assholes.

These assholes murdered my father. They kidnapped me when I was thirteen. They stole so much joy from my life.

Anger burns the fear away, until all that is left is a molten core, seething inside me.

Dean forges ahead, climbing the ladder, tossing his pack into the boat like it weighs nothing.

"How much propane was left? In the tank on the beach?" My fingers find the gun.

"This is not the time to worry about littering." Dean yanks me up the ladder, and I wince at the brute force move.

"I have a rifle, and I have an idea," I manage.

Dean follows my gaze. An evil grin spreads across his face and he closes the gap between us, pressing a kiss to my forehead.

"I like the way you think, princess." He angles his head, studying me for a short moment.

I swallow.

"But you have to hurry. Go line up the shot." In an instant, he helps take my backpack off and presses the gun into my hands.

I swing myself up onto the bow of the boat, kneeling on it, my cheek pressed to the butt of the gun as I line up the sights.

I take a deep breath. Another.

"Come on, June. Steady."

The crosshairs are there. All I have to do is squeeze.

The gun barks, recoil slamming into my shoulder, making me wince.

The explosion doesn't happen instantly. Instead, the impact of the shot knocks the propane tank into the bonfire. I pull my face away from the sight, frowning.

Then it happens.

A massive, action movie worthy explosion.

"Boom," I say, slightly dazed.

Flames billow into the sky. People scramble as the parked ATVs get caught in the fallout. Screams follow them and I blink, an echo of the bright explosion searing into my retinas. Dean says something, but I can't make it out; the recoil of the rifle must've knocked some of my hearing out.

He pulls me back to the deck of the boat, taking the gun away.

The engine roars to life, and I sit on the pleather seat where my father taught me how to fish and watch the chaos.

It's not over yet.

I have a sneaking suspicion that the worst of it hasn't even started.

CHAPTER
TWENTY-FOUR

DEAN

"WAIT, the anchor, you'll ruin the boat or dig us in." June hops onto the catwalk. Her hands are shaking, and I bite back a curse. Running to the steering column, I start to lower the motors.

"They're shooting at the boat, June, goddammit."

"Don't curse at me." She makes her way to the bow, smooth limbs glistening where saltwater still clings to them.

"I'm not cursing at—" A bullet whizzes by my head. "June, get *down*."

Fuck. She's going to draw fire out there. June must've realized it too, because she flattens herself against the boat. *Good.*

"Brace yourself." The motors drop into the water with a mechanical whine. "I'm gonna pull the boat around and give you some cover."

"No! I've nearly got it." She heaves once, twice, three times, and the anchor gives, the boat already drifting along the current out to sea. A bullet pings against the hull. Thompson's boat roars to life, the white wake rolling towards us promising to send us careening.

This is it. This is going to be how I finally lose it. With this woman determined to put herself in danger. Counting to ten isn't going to fucking cut it. Counting to ten thousand probably won't either.

She heaves again, bringing the anchor onto the ship, dark gobs of silt and mud plopping all over the white hull.

"Get out of there!" I hiss.

"No, I'm going to put it back right, otherwise we'll regret it later. Just fudging drive, Dean, I can hold on. Keep the motors light on the water or you'll dig us in."

A muscle in my temple twitches, and I slam the prop switch, tilting so the dual propellers barely clear the surface. I shake my head.

June is out there on the bow, exposed, and telling me how to do my job.

My entire job right now is protecting her. So far, I've fucked that up royally.

"Screw it." I dip the engines lower, reversing the boat as fast as I dare on the sandbar.

June's hair streams around her, tugging loose from the thick braid I watched her plait while she sat, serene, by the makeshift bonfire. Now, the inferno on the beach silhouettes her and she hangs on easily, winching the anchor cable back in place.

After what feels like a lifetime, we clear the sandbar, the white surf crashing over the dark rocks of the jetty in the distance.

The clock on the control panel shows the whole thing, from explosion to anchor, took less than three minutes.

"Let me drive." June hops down from the catwalk. Water slicking her formerly clean shirt, the wet fabric clinging to her body. I drag my gaze back to her face, to the white pallor under the tan.

"You sure?" I almost add she doesn't look so good—but even like this, clearly shaken, she is stunning. The wind tossing her hair around, a black halo in the night, her skin kissed by starlight and salt.

"It's my boat." The look she gives me would freeze hell over.

But her hands betray her, still trembling. Something dark drips onto the deck, and I stare for a moment.

Blood.

June pushes past me, her hip grazing my upper thigh. She cradles her hand, using one to steer the *Betty* out to open water and the gulf.

"Bilge pump," she mutters to herself, flicking a switch.

"You're hurt." The need to check her over, to tend to her overwhelms me. Catching me off-guard.

"Something's bothering me."

"Probably that cut on your hand."

"It's fine. Something on the anchor chain cut it." Half turning toward me, her brow furrows in confusion. "What I want to know is how the hell they knew where we'd be? That wasn't an accident, them showing up there."

Even in the soft glow of the instrument panel, I can see how tight her uninjured hand is gripping the wheel. Her knuckles are white.

"Well?" Her voice has an edge.

"It's the right question to ask." A question I've been screaming at myself since the first rumble of the ATVs over the dunes. But the follow-up question, that's the real problem.

Who betrayed our location?

"And?" Her lips are an angry slash across her face. A shiver rocks her, and she slumps onto the edge of the captain's chair.

"I don't know. But you can be damn sure I'm going to find out." And I'll make sure whoever fucked us over pays for it.

Another drop of blood splatters across the deck.

"June, your hand." I reach for it, but she pulls away.

"It's nothing."

"It's bleeding. At least let me look at it while you drive."

"How do I know I can trust you?"

"I think I'm capable of bandaging your hand."

She shakes her head, dark hair streaming over her face. "No. That's not what I mean and you know it. How can I trust your team? How do *you* know you can trust your team? I'm not an ex-Marine, but I am also not an idiot. Someone told them where to find us. Who else knew we would be at that beach, Dean?"

I nearly flinch back at the venom in her voice. Anger rises in me, bitter and heavy, hot and fast. Not at her. At the fact she is right. Unless... unless *she* is the one who made contact. Maybe when we stopped for gas, she'd been seen on the boat. It was possible.

Unlikely. But possible.

"It wasn't my team. Thompson and Thorne got away clean, went the opposite way. We'll meet up with them when it's safe." I grab the first aid kit from where it's perched precariously on top of the instrument panel. White gauze, saline, antibiotic cream, tape. She doesn't pull away when I reach for her hand, making quick work of it.

"Then who?"

"We should sweep the *Betty* for new trackers." Something I need to do now.

"What do you even mean, trackers? What are you going to do, crawl around and look for something?"

I stare at her, and she stares back.

"Maybe. I've already swept it once." The admission comes out before I think better of it.

Something in June's eyes shutter. "You have to know how creepy that is."

"I know. I'm sorry."

She clutches her hurt hand to her. "Fine. Do whatever."

Nodding, I reach under the control panel, feeling around. My arm ridiculously close to her body. The warmth of her skin sears me, even though I take care not to touch her, even though every fiber of my being cries out to take her in my arms, to set her down and make sure she is okay.

My hands feel along the grooves and channels of the navigation instruments, the fish finder, the steering column, the speedometer.

My fingers find purchase, calluses catching on something hard.

"Do you know what this is?"

June looks down and shakes her head.

"I wanted to make sure before I pull it out." Maybe not the best word choice. "Pry it out."

She doesn't seem to notice, her eyes round as saucers. "What is it?"

"It's a GPS transmitter. I fucked up. Ahh. I fucked up." I rake a hand through my hair, sick to my stomach.

And I thought... for a moment, I thought maybe June was the one who signaled the cartel. But here I am, clearly shit at my job.

The black tracker is small and insignificant looking. I crush it in my hands, leaving nothing but plastic shards.

"Okay, Rambo." A high, hysterical laugh follows.

"Rambo?" I cock my head at her. "I wasn't the one who blew up the propane tank with one shot."

"That was better than a James Bond movie," she laughs.

"I didn't know you liked James Bond, professor." I smile at her and kick myself again for thinking she leaked our location. "But you don't get better than him."

"Nah. That felt like revenge. Payback. Bond. June Bond."

I sweep the rest of the boat, taking my time to explore the cabin, the few nooks and crannies where it would be possible to stow a cheap tracker.

"It's clean."

"Are you disappointed you can't crush another tracker with your bare hands?"

Sweeping her into my arms, I chuckle as she lets out another laugh. And then shivers.

"Dammit, June, let me drive."

"No." A soft smile.

I look to the sky as though the high, wispy clouds blocking the moon will somehow have the answers.

"Can I at least I warm you up?" God, I want to. Want to take her in my arms, press her body against mine until my heat seeps into her.

She nods and I duck into the cabin and find the fleece blanket.

The soft fabric smooth against my hands. Placing the blanket around her, I release my grip reluctantly. June's teeth quietly chatter; her eyes so large they swallow the starlight.

"Adrenaline."

"Huh?"

"You're shaking again. It'll stop soon. Try and breathe. Deep breaths." I cast a look back at the receding flames billowing on the beach.

"Try and breathe? I was planning on continuing to breathe, thank you so much. Certain functions tend to cease if I stop."

I step back, relief at her sass making me weak.

I care about her. I want her more than I thought possible. The thought overpowers me. Staggers me.

I always get what I want, sooner or later.

And I want June. All of her. Not just now, but for as long as she'll have me.

A slow, deep-sounding laugh escapes me, and she turns, her lips curving up in automatic response.

"What?" she asks, bemused.

"Just thought of something funny, that's all."

"What?" she insists.

"You'll see," I say, raking my gaze over her, smirking when she quirks an eyebrow and lets out an exasperated sigh.

She will see. She'll see me. All of me.

I'll let her in.

CHAPTER
TWENTY-FIVE

JUNE

MY ENTIRE BODY ACHES. Unsurprising, since I spent the remainder of the night sleeping on the floor of a boat, rocking in the none-too-gentle embrace of the gulf. My middle is heavy, hot, and I open one eye to dawn breaking on the horizon.

Ugh.

The heaviness shifts and I swallow.

The warmth against me isn't a blanket. Isn't a pillow.

Nope. That's Dean Evans curled up against me, *spooning* me, holding onto me as though I am something precious to him.

This is niiiiiice.

"Hey." His voice is gruff, rasping against my ear, my languid body suddenly snapping to attention.

"Hi," I say on a yawn. I close my eyes, leaning into him. Maybe if I pretend to be asleep, I'll open my eyes again and wake up next to him in my bed.

Maybe all this Russian smuggler crap is just a bad dream.

Instead, something long and hard presses against my back.

My eyes fly open.

Dean pulls me closer. "Is this okay?"

Yep. It's better than okay. He fits around me like a puzzle piece, and I feel so safe. Well, except for the absolutely ridiculous erection pressing into my lower back. I don't want to be impaled, after all. And except for the mild heart attack I'm having.

Slowly, he releases me, tugging his arm out from under my head, replacing it with one of the cushions he used as a makeshift pillow.

"Oh." It's a breathy exhalation, surprise tinging it. I didn't respond out loud, and now it's too late.

Dean is up, rubbing hands through unruly dark hair, the stubble on his jaw only serving to better highlight its perfection.

"Sorry. I shouldn't have tried to…" He trails off.

"You spooned me." This kind of awkwardness should be reserved for freshman hook-ups. "You were sleeping. It happens."

A muscle near Dean's eye twitches. "I wasn't sleeping."

"I was sleeping," I tell him earnestly.

His face falls, and I feel like an idiot.

"The lure." I dive into a different conversation, dying to talk about anything but how danged awkward I am. "I figured out what it meant. The coordinates on the map, one of them said amberjack next to it. I wouldn't have known what kind of lure it was if Thompson hadn't said anything. We should go. To the where the fish are."

I really don't care about going to where the fish are. Nope. I want to go to where the clothes aren't.

Or, just as tempting, back to sleep, to cuddling in the peaceful heat of Dean's big body. But I'm awake now. The *Santu Espiritu* is within my reach. And if it is drugs, fine, whatever. At least if we find the drugs I'll be safe. Safer. Probably.

Maybe.

Bracing myself against the rocking boat, I stand. "Let's get this over with."

———

"Still no contact?" I ask.

Dean's frowning at the satellite phone, clearly rattled that Thompson and Thorne haven't checked in.

"Not yet."

"Do they go radio silent on these jobs?"

"We're supposed to rendezvous today."

"Do you want to go find them?"

"I'm not sure that would help." He's staring at the phone like it might ring at any time. "They must have a reason."

"Do you think something happened?"

"I can't think like that." He glances up at me, all dark eyebrows and eyes and two days' worth of stubble, and I want to tell him it's going to be okay.

I'm not sure it will be, so I keep my mouth closed.

"How's it going for you?"

"I found it."

It made my heart ache to look at my father's handwriting, the tiny fish doodle next to it, so I memorized the coordinates and squashed the fishing list back into my pocket and glued my eyes to the depth finder while Dean tried his team on the sat phone.

"That's great, princess."

The fuel gauge shows only a quarter of a tank left, but it's the battery that worries me. As much as I've used the bilge pump over the last two days, it could be in danger of running out of power.

If the bilge pump or battery fails, we'll have no choice but to turn the boat around. Thank goodness I remembered to run the bilge pump last night. Honestly, it's sheer luck the *Betty* isn't at the bottom of the gulf.

With a sigh, I flip the manual switch.

It doesn't start.

"Something wrong?" Dean asks, coming up behind me.

I don't answer, instead flicking the switch up and down until it finally kicks on. Relieved, I slump against the captain's chair, never so glad to hear the tell-tale whine of the pump starting.

My mind swirls with unfinished thoughts and wild emotions. One moment I want to stop the boat and finish what I started with Dean on the beach, and the next I'm wishing I never met him, because that would mean I could live my life without knowing who my father really was.

But my father is dead, and Dean is living, breathing right next to me. Somehow, he seems to sense my mood, and gives me space.

Gathering myself, I check the GPS and frown.

"Son of a bean dip," I swear.

The depth finder still shows a hundred meters. It's unlikely my father found anything that deep. I press a finger against the grayscale screen of the fish finder, bringing it to life. It picks up fish, yes, but it can pick up anything as large as the wreck on the seafloor, too… except not at this depth.

This isn't the spot, and it can't be right. It's too danged deep.

I scan the watery horizon. "Son of a bean dip mother Frito."

Dean's laugh startles me, and I whip around to find him standing over my left shoulder. "What's wrong? Are we where you wanted to be? With the fish?"

"According to the list, this is the amberjack spot."

"And you really think this is where he dropped the narcotics shipment? It couldn't have been anywhere else?"

I close my eyes, wishing I snagged the lure from the beach before I blew it all to hell.

"I think this is where he was trying to steer us." Why is it still so hard to believe he did this? Led a double life where he worked for the very people who hurt me, who kidnapped me?

"What now, princess, do we just hop in the water with the scuba gear and hope for the best?"

"No. We eat something. Drink something. Keep the fish finder on and mosey around."

He gives me a blank stare. So I stare back.

A little laugh rips out of my throat.

"You want to go fishing?" he asks.

"What? No."

"Then why the fish finder?" Dean tears into a protein bar and hands me one already opened, glancing at my bandaged hand.

Oh.

"Thanks," I sputter. "The fish finder will show us anything weird below us. Not just fish."

"Okay." He unscrews an energy drink and hands it to me too. "It's not coffee."

"I would kill for coffee right now."

"Let's hope it doesn't come to that."

The words sound like a joke, but it doesn't feel like one. "Urgh."

"Princess, look at me."

Rubbing a rough spot on the white pleather, I tug at the jagged edge of the start of a tear. Who am I becoming? I felt powerful last night, setting the beach ablaze, taking some small measure of revenge.

This isn't me.

I squeeze my eyes shut, my stomach roiling.

"June," he says my name on an exhale.

Finally, I meet his eyes, my stomach twisting uncertainly. The boat continues to rumble, untroubled by my discontent.

"This is survival." Dean puts his hand on the back of my chair. "Tell me about how you like your coffee."

"Coffee." My nostrils flare as I inhale, sucking down a great big breath and blowing it out. Another breath. The protein bar feels chalky against my teeth, and I grimace.

"That's right, coffee. Latte? Pumpkin spice? Mocha café Frappuccino whipped chip abomination?" Dean sits back down on the pallet of blankets and cushions, tearing into a third protein bar.

"I know what you're doing, Mr. Ex-Marine." I scowl at him.

"What's that?" he asks innocently.

"Trying to distract me."

"Maybe I just want to know what kind of coffee you like on mornings you're not out to sea with a," he taps his temple like he is trying to remember, "a Ken Doll? So maybe the next time you wake up next to my ugly mug, I can make you your favorite."

Something tightens inside my chest, my stomach filling with that tell-tale fluttery feeling. "You're assuming a lot."

"Maybe I am." His gaze seems glued to my face, toffee brown in the late morning light. Why does he have to be so dang good-looking? It really isn't fair.

"I like it any way I can get it," I answer.

His eyebrows shoot up.

I clear my throat. "Coffee, that is. I like it pretty strong. Americanos are what I order if I go somewhere fancier than the coffee cart on campus or my trusty coffee pot at home."

A wave rocks the boat, the light sparkling off the greenish water.

"Do you like to go to fancy places?" His jaw works as he chews the protein bar and I study him, allowing hope to swell as sure as the current around us.

"There aren't many fancy places in my college town."

"I'd take you somewhere nice." Dean clears his throat. "The real question is, would you want to go with me?"

A smile blooms on my face. "Are you asking me out?"

He returns the smile. "Caught me."

"No." I blurt. "Yes."

"I think that's what they call mixed signals." One eyebrow rises.

My chest heaves, and I put my head on the steering wheel. The protein bar sticks to my teeth and I lick them, tired and faintly nauseated.

"June?"

"Sorry, my jaw's been welded shut by this gourmet meal," I manage, but it comes out garbled.

A calloused finger traces the line of my jaw.

"If this is just... if what's between us is one-sided—we can chalk those kisses up to adrenaline." His finger dips down the line of my neck, and my instant reaction belies his words.

There would be no one-sided to this. It would burn hot and fast and so good and then it would be over, ashes and third-degree scars.

I swallow again, dislodging the protein bar. "Pull the *Speed* card."

Confusion mars his handsome face.

"You know, Sandra Bullock? Keanu Reeves? It's a classic. But they don't stay together, because whatever attraction they had was built on surviving an extreme circumstance." I point at the space between us. "This could be an extreme circumstance."

"Maybe." He shrugs, and my body comes alive as his muscles bunch. "Or maybe we could watch it together and take it slow." A cocky grin tugs the corner of his mouth.

"Dean…" He withdraws his finger, and I miss it immediately. "I just think maybe we should get through this first. You know, one thing at a time. Survive, then see what happens."

"See, that's how we're different. Helps me to have something to look forward to." His gaze heats, raking over me, leaving no doubt as to what exactly he is looking forward to. "But I understand. When you're ready, I'd love a dinner-and-a-movie night with you. Just dinner and a movie. If you're not ready to answer, that's fine. I'll wait. If it's a no, that's fine too."

It shouldn't melt me, this gentlemanly side of him.

This side of him that is soft and patient and so dang hot.

Dean is a sharp edge, his entire body promising violence when he is in action. Except with me, his muscled body is thick with the promise of pleasure. I manage another bite of the protein bar, chewing slowly so I don't open my mouth and take his.

The problem isn't him waiting for an answer. The problem is I want to have sex with him immediately and often, and that—*that* —is a recipe for disaster.

A shrill ring interrupts the calm lapping of water against the side of the boat, and Dean frowns before removing his hand from the back of my chair and digging his phone out of the pack.

I nearly turn back to the fish finder, but that would interrupt the absolutely perfect view of an absolutely perfect derrière.

"Evans." A pause. "Yep. Good to hear. Yeah. Let me check. Okay. Rendezvous at," he checks his watch, "eleven hundred."

He rattles off their GPS coordinates and my lips press into a thin line.

"How's Charlie?" he asks.

Pierce, then.

My brow wrinkles. Something about that man. Where did they go last night? Suspicion rises.

Charlie and Pierce knew where to find us. We told them about the beach, then they'd taken the inflatable boat and driven away in the middle of the night. I focus on the control gauges, the endless blue ahead, my mind running a mile a minute.

Couldn't have been him, though. Pierce is government, for crying out loud, he works for the DEA, why in the world would he have given us away? It makes no dang sense.

Dean smashed the tracker to smithereens while I watched. That's how the cartel found us. Fear punches me. The tracker was how they found us, and they almost captured me.

Still. Unease flickers through me, catching like wildfire.

Dean clicks a button on the black brick of a phone and tosses it back into the pack.

"What did he say about Charlie?" Dread spreads, tingling down my limbs and into my fingertips, tapping against my thighs.

"She's still with him, said to tell you hello."

Huh. Seems normal enough. I frown.

"What?"

"Nothing." Shaking myself, I stretch my arms high above my head, pointing my toes as hard as I can. When I look back up at Dean, his mouth hangs slightly open before closing it with a snap.

"What?" I echo his question.

"You seem upset. Worried."

"It's nothing."

A crease appears in his forehead. *Dang.* He's going to age like a fine wine. "I always teach my people to listen to their gut."

If I listened to my gut, I wouldn't have let Dean strong arm me onto this boat. I wouldn't have gotten drunk and poured tequila all over that Russian dude at the bar.

I probably wouldn't have gotten this close to finding the *Santu Espiritu.*

I wouldn't have kissed him, and that would be the biggest shame of all.

"You keep watching the fish finder," I say.

It's time to go to work. Turning the boat on is safe. Work is safe. There will be no turning me on.

"I'll watch the depth. Let's do this."

He nods at my directive, a sly smile on his face.

The quicker we find the *Santu Espiritu*, the sooner this nightmare will be over.

And the sooner I can figure out what, exactly, I'm going to do with Dean Evans.

CHAPTER
TWENTY-SIX

JUNE

THE FISH FINDER is good at its job—finding fish. Those, there are plenty of, swimming in massive schools, black rectangular blips across the screen. Shipwrecks? Not so much. I sigh. The sun's high overhead, and perspiration beads on the back of my neck.

"It should be here." I slam my hand on the base of the captain's chair.

"This would be easier with another boat, huh?" He winces. "Sorry about that."

"Don't be." I pinch the bridge of my nose.

Thompson and Thorne's boat isn't going to make it in time. They ran into some trouble with a team of smugglers waiting off the coast, and thought it better to go radio silent just in case.

Now they're too far out to get here anytime soon.

A dull beep catches my attention. At this point, I can't muster any excitement.

The thrill of discovery's long since worn off, once all the beeping only proved that there were a lot of really big fish swimming about.

Freaking amberjack.

Sighing, I'm afraid to look, disappointment already settling deep in my gut.

"Wait." Dean's voice triggers a fresh rush of adrenaline. "June, look. June."

I take a deep breath, filling my lungs, my chest expanding as I search the grayscale screen. It beeps again. This… if this is a fish, it is a mother-loving whale shark.

I continue my pass over the object, easing up on the throttle. My gaze cuts to the depth finder, which also beeps a small warning. Forty feet. Thirty feet. *Holy crapola.*

Finally, the fish finder shows we've reached the end of the object.

The keys slide in my clammy hands. The engine dies, and I stumble from the captain's chair.

"I'm gonna be sick," I mutter.

This is it. *It has to be.*

Dean calls my name, but I can't focus on him right now. No way.

The metal barrier of the catwalk is hellishly hot on my hand. Carefully, I pick my way to the front of the boat, to the heavy metal anchor that is plenty long enough to cut into the silt and sand of this shallower water.

Water that, in the danged middle of the Gulf of Mexico, has absolutely no right to be so shallow.

A drum beats in my chest, picking up speed. My heart races so fast I can hardly catch my breath. In a smooth, practiced motion, I throw the anchor overboard, where it splashes and fizzes into a cloud of white bubbles.

Immediately, the boat slows, no longer at the mercy of the current. Then the anchor bites, and I brace myself against the railing.

Mud and silt fly, clouding the water. *Dang it.*

A deep breath steadies me. I need to calm the fudge down. If I do this wrong, if this… shadow blip is what is left of the *Santu*

Espiritu, I need to do everything right. Take it slow. Stirring muck up from the bottom won't help visibility once I'm down there.

"June, did you hear anything I just said?"

"Get the diving buoy out. It's in the cabin. I need to check my tanks. Do you know how to dive?" *Idiot*. Of course he knows how to dive. He's an ex-Marine, for crying out loud.

I glance over to where he stands. The salt spray and dirt across the glass windshied in front of the captain's chair impedes most of my the view of his face, but his eyes narrow in concentration. One finger runs across the screen of the fish finder. His other hand is on the sat phone, dialing a number, rattling off coordinates to someone I can only assume is Pierce.

A pop sounds as I roll my neck, then my shoulders. Breath leaves my chest in a slow exhalation.

For all my father's faults, he steered me to our goal. I don't have time for DEA bullshit. This is the find of my career, of my lifetime.

The *Santu Espiritu* is down there, I'm sure of it.

Certainty settles in, followed by confidence and excitement. Even if my dad didn't bother to tell me about his find while he was alive, I've found it now.

My chin juts out and I inhale the tangy salt air, calm settling over me.

Only one way to find out if I'm right or wrong.

"Did you ask if I could dive?" A gruff chuckle, before Dean ducks into the cabin.

Carefully, I pick my way back to the deck of the boat. "They're to the left of the—"

"Kinda hard to miss." Dean winks, the sunlight somehow managing to flash off his all-American smile. Two sets of tanks and respirators clank against the deck.

The masks and snorkels follow, then the fins.

Grief stops me in my tracks, stealing my breath.

"You okay?" Dean pauses, the weight belts in his hand dropping to the seating.

"Yeah. I'm fine."

"This is big, June. If what you think is down there is down there, take a minute. Soak it in. This is a big moment."

"It's not that."

I swallow against the lump in my throat. "Those were his tanks. My dad's."

Dean doesn't speak. Standing quietly for half a second, long enough that I regret saying anything at all.

He pulls me into him. His arms are around me, holding me. Strong. Safe. My cheek presses against his chest, his beard tickling my scalp, and I inhale deeply, catching the sea salt and sun scent of him, before cautiously circling his waist with my arms.

Dean leans his head on mine, and I squeeze my eyes shut.

There is what we had on the beach—the hot, the heavy, the kissing and his mouth and oh-my-god-the-kissing. And it was good.

Then there is this. This is what it could be, if it doesn't burn out like a short fuse on a stick of dynamite.

Him, holding me steady. The sun beating down on us as the boat rocks beneath my feet and my heart rocks inside my chest. In his arms, I can let the stress go. I can relax. This embrace is different. Comfort. Companionship. Safety.

More than good old-fashioned lust.

The ache inside my heart eases and I pull away, tilting my chin up at him, afraid to breathe.

He takes me chin in his hand, and his soft smile nearly undoes me. "Take as long as you need, June."

My throat bobs, and I press myself back against him, marveling at the way my body fits into his, the way he seems to know what I need.

The way he isn't afraid to give it.

"Yes."

"Hmmm?" The noise vibrates against my cheek.

"I said yes." I look back up at him.

"To go in the water?"

"No, I mean yes, obviously, but also *yes*. Yes, Dean, I would very much like to go on a date with you." It will be worth it. Even when he leaves. I'll risk the hurt for more of this, more of him.

More of us.

He flashes that dazzling smile, and it takes all my self-control not to push him down and have my way with him. Self-control helped out by the fact that my shipwreck might lie mere yards away in the sand.

Excitement ramps up, billowing sails fueled by my sudden hope for the future.

My wreck. And a hot date. Two things to live for. I grin like a fool. *Like a fool in love.*

"You ready?" Dean smooths a hair away from my face.

Acting on impulse, hope and excitement bubbling inside, I stretch up on the balls of my feet, pressing a quick kiss across his lips.

"I'm ready." I turn, checking the equipment with the practiced ease of someone who's done it a million times.

Beside me, Dean does the same. I watch him from the corner of my eye, my body intimately aware of his.

I'm excited. So excited that it doesn't feel real.

"Buoy's out?"

"Yes, ma'am." There's a smile in his words, but if I look at his dang dangerous lips again, I'll keep stalling finding out if my wreck is down there, or if… goosebumps pebble across my skin. If the narcotics are.

I slip into the cabin, adrenaline and excitement overriding my fear for once, and pull out my bikini from where Dean thoughtfully put it in the backpack, then pull out my black wetsuit.

Bikinis look great, but pairing wet skin and a nylon weight belt? No thanks.

The wetsuit cuts high on my legs like a one-piece, fitting like a glove, and the reflective taping works like a charm for visibility underwater.

My father bought it for me too, and I pause as I zip it up,

wishing he was here. Wishing we were doing this together. With one last look at myself in the mirror, I duck back through the door and onto the deck.

The sun slicks across the surface of the water. Out here, far from shore and closer to the Mexican border, the water isn't the typical gray-green murk of the gulf. It's a crystalline blue and turquoise. Visibility should be good. Whatever is down there, we'll see it.

I tug the tanks over my shoulders, clipping in, heart beating loudly in my ears. "Have you heard anything else from Thompson?"

Dean shakes his head, running a hand through his stubble as he straps on his tanks with the air of a man who's done it a thousand times. His face is a blank mask, inscrutable.

I bite into my lower lip.

Are his men trustworthy? Dean thinks so. It will have to be good enough for me.

"They're safe. They know protocol when things get iffy."

Tension returns to my chest, my stomach tightening. My nerves are haywire, operating on overdrive.

Probably a side-effect of being shot at too many times in a forty-eight-hour time period.

"Okay." I shuffle to the back of the boat, noting Dean has already lifted the props out of the water.

The long fins snap onto my feet, and I pull my hair back into a tight bun. The mask strap pulls on, and the snorkel flops against my cheek. Dean sits next to me, loosening the straps on his fins with a quiet efficiency that, for some reason, really does it for me.

Hot and competent.

"What's that look for?" He grins.

A small shrug. "Just hopeful."

"Ah."

He doesn't need to know I'm hopeful about more than the *Santu Espiritu* now.

"I'm going first."

"I'm perfectly happy to let you go first." His gaze runs across my legs. "But, for the record, I don't mind if we both go at the same time."

Heat spreads through me and I squeeze my eyes shut, as though it will block out my sudden fantasy of the two of us, tangled together, *going* at the same time.

Leaning backwards, I meet the cool embrace of the gulf waters instead.

Not that they'll bank the heat in me.

CHAPTER
TWENTY-SEVEN

DEAN

JUNE POPS up a few feet off the boat, floating on her back, and I bite back a groan at the sight of her body. Tantalizing and wet, the straps of the scuba tanks amplifying her cleavage against the zipper of the wetsuit in a way that makes me want to forget about this damned mission.

Checking the tanks one last time, I test the air from the respirator. It isn't stale. Everything is fine. Yet I can't shake the feeling that something is off. That after last night, June finding this blip on the sonar fish finder was a little too easy. A little too convenient.

Could be a wild goose chase. Might be some unlucky fishing boat down there.

Or it could be the drugs, or the centuries-old shipwreck June seems to believe is waiting for her. The sun lashes against me, and I take a deep breath, the Marine Corps tattoo standing out against my skin.

I can't believe I thought June was just like Fiona. June Legarde couldn't be less like her. All they have in common is their beauty, and even that is worlds apart. Fiona doesn't hold a candle to June.

June is a dream of what could be. Brilliant, brave, her sheer determination and ambition… the total package.

"Are you coming with me, or are you going to stare all day?" June's voice cuts through my reverie, her gleeful tone triggering another smile.

Biting down on the respirator, I splash overboard.

Bubbles wreath around me, and my eyes take a moment to adjust to the darker waters of the gulf. June's legs dangle in front of me, and my hands stretch towards her, already wanting her close again. Her face appears, her dark hair already slipping loose and floating around her. She flashes me the okay symbol, which I return before catching her hand in mine.

The way it feels—her slender fingers entwined with mine, the current gently tugging our bodies, June's eyes wide behind her mask—I wish I could hold onto it forever.

The mechanical sound of their breathing and the gentle slosh of saltwater act like a balm on my soul. It's been too long since I've done this, dove without fear of what waited when I emerged.

We sink slowly, timing our descent. The boat shrinking as we swim, a shadow across the ocean floor. Schools of glittering silver fish swarm around us. Pressure on my fingers swings my attention to June, who points at something in the deeper, murkier waters.

A tell-tale fin appears, then vanishes back into the deeper water.

Adrenaline pumps through me, and June raises a hand to her head in the universal sign for shark.

Out here, in the gulf, it could be one of several varieties. Nurse sharks are fairly docile and would avoid us. Blacktips could get aggressive, as could the most likely candidate, the hammerhead.

Should've brought a harpoon. Just in case. The dive knife I nicked while she was in the cabin presses against my hip. It will have to be enough.

Still, it's unlikely sharks will bother us. Next to me, June swims surely, and I allow myself another moment to drink in the sight of her, lithe limbs and soft curves. I stroke my thumb over the side of her hand and she flashes me another okay sign. This tension between us—when it breaks, it will leave us ragged and gasping for more.

I can't wait.

Dappled sunlight colors the underwater world in light blues and aquas. More fish swim around us as we hit the seafloor, a sudden riot of colors. A brown and white striped grouper chugs along through the seagrass, startling a crab who hurries to get away from him. A school of black and white angelfish, a manta ray that wings away as fast as it can add to the wonder.

And then June tugs my hand, practically towing me behind in her sudden burst of speed.

Something looms ahead, casting a shadow on the sand and seagrass.

Tension winds my body tight, and I clench the respirator in my teeth. This is it. Either the narcotics are here and this gamble on my professor will pay off, or I'm screwed.

If it's the latter? If there are no drugs and she is just a dead end?

I'm not sure I can bring myself to let her go.

CHAPTER
TWENTY-EIGHT

JUNE

SEA LIFE GLIMMERS, parading all around us. Even the elusive amberjack make a showy appearance, massive silver bodies gleaming where the sun hits them, dazzling as they school above me, chasing smaller prey.

Vicious, nearly as long as I am, a sport fisher's wet dream.

But I turn my gaze, focusing on what lay beneath them, mostly buried in mud and muck, the teeming fish a sign that it's been here a long time, an artificial reef sunk in a devastating storm.

Dean trails behind me, as great a dive partner as I could ask for.

I close my eyes, trying to steady my body, my breathing.

At this rate, I'm sucking down oxygen too fast. Slow and steady. Relaxing will help the tanks last longer.

Something flashes in the sand, catching my eye, as we swim towards the looming structure. Pausing, I fan a foot over it, hovering, hoping it isn't just a stingray waiting to jab its next meal. More likely a shellfish, but it never hurts to be careful.

If this is the site of a massive archaeological find, I can't overlook the chance that this isn't just some pretty shell.

When nothing rises out of the sand, I dig my hand through it. Particles trickle around my fingertips, and I rub my other hand against it.

Disbelief surges. A hand grips my shoulder, and I stare at Dean, then back to the object in my hand. I can't look away from the dull, barely glimmering object.

Holding it up, I swear I hear Dean let out a laugh through his equipment. Bubbles wreath my face as I laugh into my own respirator.

The circular gold piece is heavy against my palm, the design eroded after over four centuries in the sand. The recent hurricanes must have shifted the seafloor, likely uncovering more of the wreck.

Because the gold piece…

It's a sure sign that the reef teeming with sea life in front of us is, in fact, the remains of the *Santu Espiritu.*

My heart hammers against my chest, and I close my eyes for a brief moment, attempting to regain some control over my body.

Finally, I open my eyes.

The reef is still there. Fish still swim around it, obscuring it from view. And Dean. Dean floats next to me, his expression inscrutable under the respirator and mask. I tuck the piece into a small zipper pouch hanging from my tank straps, careful to secure it.

This is it.

Elation spreads through my body, making my limbs feel even more weightless than the buoyant saltwater. My dad left clues to his life's work. To the wreck he told me stories of as he tucked me into bed at night, the ship we'd worked together to find under the hot Texas sun for most of my life. This was for *me*, not for some criminal organization.

He hadn't been running drugs.

Bubbles pour from my respirator, and I swim towards the structure with my heart in my throat. Saltwater pools at the bottom of my mask, but it isn't from the sea. I swim faster, Dean keeping pace beside me, the long fins propelling us through the water. Amberjack scattering as we approach.

A rotting wood pier juts from the seafloor and I pinch my nose, decompressing my ears before swimming down to inspect it. Dean swims on, powering through the water.

Gently, I fan a hand over its surface, sending several irritated shrimps curling their bodies away, legs fluttering in the current. Emerald-green algae and crimson barnacles distort the carved imagery, but I would know it anywhere. I bring a hand to my mouth, forgetting the respirator is there.

The *Santu Espiritu*.

The woman's mostly disintegrated face takes on an eerie, nightmarish quality underwater, the wooden hair fanning around her face covered in living creatures. She was built to withstand the onslaught of salt and sun, and she'd withstood the currents and tides of the gulf for almost five hundred years.

Blowing out the breath in my lungs, I sink to my knees on the seafloor next to the sad remnants of the figurehead.

Any lingering doubts long gone.

A career-defining moment. A life's goal achieved—and all I can think about is how badly I wish my father was here to share it with me.

CHAPTER
TWENTY-NINE

DEAN

I SLOWLY LOOP around the ship—which, I have to admit, is pretty fucking cool. June flits about the rotting wooden remnants of the *Santu Espiritu*, swimming in some kind of pattern that I chalk up to a protocol she has, or conversely, a random product of excitement.

She's beyond thrilled. Her body telegraphs joy at every turn, and she keeps bringing her hand to her mouth, even though it's already covered. Even if she didn't, her frantic thumbs up signaling and pointing does it.

Despite my secondhand excitement for June, worry gnaws at the pit of my stomach.

This is wrong.

The shipment is here somewhere. It makes more sense that June's dad would scuttle the drug sub nearby, where June would no doubt eventually stumble over it. The drug shipment? That's the least of my worries.

The stakes are higher than cocaine and opiates.

No. Whatever's hiding inside that sub should turn the tables on a string of domestic terrorist cells. I don't know how far up into the government they go: names, place, meeting times. Or most importantly, their plans. According to all the chatter, all the reasons I put my crew on this op once I'd been read in, this shipment is the key to disrupting their plans. But it won't make a fucking difference if I can't find it.

My pulse beats inside my eardrums, amplified by the near silence of being underwater. I swim out a little further past the find, confident June will be fine if I slip away for a few minutes.

A grayish rock peeks out from behind undulating ribbons of seagrass, small fish darting around it. A blanket of green moss covers most of it. I swim past it, eyes scouring the sand and silt. Ten yards. Fifteen.

Then it hits me.

Eyes wide, I stretch my arms out and scissor my legs, turning back towards the remains of the *Santu Espiritu* and that gray rock.

It wasn't a blanket of moss.

It's a fucking camo net. *Jesus.*

My fingers scrabble over the rock, pulling the thick green netting back as far as I dare. A sharp edge on the metal slices my finger, and red leaks into the saltwater in a stinging rush, but I don't care.

Fuck.

It's massive.

The sub is eight feet long, easily, half buried in mud and silt, everything but the tip painted in a flaking camouflage that would make it harder to spot from the air when pulled behind a boat.

There's no way I'm moving this on my own.

My hands carefully work over the rough surface until I find the seam and follow it to the lock for the hatch.

Opening it underwater means contaminating any evidence.

Shit.

The needle on my air gauge dips into the red zone. Less than ten percent of air left. My size, though an asset on land, always causes problems when it comes to how fast my lungs need air.

A tentative plan forms in my mind.

We have to surface. A loud roaring sound fills my ears, and a shadow passes over the seabed.

A boat.

It's gotta be Pierce.

Dread weighs my limbs down, more effective than the diving belt around my waist. Not the ideal reaction to a team member arriving, but where the hell has he been?

My eyes dart to the gauge. It's time to grab June and get to the surface.

Quickly, I pull the netting back over the tip of the sub, my fingers clumsy from the cut on my palm. Not a perfect job, but it will have to do.

Shit is about to get real interesting.

———

From the moment I catch June's attention, tapping my dive gauge and pointing up to signal starting the slow ascent, my mind works at a record pace. Which, considering it's been muddled with lust for the last two days, isn't saying much.

Breaking the surface first, the sun dazzles in my eyes. Pierce's boat looms near the *Betty*, quiet, motors off. No sign of Charlie.

No sign of my men, either.

My stomach knots. I tug the respirator from my mouth and wait for June to breach the surface.

I need to tell her my suspicions about Pierce. I need June to be safe more than I've needed anything in a long, long time.

My jaw tenses. I don't know Pierce nearly as well as I would like.

I only hope Charlie is still with him.

Next to me, bubbles pop on the rippling water, followed by a glistening head of black hair. As soon as her respirator leaves her mouth, she lets out a joyous shriek, nearly dunking me as she wraps her arms around my neck. I kick double time towards the boat, heart heavy despite her happiness.

I can't unload on her right now.

She needs this moment.

I've already ravaged the memory of her father. I won't take this from her too.

June babbles and I force a smile, trying to recover some of that initial wonder at seeing the *Santu Espiritu*.

"I knew my father wouldn't have left those clues for me for it to be what you said."

Guilt claws at me. I blink, trying to match her smile with one of my own. I need to tell her I found the sub.

This fucking sucks.

Her hands are on my chest now, eyes gleaming with excitement. Not the tears she had earlier this morning. I'd do anything to keep from seeing them again, to keep this look on her face.

Even if it meant lying through my teeth.

It's safer this way.

"Did you swim off to see the figurehead? Can you believe what great condition it's in? That's museum quality. It must've been buried for hundreds of years. I bet the seabed shifted with that last massive hurricane we had, don't you think?"

She prattles a mile a minute, oblivious in her excitement.

Ignorance is bliss.

And it is so, so much safer than pulling her in any deeper.

"Hey, is that Pierce?" She starts waving her hands in the air, and I swear. "What's wrong? Pierce! Over here! Charlie, y'all, you're not going to believe what we found."

Not a sound comes from the other boat. My chest tightens, adrenaline sparking, tingling down into my fingers. This isn't good.

"June, we need to get on the boat." My voice is low, and I knife my legs through the water, wrapping an arm around June's waist as best I can with the tanks on her back.

"Where is Charlie?" She sputters, still staring at the boat.

"June. Move. Fast," I grunt. Finally, she complies, swimming easily to the back of the *Betty*. I get there first, wrenching the fins off and hauling ass up the ladder before lifting June easily next to me.

"What's going on?" She looks so worried, her lips pursed, furrows marring her features, that I can't resist. I want to wipe it off her face. I lean in, pressing a quick kiss to her mouth.

"Don't you two make a sweet couple." Pierce emerges from our cuddy cabin.

He's been on the *Betty*.

The hair on the back of my neck stands up.

Where is Charlie?

June laughs, a nervous, forced sound, and my knuckles crack. *Relax*.

"Well, what did you find down there, Dr. Legarde?"

"The wreck." Her throat bobs as she swallows, smiling in spite of her nerves. "It's in good shape. Good enough to excavate. With a proper team, that is."

Pierce's posture is loose, his stance easy, weight distributed between both legs. His arms tense at his sides.

"And what about you, Dean? What did you find down there?" His smile is betrayed by the simmering viciousness in his eyes. He steps closer, and my hand moves to the knife sheathed on the dive belt. June must notice too, because her body tenses next to me.

How the fuck does he know?

There's only one answer to that question, and it isn't one I like. Even if I suspected.

"Fish," I tell him blandly.

Pierce laughs, low and dangerous. A muscle twitches in my jaw. Quickly, I unsnap the tanks from my back, not caring that they might topple overboard. Fuck it. They're the least of my worries. If we get out of this mess, I'll buy June new ones. Hell, I'll buy her an entire dive shop's worth.

Standing, I try to put myself between Pierce and June. The moment goes long, and Pierce telegraphs the punch before he swings.

Amateur.

"What the fuck, man?" I growl, playing dumb.

Stupid is just about the only play I have. The goddamned weight belt hamstringing me is going to be an issue, though.

"I know you found the drugs."

Behind me, June gasps, and my heart splinters.

"We found the wreck," I counter.

"What is he talking about, Dean?" June's voice is higher than usual, tight and nervous.

"What am I talking about, Dean?" Pierce echoes, a smug grin on his face.

I growl, leveraging a punch of my own at Pierce's torso, which he dodges easily. My hand flits to the knife at my waist, but some kind of sick honor keeps me from pulling it. All I have is suspicion.

Pierce read my file. Knew what he was getting into with my past.

I would be the perfect fall guy. With the shitty end to my military career, my desperation to make my new contracting firm work, the way I lost bid after bid—I was ripe for a setup. Again.

Pierce steps left, trying to circle me, trying to force me away from June.

"What is going on? Where is Charlie?" June stands, her tanks on the platform behind her.

"Charlie is currently unavailable." A muffled shout punctuates his words, and I glance at the half-open cuddy cabin door.

This is now a hostage situation. Fuck. How the hell did Charlie manage to get herself taken hostage?

Charlie has never, not once, not gotten the drop on a target. I snarl.

"What is going on? Dean? What is going on?" June pleads.

I played this wrong. I should've told June. Instead, I threw her into a trap.

"Tell her what's going on, or I will." Pierce leans left, and I aim a kick at his right side, anticipating the shift in direction. My foot connects with his ribs in a meaty thud, but a wave hits the boat and I lose my balance, falling hard onto the slippery deck.

"What is he talking about, Dean?"

"Seems to me your *friend*," Pierce loads innuendo into the word, "has been lying to you. Taking advantage of you." His eyes narrow, and he whips to June.

No. I won't let Pierce hurt her. Hell will freeze over before I let him touch her. I stand unmoving between them.

"Dean?"

"June. Princess. He's lying."

"Dean didn't tell you why he left the Marines, did he?"

I aim a mean left hook at Pierce, but he neatly dodges it. He's smaller and faster, and I'm tired from swimming for the better part of two hours, from sleeping on a boat, from running the last two days straight—I'm slow.

Too slow.

Pierce's hand twitches at the gun holstered at his side, and my pulse throbs in my temple.

"He was expelled. Like the traitor to his country that he is. He's been working with the smugglers the whole time. The drugs are down there, aren't they, Dean?" Pierce's smile is razor-sharp now, and I don't know how I missed the edge to him these last few months. "They are, and he knew they were, and he wanted to use you as a hostage, as leverage, to get the drugs back to the cartel."

"It's not down there, Pierce. The sub isn't down there." I'll lie forever if it means keeping June safe.

"You were kicked out of the Marines?" June sounds small, but I can't turn towards her. Can't hold her close and tell her everything is going to be okay.

"He was. And for fucking the enemy, for selling secrets."

"No."

It was a lie. I didn't tell Fiona shit. I'd never sell out my people, never thought her questioning was more than curiosity. I knew better than to ever indulge her curiosity.

Unlike the piece of shit in front of me trying to twist my life and hurt June.

Enough.

I whip the dive knife out of my belt. Not my preferred weapon, but it'll do.

"See? He can't even deny it."

"I just did deny it, asshole." My rage begins to spike. I would love to plunge the knife straight into Pierce's smug face, to end this bloody. "I wasn't kicked out."

I hadn't re-upped. Under a cloud of suspicion, sure.

"You knew you could never live down the rumors."

Stabbing Pierce gains even more of an appeal.

It wouldn't show June he's lying, though, and it would ruin any hope at getting my firm off the ground.

No, attacking Pierce, as satisfying as it would be, would only prove I'm a fucking traitor. The whispered allegations that follow me would be even worse if I knifed my government-issue partner.

I study the knife for a moment, the lemon-yellow handle, the balanced tip. Then throw it, my aim steady as ever.

Throwing knives, however, is notoriously unreliable. More likely to piss off your opponent than hurt them.

Still. Pierce flinches and June gasps in disbelief. The knife sails past Pierce, landing with a splash in the water.

"I'm unarmed. Let her go." I hold my hands wide.

"Dean." I can't bear to look at June, listening to the way she sobs my name.

"The drugs *are* down there, aren't they?" Pierce's gaze is avid now, hungry.

Fuck him.

"She didn't know shit. Your intel was bad." Behind me, June sucks in a breath.

Something bangs against the cabin walls. *Charlie.* Goddammit, this is a clusterfuck of epic proportions and I can't think straight with June here, in danger.

I raise my hands over my head, the barely healed wound in my side pulling tight.

"Smart. Smarter than I gave you credit for."

"June," I bark her name. "Go."

Salt spray licks across my back and June is gone, hopefully swimming to the rental boat Pierce anchored. Something like pride flickers through me, replaced by the agony of knowing she must hate me now, must think the worst.

At least she's out of harm's way.

Even if it means we'll never be together.

CHAPTER
THIRTY

JUNE

I SPUTTER, saltwater stinging my eyes, lungs burning from the effort of hauling ass across the water to Pierce's boat. Water puddles around me on the white fiberglass deck and I stay low, out of the *Betty's* line of sight. Checking the radio first, I pull the walkie set off the carrier.

The wire's completely cut. *Son of a gun.* Not that the Coast Guard could make it out to the middle of the gulf fast enough. At this rate, I doubt even Dean's Ken Dolls will make it in time.

Across the water, the *Betty's* engines rev.

A bullet pings off the side of the rental boat, and my mouth drops in disbelief. He's shooting at me? A DEA officer, who accused Dean of working for the smugglers?

Uh, what the fuck?

My mind clips along, sorting and filing information.

Dean's discharge from the Marines is due to some impropriety with a woman. Not good. Dean was scary with that knife on the boat. Which, if I'm honest, wasn't completely uncalled for, understandable even, given that Pierce has to be working for the Russians.

Why else would that smarmy jerk be shooting at me?

Which brings me to the biggest problem: Pierce is working for the Russians.

My fingers work on automatic, finding the key fob and turning the boat on.

Pierce is working for the Russians.

He has Dean.

Charlie, too, from the sound of it.

Plus, that absolute turd of a human is shooting at me. At me! A professor at an esteemed university, the woman who found the legendary *Santu Espiritu*. It's unconscionable.

Absolutely ungentlemanly behavior. The man is a criminal.

It will not do, and it will not stand.

Quite frankly, I'm sick of men acting like I don't know what I'm doing.

Anger rises in me. Conviction matching it.

A seed of a plan forms in my head.

I'm going to rescue Dean. And Charlie. Pierce will never see it coming. Because he can't see past his own dick.

Frowning, I chew my lip. No, that isn't right. He's definitely overcompensating; he probably can't even see his own dick.

I might be in shock again.

Funny how that keeps happening.

Another bullet pings, slicing into the padded captain's chair, and I stamp my foot, glaring across to the *Betty*. Shoving the engines into the water as I drop into a squat, bracing myself against the steering column.

I turn the idea around in my head. It's risky, for sure.

Perhaps not the most brilliant thing I've ever conceived of, but desperate times call for desperate measures. Ugh. I must be stressed if I'm thinking in clichés.

"Hey, dick for brains!" I scream. "If you want to kill me, you'll have to catch me first. And since I've had the drugs the whole time, you might want to rethink that plan, or you'll never find them."

I gun the boat, my heart in my throat. This entire, incredibly stupid plan hinges on Pierce taking the bait—and thus being stupider than my stupid plan.

Flawless.

"June, shut *up*." Dean looks livid, his hands behind his back, zip-tied to the railing. Pierce raises the gun, bringing it down onto the back of Dean's head. His eyes close and I half-scream, half-yelp.

Oh no, he did *not* just pistol whip my man.

Pierce slowly turns towards me, and even from here, the malice sparking in his eyes makes my blood run cold.

No, not cold. It's definitely hot. Boiling, even.

I'm *fucking* furious.

But I know the *Betty*. The bilge pump is taking on water, water that, if it isn't expelled, will be a problem.

Fortunately for me, that's exactly what I need: a complete catastrophe.

Eyeing the control panel, I memorize the layout. These rental boats are a dime a dozen on the coast. How many times did I listen to my dad detail what they kept on board, how out-of-towners were better off with him than on some of these by themselves? How the wake they created when they didn't know better was dangerous as all hell?

Ha!

Still. It'll take all my skill to keep this big lug of a boat steady and create the wake I need without swamping myself.

I crank the wheel one hundred eighty degrees, turning it back towards the *Betty*, hot on my tail. The rental changes directions so quickly it catches the other boat in a massive wake, sending it skidding over the wave, smashing into the water on the other side. I look over my shoulder. A green gush of water shoots over the bow, sending a wave of water back over it.

I pass the side of the boat, flattening out against the floor. No bullets fly.

"Ah, rang your bell a little, did I?" A high-pitched laugh startles me, and I look around for a second before realizing it came out of my mouth. Panic? I ran straight past it into sheer mania.

Love this journey for me!

Popping up for a moment, I glance over my shoulder. My heart nearly stops when I catch sight of Dean hanging limp against the railing.

"Fuck," I mutter.

I'm a good swimmer, a great swimmer even, but I need Dean conscious if I'm going to get Charlie out, too. Leaving either of them isn't an option. Not going to happen.

Pulse skyrocketing, I glance at my watch out of habit, only to realize it must've died at some point. At least it won't tell me to breathe or some bullshit.

Pierce yells something incoherent, and I chance a second look back.

His face is red with rage, apoplectic. A silvery gun flashes, and I flatten again. A bullet going wide, lodging into the door of the rental.

I pick up more speed, then cut back across, sending the *Betty* flying over the wake again. This time I don't slow down, immediately circling back behind the other boat, and Pierce takes the bait.

Stupid, stupid Pierce.

Thank you for your service, asshole.

The *Betty* splashes down hard, a third massive wave hitting it. The water's ridiculously choppy now, the two cruisers skidding across and into the waves. I shiver, goosebumps pebbling over my arms despite the sun.

This could still end really badly.

I can't think about that possibility.

The *Betty* is moving slower now, and my stomach sinks. This might get us all killed. Sunk in the same spot as the *Santu Espiritu* did, all those years ago.

I smile grimly.

It's too late now.

The *Betty* won't make it much longer. It's do or die. Literally.

I push the handle forward, picking up speed for one last chaotic circle. The *Betty* slices over my wake, the waves even bigger now.

"There's fucking water in the boat." Pierce's rage sounds over the motors, crystal clear.

"Get up, Dean, get up," I urge.

I look back, and hair lashes across my face, stinging my eyes.

Shock wrenches me at the sight.

Charlie.

She's on the deck, her blonde hair streaked with red, her hands cuffed. Pierce holds a gun to her head. Dean is still, a trickle of crimson falling across his shoulder.

I chose wrong and I'm going to get us killed.

"Fuck." The word comes out with delicious force.

The time for professionalism is over.

"I'll shoot her if you don't stop. I'll shoot both of them. I don't give a fuck. Tell me where the drugs are now," Pierce screams. Charlie fidgets beside him.

I nod slowly, gauging the level of water in the back of the boat. It comes up to Dean's ankles.

There isn't a lot of time.

I kill the motors, the wake still rocking the boats unsteadily, and I grip the captain's chair with all my strength to keep from falling over. A wave sloshes into the boat, coating my feet.

"Okay," I cry out, loud enough to be heard over the water. I hold my hands up in surrender. "I'll tell you. Just put the gun down and I'll tell you what you want to know."

Another wave from the wake smashes into the *Betty*. Water streams over the sides, and finally Dean moves. Hope bubbles inside me as I keep my eyes on Pierce.

"The drugs are in my office. At the university." I grasp around for straws, raising my chin, trying to figure out where the hell I would have hidden god only knows how many drugs in my tiny office.

The entire idea is absurd.

"There's a drink machine outside my office. It hasn't worked in years. Everything's inside the vending machine."

"You're lying." Pierce shakes the gun, water licking around his shins.

"No." Yes. Yep.

Pierce kicks at the water, sending spray up onto Dean. His fingers twitch behind him. "What the fuck is wrong with your—"

Charlie explodes into action, driving her forehead straight into Pierce's face. He staggers back, blood leaking from his nose, and my jaw drops. Without missing a beat, Charlie sweeps his legs from under him and he splashes into the water, the gun floating back towards the engines.

"You fucking bi—"

"Shut up." Charlie kicks him in the ribs. Water splashing, soaking her shorts. Twice. Three times.

Pierce coughs once, then goes quiet.

Well. He can follow orders.

"Charlie? Are you okay?" I shade my eyes with my hand, in total disbelief.

Charlie kicked his ass. Pierce's chest and legs, technically, but maybe she did get an ass kick in there.

"We're sinking, I have a concussion and I'm handcuffed. And our old friend Marine One over here looks worse." Charlie wades over to where the gun floats, aiming it at Pierce, who sits up, looking, if at all possible, even angrier.

"You wouldn't know what to do with that gun if it told you," he says, a snide look on his face. It's slightly ruined by the blood running down his cheek.

I tilt my head, twisting my lips to the side.

"From what I can see, she looks pretty competent," I yell at him.

Which is… odd. All of this is odd.

Pierce kicks out a leg, and Charlie fires the gun. Blood blossoms across the surface of the water, coiling crimson against brackish green.

"I warned you," Charlie tells him with a sweet smile.

"You shot me." He sounds shocked.

"You'll live, you asshole. Tell me where the keys to the cuffs are, or I'll shoot you again."

"Fuck you."

"Fine, the hard way, then." A second shot rings out, more blood clouding the water. Pierce screams, Charlie smiles, and my mouth hangs open as I watch.

"You're crazy. You're all crazy," Pierce whines.

Dean stirs again, coming to. Finally. Finally.

"Keys?"

Pierce's groan is loud enough to be audible over the still-running motor of the *Betty*.

I inhale sharply as Charlie digs a finger into the gunshot wound on his shoulder. "Oh, they're not there, are they?"

"Pocket. Back pocket."

Charlie pushes him to an upright position, causing another groan of pain, and my stomach flips.

"June. June." Dean's voice is raspy, slurred. Shit. He sounds awful. I drink him in, the stubble that now borders on a full-grown beard. He's so damn handsome, it makes my heart hurt. God, I hope he's okay. He has to be. "Why is your boat sinking? Why is Charlie holding a gun on me?"

I flip my attention back to my friend. Charlie's eyes are flat. Guarded. Her easy-going smile nowhere to be found. Suspicion nags at me.

"Charlie—"

"The drugs aren't in your office, June. Where are they?"

"Charlie, put the gun down." Dean suddenly seems more alert. The water laps at his knees, and he works his wrists gently, his shoulders bunching.

Distraction. He needs a distraction.

"Oh, oh my god, Charlie! Charlie," I cry out. Will I win an Oscar? No. "You shot him. Several times." I pause. "Good job on that, actually." As the words come out, it clicks. "And you ran over that guy in the parking lot… on purpose, didn't you? Who are you? Is Charlie even your name?!"

"Put the gun down, Charlie." Dean's voice is low now, warning laced through the words. Ugh, I could shake him. Hello! I'm trying to make a distraction here.

"Shut up, Dean, your way isn't working." Charlie's eyes slip back to Dean, and I let out an ear-piercing shriek.

"Charlie, what the hell? We're supposed to be friends and you're over there on my boat, which is sinking, by the way, did you notice that? And you're holding a gun on my boyfriend."

I have Charlie's full attention now, and Dean's. That delicious, cocky smile turns the corners of his mouth up, and I have never, ever been happier to see a damned dimple in my life.

"Boyfriend? Good. I'm glad you finally banged it out, June. I'm not holding the gun on him. I'm motivating you to tell us where the drugs are." She shakes her head, grinning.

"I don't know where they are." My voice is a thin whine of anxiety. "Is that all I've been to you? Some kind of drug mule?"

"June, no. Don't be like that." Charlie glares at me, then laughs. "And wait, what? That's not what that term means. At all." She snorts. "Trust me, it would be easier if you were just some drug mule. We'd just fish 'em right out of you."

"Ew," I say, cringing.

Dean mouths the words 'drug mule,' shaking his head and laughing.

I scowl at him. He doesn't seem too upset that Charlie is pointing a gun at him.

"I don't have a clue where they are, Charlie, and I don't appreciate feeling used."

Charlie runs a hand through her hair, the cuffs dangling from one wrist, flashing in the sunlight.

"Well, Evans, do you think she's telling the truth? Or were you blinded by the beaver yet again?"

My jaw drops. "You did not just say that about me."

Dean narrows his eyes at me. "She doesn't know."

"Idiots," Pierce mumbles. "All of you are fucking idiots."

"What's that?" Charlie steps on top of his thigh, causing more blood to leak into the water.

Pierce groans. "Are we going to get off this fucking boat or are you going to drown me?"

"Now that you mention it…" Charlie trails off, squinting across the water at me. "You really don't know, do you?"

"I don't. And I don't know who you are, but you aren't my friend." It sounds childish, but it freaking stings. It hurts. This whole time, for the last month, Charlie has been there. An ally in faculty meetings, a shoulder to cry on after my dad's funeral. I thought I was so lucky I'd met her and we'd hit it off right away—

"Oh my god. You've been here to find out about the drugs from me this whole time? You… you're not even an academic, are you?"

"Like that's the end of the world." Her tone is flippant, but her cocky smile disappears. "Is your boyfriend here going to attack me if I cut his ties? We need to abandon ship, Dean."

Dean brings his hands up in the air, the zip-tie gone. "Charlie, we are going to have a long talk about your methods when we get off this boat. You don't just get to decide to step all over the chain of command."

Chain of command?

"Fine." Charlie's brows rise. "Then let's move this party."

"What about me?" Pierce whines.

"Looks like you'll have to swim." Charlie takes a leap off the sinking boat, splashing into the water, gun tucked into her bra.

Dean stares at Pierce, who moans softly, bleeding from two bullet wounds. "Fuck."

Water laps Dean's waist and he bends down, tugging Pierce over his shoulder.

"Leave the traitor there, Dean," Charlie calls out before ducking under a wave, surfacing closer to my boat. No, the rental boat. My boat is now half sunk, about to join the *Santu Espiritu* at the bottom of the sea.

Dean grunts, stepping off into the water, towing Pierce behind him.

Trembling, I sit down heavily on the captain's chair and close my eyes.

I've been played, by a woman I thought was my new best friend.

Dean... Dean knows her. Knows Charlie. They're working together. The knowledge curls inside me, a snake waiting to strike. I shouldn't jump to conclusions, but when the conclusions in question are jumping out of a sinking boat—

None of it quells the rising relief in my chest, though. I'm alive. Dean is alive. Charlie is alive, though a complete stranger.

I found the sunken treasure ship and sank my own.

Dean is alive.

I'm alive.

I open my eyes, the sun glancing off the water. I frown, curious what it is that's caught my attention. Probably Pierce's foot. Dean is foolishly hauling him across the water to the rental boat.

Charlie hauls herself from the ladder.

"June, I should probably apologize." Water puddles at her feet. "Dean and I don't always agree on our methods. I didn't mean to scare you with that, I'm sorry. It's nothing personal."

"Not now, Charlie." My frown deepens, whatever it is I saw tugging at me, demanding attention.

Something about the water.

Pierce's toes stick out from it as he floats along behind Dean.

"Okay, don't talk to me," Charlie mutters. "I saved the day, but go ahead and be mad." Out of the corner of my eye, I see Charlie shake her head, wringing her hair out.

The water changes around Pierce, frothing with movement.

A triangular shape cuts through the top of the foam before disappearing.

"Shark," I scream, my body going rigid with shock and a new round of adrenaline. At this rate, my kidneys are going to shrivel up into dried beans. Perfect for canning, less perfect for daily use.

Dean swims faster, and a second, bigger fin cruises behind him. Pierce is leaving a blood trail, leading the way to the human all-you-can-maul buffet.

A pistol thunders next to me and I swing my attention to Charlie, who peppers the water with bullets.

"Stop it. You'll hit one of them," I yell at her.

"That's the point." Charlie frowns as the trigger clicks, the magazine empty.

"What the hell is wrong with you?"

Dean's still doing his best to swim faster.

Terror grips me. What if the sharks don't go for Pierce, but for Dean?

Am I really this close to a flipping chance at happiness, only to have a shark rip it away?

"Why does this remind me of *The Old Man and the Sea*?" Charlie's head is angled at the water. "Except like, way less boring. Never liked Hemingway."

I gawk at her.

Maybe there *is* something I can do. Spinning on my heel, I turn into the cabin of the rental boat, ignoring the walls pressing down on me, caging me in. The cushion thuds against the floor, the storage compartment torn apart in my search. Finally, I look up, heart pounding in my ears.

There it is.

My hands wrap around the cold metal surface of the harpoon, and I race back through the tiny door, slamming behind me. I pull the diving mask off my neck, strapping it back into place.

"Wait, no, June, don't." Charlie tugs on my arm, but I shrug her off.

"Just don't fucking shoot at me, asshole."

Charlie stares at me, clearly shocked by my vocabulary.

Worth it.

I grip the hot railing tight as I step up onto it, the harpoon in the other hand. Finally, I straighten, eyeing the three fins now bobbing around the two men.

"June!" Charlie yells. "Be careful."

"Like you care." I launch off the side of the boat, splashing into the water, slicing through it as fast as I can, harpoon in my fist.

This might be the stupidest thing I've done yet today.

I'm going for a new record. Good for me.

Not only is there a chance harpooning one of the sharks will cause a massive frenzy, making the situation more dangerous, but there's also a chance one will attack me.

Too late now!

My arms cut through the water, legs propelling me on a burst of energy I could've sworn I ran out of. Lactic acid builds up, burning my thighs and calves. I push the pain out of my mind.

Fuck this. Fuck Pierce. Fuck the damn sharks and fuck the smugglers.

I focus on the anger, on all that hot resentment building inside me.

Fuck Charlie for lying to me. Fuck my dad for lying to me.

Fuck 'em all.

The water is choppier now, the wind kicking up the waves. I cut through them, trying not to grind the snorkel to bits in my mouth. A deep inhalation brings saltwater into my lungs, and I blow out fiercely.

Seconds seem to turn to days.

And then, there they are. Dean's legs churn the water up behind him as he struggles to keep Pierce afloat.

Three hammerheads circle. There's at least half a dozen more right below. I've got one shot. I'll have to use it well.

I slow, dog paddling next to Dean, my gaze firmly fixed away from his body. I'm hell bent on protecting it.

One of the sharks picks up speed, maw gaping open, rows of razor-sharp teeth aiming for Pierce.

I hesitate. He would deserve it.

Instead, I kick out a leg, connecting with its sensitive eye. It swerves, diving back into the murk. Now just two.

Dean and Pierce are closer to the boat now, and I can hear the sound of the motor.

Charlie is going to leave me. She's going to leave us all.

I swim toward the noise, keeping my eyes firmly fixed on the sleek predators around me. Dean must be close to the ladder, but they'll have to figure out how to get Pierce on board.

I've got to keep him safe. I can't lose him, not when I just decided to go on a date with him. And how long has it been since I've been on a date?

Too fucking long, that's how long.

I deserve a date, goddammit. No hammer-fucking-head shark is going to bite its way through my date with Dean.

Another shark approaches. I kick my legs and swim towards it, my teeth clenched around the snorkel. It breaks the surface, then dives back down.

Yeah, you should be afraid, bitch.

I paddle closer to the boat, the harpoon still at the ready. As long as there is a threat to that kernel of happiness I felt this morning, there's no way I'll stop.

Something bumps me, then tugs at my waist. My heart stops and I elbow back on reflex, crunching into cartilage.

Please don't be a shark.

But it didn't hurt. Could be shock. I swivel as fast as the current allows.

Dean.

He tugs me along now, pulling me behind him until my brain catches up. *Pierce must be on the boat.* Coming to my senses— what's left of them—I swim, the sharks finally scared off by the noise of the motors.

I cut through the water, Dean still pulling me behind him, his hand heavy against my arm as he eventually pulls me onto the boat.

Someone gently extricates the harpoon from my hands, and I pant on the deck, shivers wracking my body. Pierce is handcuffed, turning paler by the second as blood leaks from the bullet holes in his shoulder and thigh.

My leg connects with his shin and he opens his eyes for a moment, a wicked smile on his face.

"She's just your type, isn't she, Dean? Mean, and probably a sleeper for the other side. Just like her dad."

Dean swings, a sickening thud sounding as his fist connects with Pierce's jaw. "I saved your ass. Talk shit about her again, and I'll throw you back to the sharks myself."

"Nah, you need me. Turning in a dirty agent?" Pierce laughs, a hoarse, wrecked sound. "Better than telling Uncle Sam you killed me, especially with your record."

"He has a point, Dean." Charlie turns the wheel, steering back for land. "Besides, I think June's traumatized enough."

Dean's eyes widen, and he kneels next to me. There's a welt on his forehead, and I reach for it.

"That looks bad." My teeth chatter. I'm so damn cold.

"Fuck, princess."

His arms wrap around me and I close my eyes, snuggling into his neck. He's so warm.

"I ninja-kicked a shark."

"Yeah, you did."

"I saved the day."

"You sank your own boat."

"Same difference." I look up at him, a soft smile on my lips. I like him so much. Even if he lied about Charlie. That was before I knew him, or about the pieces he put in place to stop Pierce from doing terrible things. He never lied about who he was. Charlie, on the other hand…

"The *Betty* didn't make it, but I saved you," I say.

"Yeah, I think you probably did."

I expected an answering grin, the cocky one I can't resist, but his expression is serious, thoughtful, even. Dean rubs his cheek against the top of my head and I sigh, pulling myself closer to him.

Maybe I'll get that date after all.

CHAPTER
THIRTY-ONE

DEAN

A HOSPITAL MACHINE BEEPS, and the steady drip of the IV in June's arm half lulls me to sleep. Cream walls, white bedding, a whiteboard with patient care notes on it.

Thank God the only thing wrong with June is dehydration and shock.

I'd never forgive myself if anything happened to her today. Not today, not ever. But in my line of work, that seems to be a near guarantee.

Selfish. I'm so fucking selfish for wanting to be with her. All I can give her are lonely nights while I travel, working. I've seen it too many times, partners left behind, scared and in the dark about where their loved ones went. What they did in the shadows.

June deserves so much more than that life.

The door to the room creaks open and I shoot up, hand on the pistol I refused to part with. The cartel still coming.

They don't like loose ends.

I watch the door as a brunette bustles in, dressed in slacks and a button-down.

"Charlie? What happened to your hair?" My secret weapon,

the most unpredictable member of my team, living up to her reputation, as always. I'd be amused if I wasn't still pissed at the way she handled the entire situation with Pierce.

"It's a wig. Wake her up." Charlie expertly unhooks the IV. "You still armed?"

"Always."

She nods, and I wipe my bleary eyes. "We need to get her out of here."

I spring into action, collecting myself. "They're coming?"

Another nod. A machine screeches, angry it can no longer track June's heartbeat.

"Pierce is gone," Charlie says.

"Fuck."

"You should've left him there." She looks at me.

"You know I couldn't."

"I know."

June sits up, awake, her hair wild, eyes wilder. "He's gone? How?"

"I left his room for a second." Charlie looks chagrined. "I assume he had help."

I smoothed a hand over June's forehead and she swats it away, glaring at me. "Wait a minute. Why is she still here?"

"You were in shock. You've been asleep for four hours," I say.

"Answer the question."

I hesitate. "Charlie is part of the team."

"Obviously."

"Listen, June, I'm sorry. I know it's a lot to take in."

"And I want you to hurry the hell up." Charlie pats the brown wig.

"You're upset." My eyes dip toward Charlie.

"She lied to me. You both have been lying to me. Of course I'm upset."

"We did what we had to do to keep you safe." Something I would do again and again if I needed to.

"And find the drugs," Charlie adds.

"And find the shipment," I agree, and June's eyes squeeze shut.

"We have to go. We don't know if he's coming back for you." Charlie's voice is tight.

"How did he get away? Can't you track his phone or something?" June undoes the blood pressure cuff, and Charlie's face remains a blank mask.

"Here," Charlie says, and puts her field training to good use by quickly taking the IV needle out of June's arm and sticking a Snoopy band-aid on her.

"I don't have a court order to track his phone. Yet," I finally answer, shooting Charlie a warning look.

June swings her legs over the side of the bed, then sags slightly.

"Slow and steady." My heart clenches at the sight, the fight in her struggling against the bone-deep weariness I feel too. "You have a safehouse for us?"

"Yeah, of course." Charlie's lips are an angry slash against her face and I study her, surprise widening my eyes. She's hurt by June's clear mistrust and anger.

It isn't often Charlie gets to work undercover with good people, people like June. Even someone as hardened as Charlie isn't immune to feelings.

"We need to move. We can't risk staying here," Charlie urges.

"If you were better at your job, maybe we wouldn't have to." June's tone is clipped. Angry.

Charlie steps closer, her brows knitting together. "That's not fair, and you know it. Everything I did, I did because it was the best option. I kept you from getting shot and captured. Yes, I lied to you. Does that mean we weren't friends?" Her mouth twitches into a frown. "I think you're the only one who can answer that question."

"You were always my friend, Charlie." June's words are soft. "I shouldn't have snapped at you. But you lied to me, manipulated me, even, and that hurts. You aren't who I thought you were."

"I did what I had to do." Charlie moves toward the door.

I step closer to June. "None of us meant to hurt you, princess."

"I think you believe that, both of you. But it doesn't mean you haven't, does it?" A sad smile crosses her face.

June stretches, and I reach out to her. My heart swells as she takes my hand.

"Do you have clothes for me?"

I shake my head, a fresh wave of guilt washing over me. All she has on is a hospital gown. She makes it look damn good.

"Here." Charlie thrusts her purse at June. "I grabbed some things from your house for you... before all this, I mean. When I saw the Jeep wreckage…" Charlie's throat bobs, and she shakes her head. "You might not want to go back there for a while. June, I meant what I said on the boat. None of us got into this job to hurt good people. Like you."

June squeezes her eyes shut, and I rub her back. "We'll get him. We'll get him and then you'll be safe." It's all I can offer.

Wordlessly, June extracts a pair of beat-up jeans and a shirt that reads, *Divers Know How to Go Down.* I make myself look away as she tugs on the clothes.

"I'm not staying at a safehouse." She laces up a pair of sneakers.

"Yes, you are," Charlie snaps.

"No, I'm not. I'm so tired of hiding. Did you know they kidnapped me, Charlie? When I was a kid. I've been hiding my whole goddamn life." She gestures around, resigned. "And look where it's gotten me. Nowhere. Trouble found me anyway."

My stomach falls. That's what I am to her. Trouble.

I can't let her down now.

"She can come."

"She's not coming." Charlie tugs on the mouse-brown wig.

"I already called it in, Charlie. Coast Guard should be heading for the site any minute now. We should both be there." A muscle twitches in my temple. "June should be there. She'll be safe with me."

Another machine beeps.

"Coast Guard? You did find the drugs." June's voice is small. Full of hurt. "They were by the wreck, weren't they? That's where you swam off to."

She sags back onto the hospital bed, eyes downcast. Her face so sad, so beautiful, it almost breaks my heart. Her palms press into her eyes, a ragged breath shaking her chest.

My heart twists, and I can't stop myself from moving. The bed protests as I sit next to her, gathering her up in my arms. Her cheek rests against my shoulder, hot tears leaking onto my skin. My shirt soaking them up, but it isn't enough.

I wish I could soak up her pain.

"He was running drugs. You were right." The words gasp out of her, barely audible. "I didn't want to believe it. I am an idiot."

Charlie turns away, facing the door, giving us privacy. The small but unexpected gesture surprising me.

I rub June's hair, savoring the silky slide of it against my fingers. "June."

"No, don't. You can't make it better. After they took me, he was so angry. So angry. Because they forced his hand—through me. I can't believe I didn't see it. I feel so stupid. Of course he went to work for them."

"You weren't stupid. We can all be blind when it comes to the people we care about." I know that firsthand. My lungs hurt. "You were leverage for the smugglers."

"Why my dad? Why us?"

I sigh, sending strands of her hair floating into the air. "Access. Your dad was ex-mil, knew the area, knew how to handle himself. You were an easy target. Opportunity and occasion." I rub her back, holding her close, her quiet sobs wracking her body against mine. "He did it to keep you safe, June. It's as easy and as hard as that."

"It doesn't make it right. None of this makes it right. I can't believe the stupid shipment was there."

Words fail me. I have no idea how to make this better. There's no way to stop her from hurting. Every fresh tear against my skin burns, acid regret.

"I should've told you. I tried to."

Damn it to hell, but I fucked it all up.

Minutes tick by, unaware that I wish time would stand still. That the world around us would vanish, that I could hold her against me, could help her shoulder this pain. Together. Until she was ready to face the future. With me.

Finally, June stands, pushing away from me. She brushes her long dark hair back off her shoulders, fire and fury in her eyes.

"I'm coming with you." She shoulders past me, pausing at the door.

"You're coming with us," I agree.

"No, you *will* let me come, because the Coast Guard will almost certainly destroy the archaeological site without me." Realization dawns on her face, her mouth a soft "o" of surprise. "I'm coming?"

I nod once. She's fearless. It makes me proud; I have no right to be. I had no hand in who she is. Today's been tough. She's seen some shit, and she came out even stronger.

She sank her own damn boat to save my ass.

Charlie sighs. "For the record, I think this is ridiculous. She's a civilian, Evans. A fact you should try and remember."

"I'm a civilian who blew up a propane tank with one shot and ninja-kicked a shark, Charlie. Call me June Bond if it makes you feel better."

Charlie snorts.

"Well, are we leaving, or are you two going to stand around all day and argue?" June crosses her arms over her chest.

Charlie grumbles something else about civilians, then pulls the door open and strides down the hallway, her brown wig bobbing as she walks.

June follows behind her and I tuck the pistol back into my shoulder holster, taking the rear position. A second call to the Coast Guard, and they'll wait another ten minutes to let us board. Thompson and Thorne are already on board.

Ten minutes, and we'll be back on our way to the site that nearly killed us all.

CHAPTER
THIRTY-TWO

JUNE

SHIVERS WRACK MY BODY. The adrenaline's still forcing its way out. My teeth chatter, and a concerned member of the crew brings me a thermal blanket and a mug of hot tea. I swear I'll take them a basket of cookies once it's safe to go home and bake them. Well, buy them. I won't have time to bake them, not with all the work I'll need to do on the *Santu Espiritu*.

First up: finding and funding a replacement for the *Betty*.

Thompson stands next to me, leaning on the railing of the cutter, looking off to the distance, and I study his face. He's handsome, that blond-haired and blue-eyed athletic quality that would have most women swooning.

Still, he has nothing on Dean's rugged looks.

I frown.

Dean, who got what he wanted from me. He found the drugs.

I have no right to hope for anything else from him.

He found the drugs, because my dad was a bad guy.

It makes me sick, and my knuckles whiten around the cup. The proof is undeniable. It's all around me, in the way all these government and military types hold their weapons, in the way the

Coast Guard cutter glides through the water, straight to the shipment they want to seize. Charlie would probably feel right at home here, but she stayed on shore at Dean's orders.

I sip the tea, holding it in my mouth, letting the warmth coat my throat. The sky a steel gray now, thunder threatening in the distance, the water choppy and rough. I used to love this weather as a girl, loved to watch it roll in and threaten violence from the skies.

Maybe I'm tougher than I give myself credit for.

"He likes you," Thompson finally says.

"Who?" I pull the blanket closer around my shoulders.

"Nah, you're smarter than that."

I nod. "It's going to rain." I'm too raw for this conversation, my nerves scraped bare by the revelation of my father's involvement. By the knowledge that I'm out of my depth when it comes to my feelings for Dean Evans.

"Do you like him?"

What is this, fifth grade? The question almost slips out, but I stop myself. Another shiver shakes me and Thompson reaches out, clamping my shoulder. I look up at him, hair whipping out of my hastily tied braid. Trying to focus on anything but the reality of where we're going.

More hair lashes across my face. *Ahhhh.* I will never go anywhere without my no-slip grip rubber bands again. Part of me is surprised my hair hasn't poked someone's eye out at this point.

"You don't have to answer. But I know him. I've known him for years. He's saved my life a few times." Thompson jerks his chin to where Dean stands, glowering at me. "He's got it bad for you."

"It doesn't matter." My throat is tight.

"Of course it matters."

"But he'll leave when this is over, and I'll be left with what?" I blink rapidly.

Thompson sighs, pulling me into him. "Don't cry. I can't stand it when pretty women cry."

I make a noise somewhere between a sniffle and a laugh. "I'm tired of being scared. I'm tired of trying and getting hurt."

He lets me go, pushing me away and resuming his lean against the railing. His biceps flex as he braces against a wave. Tea sloshes over the top of the cup.

"I think we're all tired of that." His eyes look old, the good humor replaced by something darker. "He's got walls up. The last woman, she did a real number on him."

"I'm not her." I'm sick of hearing about this other woman.

He chuckles again, a dark sound. "All I'm saying is if you like him, you should try. At least a little bit. I think he'll meet you halfway."

"I don't want halfway."

Thompson reaches out, tucking a strand of hair behind my ear. "You don't have to worry about halfway with Dean Evans. He's all or nothing."

He studies me, eyes lingering for half a second too long on my lips. "It's a good thing he found you first."

I have nothing to say to that, so I take another sip of the lukewarm tea. He dips his head and walks away.

The sea rolls under the boat, gray-green and inscrutable. Leaning my elbows against the railing, I turn Thompson's words over in my head.

I like Dean.

A lot.

He's a good man: smart, funny, kind, with a drive that matches my own.

We'll probably have the shipment in the next hour. And then what?

We have a few nights together, if we're lucky, and Dean and his merry band of man-meat will be on their way to their next job.

It's a surefire path to heartbreak, continuing this *thing* between us. I don't aim for things that aren't possible.

Well, except for the *Santu Espiritu*. No one seemed to believe I'd find that, and look how that turned out.

Self-satisfaction curls in my chest, purring like a happy cat.

At least I have that. At least I found the *Santu Espiritu.*

I always thought I'd be happier after I found the ship, like finding it would solve all my problems.

It didn't.

Maybe I should try for one more slightly impossible thing. Maybe I should just see what happens with Dean instead of over-analyzing everything.

White-capped waves break against the dark surface of the water, and my hands are steady on my cup. The shaking stops. The teabag's tag blows in the wind, and I let my mind drift.

"What'd Thompson say to you?"

I startle, so lost in my thoughts I didn't Dean walk towards me.

He steps closer.

Despite all my best intentions, the walls I constructed in my mind, the arguments against this, against him, fail completely.

I'm happy to see him.

"Was he an ass?" There's an edge to his voice now, so sharp it might cut me if I let it.

"Not at all." My voice is soft.

Dean stiffens next to me, a muscle twitching in his jaw, and I avert my eyes. Everything about this man appeals to me. But why should I be the one to fix him? It isn't my fault the last woman he loved did a number on him.

"Listen to me, princess."

"June," I correct, staring at the ominous gray horizon.

"Thompson is a sweet-talker." He clears his throat and I cough, covering up a laugh, and turn to him, an eyebrow raised. "I don't know what he said to you, and frankly, it's none of my business, but just, you know, he's a ladies' man. I saw him touch your hair."

"For crying out loud." Great. I'm falling for a man who makes a living doing all kinds of government dirty work—and is also an idiot. "You're right. It's none of your business."

He blinks, schooling his features into blankness.

"Do you want me to tell you what we talked about?"

"Maybe," he says cagily, eyes avid, betraying his interest. His big hands fist at his sides. I avoid rolling my eyes, but just barely.

"Maybe?" I echo.

"Okay, yes. Yes, I do want to know." He nods once, his eyes dipping to my lips, to the where my *Divers Know How to Go Down* shirt stretches across my chest.

"He told me you like me, and that you're a good guy, Dean Evans." My skin is electric, tingling in anticipation, my whole body primed to feel his hands on me.

My calves tighten as I raise up on my tiptoes and kiss him. He stiffens in surprise before his arms wrap around me.

Thunder rolls overhead and he deepens the kiss, his hands running through my still damp hair. My lips part, and I press myself against him. The hair on his jawline softer now, the harsh stubble gone. I revel in it, stroking his face, the blanket forgotten. The shivering stops as his tongue sweeps against my lower lip, and I moan into his mouth. Wanting his tongue in other places.

A crew member wolf whistles, a few others joining in.

Breaking the kiss, I grin at him and he turns, scowling. The Coast Guard applause dies at his expression.

"Do you want to know what else he told me, Dean Evans?"

I can't take my eyes off him, off the desire in his expression. Loving the feeling of him around me, caging me in against the railing, his massive, strong body protecting me. The way he protected me this whole time, and not just physically. Letting me believe in my father's innocence, letting me draw my own conclusions, then holding me tight as the truth came crashing down.

Part of me wants to be mad at him for ruining my memories of my father—but none of it is his fault. My father is in the past. What he did… it's unconscionable.

But Dean isn't in the past.

Dean is flesh and blood, standing in front of me. He is now. *And maybe…*

"Well?" I prompt when he doesn't answer.

He shakes his head, bringing his forehead to me.

"He told me to meet you halfway." I press another quick kiss to his lips.

"Is that so?" His voice is somewhere between a growl and a rasp, sending goosebumps pebbling over my arms. Tepid tea sloshes over my hand as the boat hits another rough wave. The first raindrops splash across my cheek and nose, and he wipes them away.

"I have a problem with that, though." I tilt my chin.

"Oh." Disappointment laces the syllable.

"Yeah. I don't want halfway."

Another wave hits, and his body rocks into mine. I groan, softly, eyes half closing at the pressure.

"What do you want?" His lips are at my ear.

"I want to go all the way." Fire races through my veins as I say it, my own words catching me off guard.

It feels good.

He kisses the side of my neck, and the rain begins falling in earnest. My eyes close.

"It's going to have to wait until we can get off this boat." Dean presses another kiss against my neck. "Because when I take you, it's going to be loud." He whispers it like a promise. "I'm going to figure out what makes you scream, and I'm going to do it over and over again."

"Oh." I blink. "Okay, sounds good to me."

"That's all you have to say?" he asks, laughing. He pulls back, and I drink him in, the aggressively masculine jawline, the heat in his eyes. The way his body feels against mine.

"What's wrong with what I said?" My nose scrunches. "I said yes. That sounds nice."

"Nice?" he chokes out.

I nod.

He lets out a loud laugh.

"Then let's get you out of this rain. I don't want you catching a cold, not with what I've got planned." He grins, and his wicked smile makes my knees weak.

"Do you think they'll turn the boat around? This could be an emergency, you know." I'm babbling again.

"What kind of emergency, princess?"

"Pants. Let's tell them I have a pants emergency."

He laughs louder and picks up my blanket.

"I doubt they'd do it, even for you, princess." Dean leans close again, tucking the blanket back around me. "It's okay, though. Just keep imagining how good it's going to be when I get you off… this boat."

He winks, and it's all I can do not to jump back on him.

"I'll get you some more tea," he says, tugging me into the safety of the cutter's cabin.

Tea, for once, isn't going to hit the spot.

CHAPTER
THIRTY-THREE

DEAN

THE SUB SURFACES, divers popping up around it, and my eyes dart around until I find June's dark hair. Rain drizzles steadily, the gulf's surface frothing and dangerous. Still, she wears a massive smile, waving at me from the water.

The Coast Guard allowed her to borrow one of their underwater cameras after she relentlessly hounded them about it. Dropping words like "priceless artifacts" and "go down in history for ruining an archaeological treasure," and my personal favorite, "lawsuits from UNESCO, Spain, Mexico, and my university."

When she mentioned the words "international incident," I had to turn away so no one would see me laugh at the brow-beaten expression on the captain's face. She finally relented, allowing June to accompany them once she provided digital proof of her diving and research credentials. No military officer wants to be in the news for fucking up an archaeological or historical site, and June knows it.

I am so fucking proud of her.

They insisted she wear one of their wetsuits, and I can't take my eyes away from her as she loads into the Zodiac boat and motors back to the cutter. The wetsuit fits her like a glove, all curves and muscle. The zipper down the back teases me, reaching from the top of her neck to the round curve of her ass.

The sub clangs as it hits the deck of the cutter. Stepping forward, I help the remaining crew secure it to the boat. My fingers itch to open it, to finally get closure. There's a fuck-ton of evidence in it, and from the weight the winch registers, more than drugs.

Good.

Pierce's involvement stinks.

Where there's one bad agent, there are usually more.

I swallow, rubbing a hand across my beard. It's one of the things Thompson and I worry about. Us contractors, we don't get the same benefit of the doubt.

Which means we need to be really fucking careful not to blow the tentative contracts we have.

We're good at being careful.

I wince. Usually.

This sub might be the key to something that's been forming for years. The same thing Fiona hinted at before the military rubbed her foreign agent affiliation in my face. Before they said leave or be fired.

Stomach clenching, I rake a hand across my scalp.

Either the evidence is in there and we have an uphill battle to fight, or it isn't and we have a lot more fucking work to do.

A crew member hands me a crowbar and Thompson, opposite me, catches my eye and nods.

"Do it, Evans."

"Could be classified."

"It's not officially classified until an analyst wearing a pocket protector decides it's classified, and you know it. Besides, if it's what we think it is, it's time-sensitive." His words are loaded with meaning.

The crew member shifts nervously next to me, and I fix the man with a hard stare until he wanders off to a safe distance, eyes firmly on the sea. The captain remains, a grim expression on her face.

The crowbar fits neatly into the slit of the metal hatch and I grunt, leveraging my weight on it. Mud and silt drip onto my shoes, cold and wet. The hatch pops open with a metallic clang, and the captain hands me a flashlight.

"Thanks," I say gruffly, clicking it on.

The high beam illuminates the interior. Dry. Everything in it is dry. Drugs, packed neatly in taped up bricks, stacked all together. Not as much as I assumed. *Minor drug shipment.* Sweeping the beam along the interior, something else catches my eye.

"Thompson, come look." I push aside the drugs with the flashlight, careful not to smudge any possible fingerprints.

A metal crate. The tell-tale symbol painted in fluorescent yellow on the box.

"Fuck." Thompson breathes. "You were right."

"Captain, we need to call this in," I say, hoping to god the metal crate is sealed correctly.

She takes a long look at the box, eyes widening. "On it."

I swallow. *This is it.* Exactly what I worried the analysts were hinting around at, the intel that I didn't quite scrape a high enough classification to access. It must be what the redacted cables referred to, and it's my worst nightmare.

Proof the domestic terrorists my team's been tracking are working with the Russians, and worse, planning something huge.

Domestic terrorists don't just order up weapons-grade uranium for shits and giggles. No, this brand of white nationalist doesn't go to this much trouble just to make a few threats and parade around chanting hate speeches before going home. They need to be dealt with, and they need to be dealt with quickly.

I breathe out slowly, pinching the bridge of my nose. This needs to be handed off to all the right agencies immediately.

I glance over to where June stands, a towel wrapped around her, something steaming in her hands, the wild look of excitement on her face, and resolve cements in me. This will get reported up correctly as soon as I can. HQ will figure out the next move, the next mission. I've done my job for the day.

June's lips curve into a smile, and she sips her drink.

The night, however, is still mine.

———

Thank god the crate was secured properly. It took the rest of the afternoon to clear the sub correctly, with people in full gear, their equipment crackling as they swept us for leaked radiation. And my mind has been working overtime, chewing over the facts of the case. But the evidence is in the proper chain now. I saw it off, signed the papers, ordered Thompson to write the report and brief the rest of the squad.

All the while thinking of June. The way she regaled the crew with stories of the *Santu Espiritu*, how she charmed them into letting her borrow their computer to email the photos she took of the wreck to her supervisor. To a news agency. To pitch a massive non-profit on assisting in the marine dig.

And now she sleeps peacefully in my replacement Jeep, her lips softly parted, face slack and sweet. So damn beautiful, and somehow, at ease with me after everything. Trusting me enough to sleep next to me again. Or at least, tired enough to. She fell asleep almost immediately, slept through the first pitstop I made too.

Excitement and nerves push to the forefront, left leg shaking as I drive. The ship docked in Corpus Christi, necessitated by the contents of the sub and the amount of manpower needed to clear the ship.

And I called ahead to our destination, waiting to be let off the cutter—thought I'd play it cool.

It isn't a government safehouse; not convinced requesting a safehouse here would even be prudent. No telling how far the corruption reaches. Besides, I want to do something nice for June.

I could be her safehouse, if she lets me.

I glance back at the packages I picked up in the backseat. Luckily, government contracting pays well. A knot forms in my stomach, and I clench my hand on the wheel.

What if she doesn't like it?

Then I'll get her something she will.

The second package, weapons, courtesy of Thompson slipping out and ordering them for pick-up as I processed the first tranche of paperwork. While June processed and catalogued the photos she'd taken.

We worked wordlessly, side by side, no need for conversation. Companionably. Occasionally, her knee would brush mine and it took all my restraint not to carry her off to one of the cutter's bunks.

"Hey." Her voice is gravelly with sleep as she sits up, rubbing her eyes.

"Hey yourself."

Destination looming on the horizon, I can't help the grin creeping across my face.

"What's that?"

"Well, it's not a safehouse."

"I can see that."

"I got us a suite. It'll be safer—that is, if I stay with you. We can't be sure Pierce is done with you."

Her expression tightens.

"I can get us adjoining rooms, if that would make you more comfortable." God, did I push her too far too fast? I wanted to make things right between us, not mess them up more.

"Dean…"

I clench my teeth, waiting for the blow.

"It's beautiful."

The sun sets behind the hotel, casting oranges and pinks across the sky. The glass exterior seems lit from within by the golden pink light.

"Do you want an adjoining room?" I can hardly breathe with

wanting her, but her comfort comes first. "I don't want to," I clear my throat, "take advantage of your adrenaline."

June drags her eyes away from the golden hotel. Her lazy smile has heat rushing through me. The light catches her dark hair, making it shine, and I shift against the seatbelt.

"Hmmm. I seem to remember you made me a promise."

I hardly dare look at her as I park the car as close to the hotel as I can.

"I did?"

"Mmhmmm." Her fingers trail along my jawline. "Something about screaming?"

"June, I... I don't want to push you, if you're worried about the, you know, the *Speed* thing." I cut my eyes to the packages in the back again, feeling idiotic.

A throaty laugh causes me to look back to her. "That's what's stuck with you? My one comment about Sandra Bullock and adrenaline?"

"I'm trying to be a gentleman here." I am, goddamnit, but she's undoing me at every turn.

She unclips the seatbelt and leans in close. She's dangerous, a firecracker, and I'm ready to light the fuse.

Her eyes sparkle in the dusky light. "Maybe I don't want a gentleman right now."

"Good." My control breaks, and I grab her, pulling her onto my lap. She squeals as my hands wind around her waist, the ample curve of her breast. For a moment, our breath mingles, and then she pulls back, leaving me raw. Wanting.

"I definitely don't want a gentleman. But I do want a hot shower." Her stomach grumbles. "And maybe an entire cow."

"As you wish." I smile, running a hand through her hair.

She crawls back over to her seat, making a surprised noise as she catches sight of the bags in the back. "What's all that?"

"You can't wear that to dinner." I nod at her ripped jeans and tight graphic tee.

She flutters her eyelashes. "What, you don't think divers can go down?" Her eyes dip to my crotch, and she licks her lips.

In one swift move, I capture her mouth, my hand against the base of her throat. Thumb massaging the smooth column of her neck, she gasps as I press against her mouth. Taking advantage of her surprise, I suck her bottom lip until she gasps again.

"I think I'm ready to find out," I murmur, tracing her swollen mouth with my finger.

"Oh."

"Shower first. Then dinner. Then…" I trail off, mind flashing on the fantasy of her beneath me, wondering what it will sound like when she cries my name.

"Then bed," June finishes. "Rest is important."

She opens her door, and I slide out of the driver's seat, adjusting my pants before grabbing the bags from the back.

CHAPTER
THIRTY-FOUR

JUNE

THE LOBBY IS BEAUTIFUL. Full floor-to-ceiling windows highlighting the ocean view. Modern wire chairs hang from twenty-foot ceilings, laden with thick, creamy cushions. Long, elegant lights drip down to us. I can't help but fidget. My crappy t-shirt and ripped jeans are totally out of place here.

Dean squeezes my hand reassuringly.

"John Brandon, checking in."

I narrow my eyes. *John?* If that's his cover name, it isn't an exciting one.

"Excellent, sir. ID?"

Dean sets the bags on the floor, fishing out a card from his wallet, and I squint at it. *John Brandon. Huh.*

"We received your reservation this afternoon, but there was a problem with the initial booking."

"What was the problem?"

Dean squeezes me against his side, his big hand splayed possessively against my hip. I want to rock into it, press into him until there is no air left between us.

The man behind the counter clears his throat. "You selected

double beds, but our only available suite has a king and a pullout couch. Will that suffice?"

Dean tilts his head at me, an inquisitive light in his eye. Only one bed? Not a problem for me.

I nod.

"It's fine."

"Excellent." The concierge types a few things in his computer. "I see your dinner reservation is at nine tonight, please be aware the dress is dinner jacket and tie. We hope you enjoy your stay."

"Oh, we will." Dean drags his thumb lazily against my hip, and I bite my lip. My entire body on fire with need. He swipes the keys from the concierge, leading us over to the elevator bank.

The doors open, and I follow him inside. Without taking his eyes off me, he presses the button for the top floor. I step towards him, his hands moving to my hair, thumbs running across my jawline in tandem. His mouth dips towards me, and I breathe deeply, inhaling his scent.

The elevator chimes, and the doors open. He smiles, his eyes promising me everything I want. Everything I can take.

He moves down the hallway with purpose, stopping at the corner door, keying in. Bringing the packages inside. I pause at the threshold.

The suite is opulent, that's the only word my mind can think of to describe it. The king bed dominates the space. A dining table set up in a side room, a small luxury kitchenette next to it. The lights glow a soft golden yellow, giving the whole room an impossibly romantic feel.

There's a huge soaking tub, stocked with my favorite scent: all lemongrass, all the time.

"Did you do this?" The door shuts behind me as I point at the shampoo and body scrubs, the lotions and soaps and soaking salts.

Dean appears behind me, his hands rubbing across my sides. He kisses the side of my neck, and I lean into him. "Maybe."

"Dean."

"Did I do something wrong?"

"It's a little weird that you know so much about me already." I squint at him. "For example, my favorite shampoo. And I know next to nothing about you."

"Was the shampoo too much?" He presses another kiss against my neck, and I arch into him.

"Dean, I'm trying to be serious."

"I tell you what—why don't you shower, get cleaned up, then I promise to answer any questions you have over dinner."

His thumb circles the back of my neck, sending shivers down my spine.

"You don't play fair."

"We can talk now if you'd rather."

I take a long look at the bathtub. A long, hot bath sounds so good.

"It can wait." I laugh.

He spins me around, pressing a kiss to my lips. Then he pushes me gently forward, and I laugh again. "Bathe. Relax."

I move to the tub, bending over, turning the faucet on. Steam begins billowing into the room, and I start to shimmy out of my pants.

A low noise catches my attention and I stop, self-conscious.

"Don't stop on my account."

"Didn't think you were the type to want to watch."

"I am now." His voice is rough against my senses, rasping in all the right places. His fingers curl against the doorframe.

"Go." I swat at him. "I'll be out quick and then you can shower." I crinkle my nose.

"Or I could join you."

"No." If I let him in now, we'll never make it to dinner. I want to ask those questions, dammit. And eat a steak. I'm starving.

If I never see a protein bar again, it will be too soon.

He bows his head. "Take your time, there's a second bathroom. Blow dryer and other stuff is in the top drawer."

"Okay." I watch as he closes the door behind him, suddenly

stunned by my circumstances. From being filthy on my boat, which now sits at the bottom of the gulf, to staying at an impossibly romantic hotel… then there is the incredibly sexy man who wants me.

Who I want right back.

We're gonna do it. If I fist pump a little, who cares? No one's here to see how dorky I am but me.

I open the top drawer and find a blow dryer, a curling iron, and a green velvet bag stashed inside. A quick peek inside shows a collection of my favorite cosmetics.

"Wow," I murmur.

It should make me uneasy, how much he knows about me, that he's been basically stalking me—with good intentions, sure. Considering the circumstances, I'm mostly relieved to have some familiar creature comforts.

I purse my lips. Charlie's probably the one who tipped him off to these details, anyway.

It was beyond thoughtful of him to do it. A wee bit creepy, but kind.

Besides, I'm throwing caution to the wind, dammit.

He promised to answer all my questions, didn't he?

And I'll start by asking who the hell John Brandon is. Then move on to the goddamn radiation team. Maybe even cover favorite movies and deepest fears. My lips press into a frown. He already knows my deepest fear—I've been living it for the past forty-eight hours.

But for now, I'll revel in steam and good-smelling soap and hot, hot water.

If I play my cards right, I'll get answers and maybe even an orgasm.

———

There's a light knock on the door as I finish applying a second coat of mascara and study my reflection. My eyes look huge, lips a dark red. Way more makeup than I usually wear. This is high-octane fancy makeup, used only in case of emergency.

Needing an orgasm? Definitely a case of emergency.

"June?" The door creaks open, and I frown at my reflection.

"I locked that."

"Ah, yeah, sorry about that." Dean's low voice sends desire running through me again. "I have a dress for you, if you want to wear it. If not, we can go down there wearing regular clothes and they can go fuck themselves. Up to you, princess."

I snort and stretch out a hand to grab the hanger. Dean stays behind the door, the picture of politeness. *Yeah, right.* I've seen what he's made of and I'm not buying it. Still, I appreciate the gesture.

I hang the garment bag from the hook on the back of the door and unzip it, inhaling sharply. Silky fabric, a shade between gray and green, whispers as I touch it, soft and sensuous beneath my fingers. A thick paper bag hangs from the top, and I pull out lacy black underwear.

My eyebrows shoot up. *Wow.* Yes, I needed underwear, but for him to buy it for me? Presumptuous. And a little bit sexy.

I put the underwear back in, gauging the dress. It's the right size, shimmering in the bathroom lights as I carefully unhook it and slide it overhead. Tugging it down, I arrange myself in it, then study the effect in the mirror.

Dean Evans, eat your heart out. It's a far cry from a dirty bikini and a filthy sundress. This is… sexy.

Maybe not exactly what I'd pick, with the slit up to midthigh and the drape in the front putting my cleavage on display. Okay, so nothing like what I'd pick.

But hell. I feel *powerful.* And I've felt too little of that lately.

Dean clears his throat. "Do you like it? I told the saleslady to pick out shoes, too, when I called in to buy it." Two black heels dangle from his fingers in the crack in the door, and I slip them on.

"You're really quiet… We don't have to go down if you don't want to. If this is too much." The strain in his voice is clear.

I swing the door open and my jaw drops. Dean is in a black suit, tailored to show off his broad chest and wickedly muscled arms. No tie, his tanned skin highlighted by the white dress shirt open at the collar.

He left the gray and black stubble, but tamed his hair with some gel.

Maybe I'm not hungry for dinner after all.

CHAPTER
THIRTY-FIVE

DEAN

I CAN'T TEAR my eyes away from her.

"You're the most beautiful woman I've ever seen." The words come out unplanned. "Stunning."

A rosy blush blooms on her cheeks. "You clean up pretty nice, too."

The image of her in that dress is branded in my consciousness. No matter what happens between us, I won't forget this moment, how she looks in that dress, how she makes me feel.

How she looks at me, like I'm worth something, like she wants me.

I can't stop staring.

"Who is John Brandon?"

Jealousy surges before my senses reclaim my brain. "It's me. It's a light cover. Not my real name."

"Oh, that's good. Dean Evans is your real name, right?" She fiddles with the slit of her dress, exposing more smooth thigh. I inhale, stepping closer.

"Yes."

"Good. That would be really awkward, if I've been fantasizing about you and I didn't even know your real name." She grimaces, and I chuckle.

"That right, princess? You've been fantasizing about me?" I want her. I want to run my hands across that smooth skin, explore every inch of her.

"I'm the one asking questions," she says, arching an eyebrow.

I snort. "As you wish."

"Is this what you wanted to do, growing up?" Her eyes are narrowed, that intelligent focus all homed in on me.

I have to fist my hands at my sides to keep from touching her. She needs this. I've waited this long. I can wait longer.

I exhale.

"Yes. I wanted to save the world. I wanted to help people. It didn't turn out like I wanted, like I expected. But I like to think I've made a little bit of difference." My voice breaks a little, and I step towards her. The curve of her breast rises as she inhales, her breath coming faster.

Good. I want her to want me as much as I need her.

"Why didn't you tell me you were discharged from the Marines?"

"I wasn't. Not really. I left because they didn't trust me anymore, not after Fiona." It doesn't even hurt to say her name, not like it used to. "I didn't think you needed to know."

The scent of lemongrass and vanilla curls off of June, intoxicating.

Every fiber of my being wants to throw her down on the bed and rip the fabric of that dress straight off her, watch her flush red as I fuck every last bit of hesitation out of her.

"Pierce is just the tip of the iceberg, isn't he?"

She's brilliant, the way her mind works, how she pieces together information quickly and with only a few details.

"Yes." I can't help myself. I run a rough hand down her side, my callouses catching on the fine silky weave of the gown. "You look incredible. You *are* incredible."

She blushes again, and I'll never get tired of bringing that color to her cheeks.

I want to do it every day, as long as she lets me.

"Ask me anything." My other hand reaches her hair, where she's shaped it into loose curls.

It'll look damned good against the white pillows while I make her come, again and again.

I make myself wait.

The distance between us is nothing. We breathe the same air, both our chests rising and falling rapidly.

Standing.

Waiting.

I'm not sure who will break first.

"Dean?"

"Yes?" I pin her with my gaze, letting my need show.

"How hungry are you?"

Hope wells, followed by a surge of pure lust.

"Depends on what's on the menu." I meant it as a joke, trying and failing to maintain control. Her face falls though, and she looks down. "Are you hungry?"

"I had a sandwich. On the cutter."

"Are you trying to tell me something?" I can be fucking patient. Her needs come first. Always.

"Do you think we could order room service?" Eyes heavy-lidded, she steps closer, putting her hands against my chest, her thumbs somehow finding my nipples. I groan as she rubs against them. "Later?"

"Yes. Fuck, yes, June."

"Good," she whispers, her hot gaze pinning me in place. My entire body stands at attention, waiting to see what she'll do next. She traces the ridge of my abdomen, and she's walking a fine line.

My control is good, but I'm on the edge.

The black lace panties were a bad idea. Seeing her ass in them, her pussy, is the only thing I can think about.

"Why?" I have to ask it. Have to make sure we're on the same page. "Why do you want to order room service?"

She breaks away from me, and the loss of her warm body against mine is one of the worst things I've ever felt. The bed creaks slightly when she sits on it. She crosses her legs, the silk fabric of her skirt falling away from her body.

I want to kiss every inch of those legs. I want to spread them around my face and fucking feast on her.

"Because you promised to make me scream, over and over again, and I'd like to think you're a man of your word."

"I'm a fucking man of my word, princess. You want to scream? I'll make you scream." I kneel next to the bed. Her breathing's gone ragged, her eyes wide and vulnerable despite her confident little speech. *This woman.* This woman will undo me.

And I'll savor every moment of it.

CHAPTER
THIRTY-SIX

JUNE

DEAN RUNS a finger across my thigh, and I shudder. "You're shaking." He stares up at me. "Is this alright?"

I nod.

"I need you to tell me yes or no, June."

How is this so sexy? The way he looks at me sets me on fire, the way he reins himself in, makes sure I'm comfortable.

I love it.

An incomprehensible noise comes out of me when his warm mouth meets the inside of my thigh.

His hands track down my legs, fingers running lightly over all the sore spots. Carefully, gently, his big hands make quick work of unstrapping the pretty black shoes. I close my eyes, savoring every touch, wanting to live in this moment.

His hands rub against my thighs. *More, I want more.*

"June? You didn't answer."

"Yes. I want you. Please."

He unleashes himself, gripping my ass with both hands, hoisting me up so I can wrap my legs around him. *Off.* I need his coat off. Right. Now.

I press a kiss to the rasping beard on his throat as I tug it off.

The shirt next. I need to see his chest, that sculpted muscle. I pull at it, feral, and the top button pops off.

"Oops."

Dean laughs, setting me down and quickly unbuttoning the rest. My gaze lingers as he reveals his perfect torso beneath.

"So, like, do you work out all day? Is that part of the job?" I trace the edge of his muscle, and it ripples under my touch.

"I work out a lot. Why, do you like it?" He flexes his arms, and I tilt my head, a hand at my chin. Pretending to consider.

"It's alright."

"Alright?!" Mock indignation colors his voice.

"It'll do." I shrug, feeling the weight of his gaze on my breasts.

"You'll pay for that one." Shirtless, he gathers me back in his arms, only the thin silk of the dress separating our bodies.

His lips part, pupils dilated. He finds my nipples through the thin fabric, and he rolls them expertly between his fingers until I moan and squirm against him.

"More."

He dips his head to my chest, teasing a nipple with his tongue through the fabric.

I'm aching. I've wanted him since the minute I laid eyes on him, and I'm dripping wet already in anticipation.

"I need more, Dean," I tell him, already coming undone. "I need you inside me. Now."

My legs tremble against him.

"No, princess. I'm not going to fuck you like an animal the first time. I'm going to take my time with you. You're not going to want anyone else after me."

I snort, but it's not funny. "Is that right?" My voice is shaky.

Cradling my head, he lays me back on the bed, supporting himself on his elbows, tracing, my cheekbone with a thumb.

"I've been dreaming about what you'd look like in bed. You're even better than anything I could imagine."

My chest tightens, desire winding through me, hot and needy.

I reach for him, and he meets me halfway, our mouths gentle at first, until need wins out. I'm on fire, and I wasn't lying to him: I need more, and I need it faster.

He goes achingly slow, peppering kisses across my neck, my collarbone, tracing a path back to my lips.

I raise my hips against him, craving the pressure of his cock, trying to find release. "Dean," I plead.

He breaks the kiss.

"You said you'd make me scream. I don't want it slow. I want you. Now."

That cocky grin reappears, and he tugs my dress up. I wriggle on the bed, helping him pull it over my head.

His expression grows hotter.

"You're not wearing the underwear."

"No."

"You didn't like them?"

"I didn't want to wear any."

His eyes darken and I reach down, rubbing my hand against the hard length of him.

"You were going to go to dinner without underwear."

I nod and he squeezes his eyes shut, his cock throbbing against my palm. I stroke it again and he groans, pressing into me.

Opening his eyes, he stares at me.

"You're so beautiful." I stroke him again. "I'm so lucky, June. I want you to enjoy this." His sudden, devilish grin makes me gasp, my core clenching on nothing.

"Tell me what you need."

"You."

He rubs a finger along my lips and I open my mouth, sucking on it. He groans, and I release his finger. My own fingers move up, and I unbuckle his belt as fast as I freaking can.

He palms my breasts again before sucking at the tips, making me moan and arch off the bed.

"You like that, June?"

"Not enough," I gasp out, though I swear, the man has me close already.

A low growl reverberates in his chest at the challenge, and I let out a yelp as he shoves my knees wide, licking along my exposed pussy.

"You taste so fucking good, princess," he tells me. "So wet for me. Such a pretty pussy, just like the rest of you."

He looks up at me between long licks, and I'm about to die.

I'm babbling, my hands tangling in his hair, pressing him close, urging him to do more.

His tongue circles my clit, and when he sucks on it, slowly increasing pressure, the room around me explodes in light and heat.

Someone's yelling.

It takes me a minute to realize it was me.

"You came so good for me." He's kissing down my thighs again. "Screamed and everything, princess."

I make an incoherent noise. A sheen of sweat shines on my chest, and I gasp as Dean's fingers slide inside me, stretching me.

"So fucking tight and perfect."

"Dean, Dean," I mutter, and I'm not sure if it's a curse or a prayer as he lowers his mouth to me again. He crooks his fingers as he sucks my clit, and his name turns to a stream of panting curses as I come again, the second orgasm hitting me hard and fast, leaving me incredibly breathless.

Dean must have used his own treasure map to make that happen. I grin down at him. "No one's ever found that spot before."

"I'm going to ruin you for any other man. You're mine, now, June."

"Okay," I agree. "Keep doing that and you might kill me, though."

"You want me to stop?" He's got that cocky grin on his face, his lips shining with my wetness.

It should not be that sexy.

It is.

"No. Don't you dare," I tell him. "I want the rest. Get in me."

He finds a condom in record time, and I stare at him like a pervert while he slicks it over himself.

I can't stop creeping on him. It's like they made him at a Build-A-Man Workshop just for me. *Yes, please, I'd like the one shaped like a Dorito.*

"See something you like, princess?"

"Yes, and I want it now." I make gimmee hands at him, and he huffs a laugh before climbing over me.

His big body pressing tight against mine, and I savor each sensation, all my nerves raw and ready.

"Mine," he says, kissing my earlobe. He thrusts, and we both cry out as he seats himself fully inside me.

He pulls out and I claw at his back, absolutely out of control now.

It feels right to give it up to him.

"Had to get that perfect pussy ready for me," he says, his voice hoarse and low.

His beard tickles my cheek, and he kisses me hard as he rocks into me.

He's big, really big, and I feel stretched and delicious in all the right places, and I swear, his dirty encouragement is making it even better.

I didn't know I was into that.

"Keep talking," I moan. "I like it."

"Yeah, you fucking do, because you were made for me, June, made to be my princess. I'm going to make you feel so good." He thrusts deep and I cry out at the force, hiking my legs higher around him. "You want to take me so deep, don't you? So fucking perfect."

His dark eyes are wild.

I need him, oh my god, so badly. I grip his shoulders, trying to pull him closer, to make him go faster.

He does, and I'm so close. "So close."

"Fuck, June."

He lowers his head, and when his hot mouth clamps over my nipple again, I shatter into a million pieces.

CHAPTER
THIRTY-SEVEN

DEAN

I CAN HARDLY STAND IT, barely able to lie still. My cock aches with the need to come, and it's taking all my fucking control not to.

I want to last for June. I want this night to last the rest of my fucking life.

June straddles me, her eyes closed.

I've made her come three times, and still, she's insatiable, and with her spread out above me, I think I might be the luckiest man alive.

"My June."

I rub my cock between the slick heat of her legs. I can't help but reach out for her beautiful, perfect breasts, pinching her pink nipples until she moans, low and throaty. Her hair falling in waves down her back.

I've never seen anything so incredible. She slides onto me slowly, rocking her hips back and forth. I grab her hips, guiding her, as she presses her body down on top of mine, seizing my mouth with hers. Claiming it.

Claiming me.

My chest tightens. This isn't enough. It will never be enough with her. The way she tightened her legs around my head when she came, the way she looks at me with trust and desire.

She's all I want.

Gripping her hip in one hand, I wrap my other arm around her torso and flip her onto her back. Pressing a finger to her clit, she moans, making a small, needy noise that has me riding the edge of her orgasm.

"I can't wait any longer, June."

"Want you to come," she pants. Her head falls back, her long brown hair tickling my thighs.

When she tightens around me, her core fluttering, I know I'm done for. Her nails scratch down my back and I follow her, kissing her, saying her name as I finally come.

This is bliss.

She's bliss.

She's mine. Mine. I'm not going to let her go.

I need to hold onto June so hard I'm afraid I'll break her.

CHAPTER
THIRTY-EIGHT

DEAN

I CURL INTO HER, savoring the sharp smell of her citrusy shampoo, the soft curve of her body. I can't stop touching her. Even now, I run a finger across the smooth expanse of her hip, the dip at her waistline.

She sighs, and I wrap my arm around her more firmly, the bottoms of her breasts teasing my forearm.

"Are you hungry?"

A soft laugh brings a smile to my face. What I wouldn't do to hear it again, to hear it every day.

"Yeah, I'm starved."

"I'm an asshole." Fuck. "Sorry." I should've insisted she eat. My lips find her neck, pressing an apologetic kiss to her skin. When she arches into me, my momentary regret dies in an instant.

"You're so fucking responsive."

She grins up at me, a feisty glint in her eyes. "You make it easy. That was… holy guacamole, Dean."

"Guacamole, huh?" I laugh, tickling her side until she's laughing too. "Damn, if it's guacamole, you must be serious."

We're both laughing, June's delighted giggles as good as the little moans she made when I was making her come.

I need to savor this. This kind of happiness, this bone-deep satisfaction—it doesn't last long.

"Do you still want to eat downstairs?" She smiles at me, and I'm momentarily silenced by how beautiful she is.

Awestruck she's bare in my arms, that she trusts me with her gorgeous body.

Maybe even with her heart.

"Maybe we can order it up. You okay?" June frowns, and I tug her closer, pressing a kiss to the worried wrinkle in her forehead.

"I'm good. Great."

The feel of the slow rise and fall of her chest, the steady thud of her heartbeat against mine... I close my eyes, tugging her closer, tucking her head under my chin. I stiffen.

"Why, are *you* okay?"

"Oh, I'm okay. Way better than okay. That... that was ridiculous. Incredible."

A satisfied smile curves my lips. "Incredible, huh?"

"I didn't know it was possible to do that."

"To come that many times?"

"To find the g-spot. You deserve an award."

I grind into her. I'm not hard again yet, but I might be soon. "I can think of an award."

She slaps my back lightly, and I feel her laugh before I hear it. "Don't get cocky."

I grin into her hair. "I already did."

"Mmmm." She writhes a little, enough that it gets my full attention... until her stomach grumbles.

"I need to feed you." It doesn't bother me. As much as I like lying here with her, being silly and cuddling, I want to take care of her.

I want that privilege, too.

"What, are you going to like, spoon food into my mouth? Order for me?"

Feisty, even now. I love it. "Is that what you want?"

She makes a small noise of disgust. "No. What I want is a massive steak. Medium rare. And a baked potato. With everything on it. Extra cheese. And a Caesar salad. Maybe a glass of red wine."

"How about a bottle? Some bread and butter?"

"Oh, you know the way to a woman's heart." She flutters her eyelashes playfully, but I nearly stop breathing. This is exactly what I want.

More than just this night, this perfect moment.

I want her heart.

"Butter. Noted. The way to June's heart, butter and bread." I frown at her. "Kinda kinky. Maybe not the best toy—"

"Shut up, Dean," she squeals, slapping at my arm playfully. "That's not what I meant."

"I know, princess." I plant a kiss on her smiling mouth.

God, she's irresistible.

I sit up and grab the sleek plastic phone. I'll order all she wants and more.

I close my eyes.

I'd give her the world.

CHAPTER
THIRTY-NINE

JUNE

I ROLL TO MY SIDE, luxuriating in the heaviness of my sated body, the soft, warm swaddle of sheets around me. Dean's voice, still so gravelly and sexy, is made even more so as he repeats my order perfectly.

My cheek rests on the inside of my arm, and a faint bruise purples the inside of my elbow compliments of the IV.

I must be out of my mind.

It's not just lust with Dean. This thing between us is already more than chemistry.

Must be the *Speed* rule.

We survived together. We're bonded. I know him better than I've known most of my former boyfriends.

Heck, maybe even most of my friends.

Biting the inside of my cheek, my chest heaves on a lengthy sigh. Shouldn't I be freaking out?

Dean casts me a look over his shoulder, one eyebrow raised. He reaches back with one hand, still on the phone, rubbing it over the bare skin of my thigh, rough callouses sending goosebumps down my arms. I shiver, and his questioning gaze darkens, turning to lust.

My heart squeezes.

His hand stills, then resumes long strokes on my hip. Finally, he murmurs, "Thanks," and replaces the phone on the cradle.

The bed barely moves as he rolls towards me, his hand moving from my hip to my face.

I can't help it, I close my eyes, leaning into the simple touch of his palm on my cheek. Something about it breaks my control, different from when I fell apart with him inside me.

This, this sweetness, will be my undoing.

"Food should be up in half an hour."

"That's fast." I don't open my eyes.

"Do you need something now? We could crack open the mini-bar. I should've thought to get snacks." Dean stands, the cold air on my cheek has me looking up at him as he stalks over to the kitchen area in the other room. His ass a masterpiece.

"Wait."

He stops, turning over his shoulder. *Swoon*. His abs ripple, his muscles standing out in his legs like some kind of art class anatomy sculpture. Except way, way hotter than an art class model has any right to be.

"What is it?"

"Just checking you out." I grin, a small laugh escaping and happiness bubbling out of me despite my best efforts at not taking this—this thing between us—too seriously.

He flexes, and I throw the back of my hand over my eyes.

"It's too much." I'm only half-joking.

"Oh yeah? I'll show you too much." He crosses the space to the bed in a few steps, landing on top of me, bracing himself with his elbows as he hovers over me. I squeal, then laugh.

The sound cut short by his lips on mine, claiming them. He kisses me slowly, pulling me up to sitting, holding my back as he deepens the kiss. My hands wrap around his neck, tangling my legs around his waist.

His hands are so strong against my back. Careful and powerful. I relax into him, lost in him.

A shrill beeping startles me, and I break away from him. This is addictive. The rush from his kiss, the warmth of his caress. The phone rings again.

Shaking my head, I try to clear it. "Think there's a problem with room service?"

Dean's eyes remain on me, continuing to run calloused hands across my back. Gripping my ass, he pulls my naked body even closer to his before kissing the sensitive spot below my ear. *He found that spot pretty quick.*

Finally, the noise stops.

Arching against him, the proof I turn him on, too, nudges me. Demanding my attention.

The phone rings again and I sigh, stiffening in his arms.

"I think you should answer that."

"Do you really want me to?" His mouth finds the peak of my breast, and I go limp again.

"No."

He moves back to my mouth, doing something with his tongue and teeth that sets my whole body on fire. Again.

The phone ringing finally wins out. I crack an eye open and glare at it.

"Dean... I think you should answer it."

"I don't want to."

"What if it's an emergency? What if it's about my steak?"

He grins. "Well, that would be an emergency. Fine." Carefully, as though I'm made from spun glass, he sets me on the bed, pulling the comforter over me. "Don't forget where we were."

I stretch my arms overhead, noting with satisfaction how his eyes track the simple gesture before he groans and picks up the phone.

"Hello?" A moment passes. Tension floods his body, his expression changing. "Got it. Where?" He faces the opposite wall, turning away from me.

I fiddle with the sheet's embroidery, pulling at a loose string.

"Okay. No, I understand—" A long pause. "Yes, ma'am. Understood."

My stomach falls, and I throw the covers over my head.

The hollow plastic sound of the phone being replaced on the cradle, then footsteps as Dean walks away from the bed. The sounds of fabric, a zipper, echo in my ears.

Why is it suddenly hard to breathe?

My throat constricts, and I pull my knees into my chest. A deep breath in, amplifying the blood pounding in my ears.

"Hey." Light streams in where Dean pulls the sheets down, and I blink up at him. He's dressed, black pants, black shirt. Black boots in one hand, ready to be laced up.

Leaving. Not in a week. Not tomorrow, but now. He's leaving me *now*.

"Hi." I tug the sheet down, wrapping it over my chest.

"I have to go." His forehead wrinkles, and I resist the urge to press a finger to it, to wipe the worry away. "Thorne's off chasing a lead, but Thompson is here, down the hall. He'll be looking out for you."

"Oh." It's soft. This is what life would be like with him. If he even wants to be in my life. He couldn't do long moments in bed or at dinner, forget long weekends or cozy nights at home.

He wants to save the world. Maybe I could get used to that. But… this, this is a little fresh.

"June." He presses a kiss to my forehead. "There's just a chain of custody issue. I'll be back as soon as I can." He rakes a hand through his hair, a self-assured grin on his face. "Feel free to eat my food."

"You don't think you'll be back tonight? I could stick it in the fridge." I don't want to sound desperate. Don't want to seem weak, can't bear to feel weak. But I want him to stay, to wake up in his arms in this beautiful room that isn't a boat. To roll over and wrap my legs and arms around him and have it mean something.

"I don't know. I wish I could tell you otherwise, but I just don't." His hands ball into fists. "I'm sorry. Trust me, I don't want to be anywhere but here."

"Be safe."

He starts to reach out, and for a split second, I think he might touch me, might know that I need soothing. Instead, he rubs the freshly clipped salt and pepper stubble on his jawline.

"I will. Oh, by the way, check the closet. There are some everyday things in your size, and there's a cheap cellphone in there too. Don't leave the hotel. If you need something, Thompson's number is programmed in the cell. He'll arrange to have whatever you need transported to you. My number's in there too, but Thompson will be faster while I'm fixing this bullshit."

"Okay, got it." Moonlight dances across the bay, visible through the sliver of window not quite covered by the drape.

"June?" His voice comes next to my ear. Dean stands over me, delicious and dangerous-looking. "I'm really sorry about leaving. Listen… this," his throat bobs. "This meant something to me. You mean something to me."

"Oh." My heart does a funny flip. "That's good." Maybe there is room for me in his life, after all. I allow myself to smile, beaming up at him.

"Why?" A lopsided grin turns the corner of his mouth up.

"Because you mean something to me too." The words come out small, tentative and true. "I want you."

"Again?" he says, a teasing smile on his face.

I nod, my smile growing. "And you know, maybe after all this is done… we could try to figure out long distance. If you want to test out the *Speed* theory."

"Keanu Reeves and Sandra Bullock?"

"You remembered." I smile.

"I'll remember nearly everything about this. About you."

His hands curl into my hair, pulling my mouth into his, stealing my air, leaving me gasping. We break apart, breathing heavily.

Dean locks eyes with mine. "Don't go anywhere. I'm coming

back for you… and then we can figure out long distance. Or…" His voice trails off. "We'll figure something out. Rest up." He winks as he presses off the bed, the coverlet dimpled from his hands. He swaggers out of the room, the door clicking shut behind his muscled butt.

I'd like another piece of that cake.

CHAPTER
FORTY

DEAN

I FLASH my credentials at the armed guards outside the base and they wave me into the squat concrete building, but I pause, glancing around. Something feels off. Nagging at me, tugging at my awareness. Palm trees sway in the heavy breeze, stars twinkling overhead. I can hardly concentrate. My mind never leaving June.

How she felt, naked and warm, in my arms. The way her hair smelled, how it felt tickling across my shoulders.

Charlie hardly said a word on the way over, taciturn and surly. But even she seemed to notice my mood, giving me space.

"You okay, man?" one of the guards asks, and I nod, stepping into the cold interior of the building. A few turns and I'm at a reception desk, Charlie behind me. A sad potted tree wilts in the corner, no doubt undone by the bureaucratic nonsense detailing its watering schedule.

"Sir?" A young private mans the desk, black braids pulled back in a tight bun, an even tighter smile on her face.

"I got a call about a chain of custody evidence issue. Paperwork." I aim for a charming smile. Judging by her lack of response, it's a swing and a miss.

"Who called you?"

"Staff Sergeant Penelope Briggs."

She frowns at the name, and my nerves jangle.

"Dean." Charlie's voice is low. "Please tell me you called it back in."

No. I'd been too distracted. I shake my head, blowing out a breath.

"I'll see if I can find her." The woman makes a few keystrokes on her keyboard, peering at the screen. "What department did you say she worked in?"

"It's about the evidence found in the gulf today. It came in with the Coast Guard cutter," Charlie answers for me, shooting me an exasperated look.

I rap my fingers against the top of the desk. Unease threading through me. A staff sergeant shouldn't be hard to find. Not even on a base this size.

"You may not have access to the whole file." What we found has surely been classified at the highest compartment at this point.

"Sir, that's correct." Her frown deepens, bordering on a scowl. "The file is classified. But it hasn't been flagged for review."

"What do you mean?" Charlie asks.

"There are no problems with the chain of custody. And there is no Penelope Briggs in our database. I can call my staff sergeant down, if you need to speak with him."

The words hit me like a physical blow and I exhale, the air whooshing out of me.

"Sir? Are you alright? Do I need to take it up to command?" Her eyes narrow.

"Yes. We need to take it up. And we need to send people over to the Wildwood Hotel. I need a secure line." I need to call the DEA. Need to clear somethings up, make sure they know Pierce is dirty.

"Dean." Charlie's voice is urgent. "I'm going to call Thompson. Thorne can turn back too, he can't be too far out of pocket."

"No. We need Thorne after Pierce and the next drop location. Call Thompson." My skin is on fire. June is alone. Thompson is there, yes. But this… getting me out of the room with her, dividing the two of us could be an attempt to get to her.

And Pierce is a loose end I haven't tied up. I'll pay for it, for not turning him in as soon as I could, distracted by feeling.

Nausea churns in my gut, and I swallow it down. I don't have time for that.

June is in danger, and I fucked it all up.

CHAPTER
FORTY-ONE

JUNE

THE WINE ISN'T GREAT. But after half a bottle, I hardly care. I swirl it in the glass, watching the light from the TV bounce off the crimson liquid. My steak is long gone, and I'm not sure if I even remembered to chew.

Earth-shattering sex gives quite the appetite, apparently.

After Dean left, I tripped over the gorgeous green-gray silk dress wadded up unceremoniously on the floor, floated happily into the bathroom, and ran a scalding tub full of lavender bath salts.

I only made myself get out when I worried I might be turning into boiled crab.

It would be embarrassing if room service showed up to discover I'd turned into a giant crustacean. Better than a roach, I guess. Thanks for the nightmares, Kafka.

I snort at my own unsaid joke, still so happy it almost hurts.

I lean my head against the back of the chair, the room too bright. My eyes close and I remember the way our bodies crashed together.

Like we're some inevitable force of nature, tangling together perfectly.

I don't regret for one second that we had sex. I don't regret helping him find the narcotics, and finding the *Santu Espiritu* is a memory and feeling I'll treasure more than the ship itself.

Probably. Maybe.

Finding Dean might be just as good, and I didn't even know I was searching for him.

He cares about me. I mean something to him, he said we'd figure out how to make it work. A happy sigh parts my lips, my heart aching with hope.

The napkin scratches across the still-sensitive skin of my lips. Then floats back to the table, settling between the dirty dishes and covered plates of Dean's food. Tugging the hotel robe closer, I smirk at my glass.

Finally, I pick up his uneaten order and shove it in the mini-fridge.

The TV on the wall mirrors my image: tousled hair, black streaks where my fancy makeup ran from the boiling bath.

Somehow, probably thanks to the combination of a massive meal and the emotional lubrication of red, red wine, I'm convinced.

Dean Evans cares about me. He cares for me.

He *like* likes me. I snort.

We're going to make it work.

Walking into the white expanse of the bathroom, I turn the curling iron back on. No reason not to fix my hair, my face, before he comes back. Cool water splashes over my cheeks, helping bring down the effects of the wine.

I want to look pretty for him.

A deep, shaky breath wracks me. *God.* I haven't really even processed everything yet.

The *Santu Espiritu* is there. My father, for all his many faults, left me a roadmap to it, and I did it.

Realization dawns, my eyes widening. I stare at myself in the mirror.

What if he dumped the sub there on purpose? What if he trusted *me* to do the right thing? To be the person he raised me to be, even if he wasn't the man I imagined?

Regret coils tight around me.

Still. I found it. The what ifs thundering through my skull pause, and I hang onto that feeling of victory, wrapping myself in it like armor.

I reapply mascara, opting for waterproof, just in case, and nearly succeed in stabbing myself in the eye when a fist raps against the door.

"Room service," a muffled voice sounds.

I swallow, nerves jangling. Just room service.

Slowly, I place the mascara on the counter, staring at the reflection paling in front of me. There's no reason for them to be back.

My heartbeat thrums in my neck, my head.

No. It's probably just room service. I'm being paranoid again.

Dean left Thompson here. Besides, the narcotics sub and everything in it have been scooped up and processed, safely locked away. No one has any reason to want anything to do with me now.

Carefully, I walk over to the door, peering out the peephole. A uniformed shoulder and beyond that, a bouquet of roses, a bottle of champagne and a saran-wrapped plate of chocolate-covered strawberries is all I see.

"I didn't order anything."

"Oh, well the card here says it's from a… John Brandon? I can just leave it here."

"Oh. Okay then."

John Brandon, ha. What a terrible cover name.

There's no sign of Thompson in the hall. Surely, if this was a threat, Thompson would've stopped it.

"Okay, have a good night, miss." The uniformed man walks

down the hallway, favoring one leg. He leaves the cart sitting in front of the door, brimming with all the sentimental things.

It's so cute and unexpected of Dean I can't even stand it.

Hesitantly, hoping, I turn the handle, the door softly clicking as I open it. I step into the hallway on cloud nine.

An arm crashes into my body, and I'm thrown back into the room. I wheeze from the impact, my chest aching with the force of the tackle.

Shit.

My hand snaps back as I try to break my fall, landing on the first room service cart and the half-finished bottle of wine.

"Unf," I say.

It's the same man in the uniform. But now, now I can tell he's the one we ran over in my car. The same eye I rinsed with tequila stares at me now, furious.

The Russian hitman. Smuggler.

Bad guy.

Whatever.

Gun in his hand, a towel over it and his forearm. If I wasn't crumpled on the floor, I'd be half convinced he was performing in some laughably bad action movie.

It's surreal.

"Want me to tie her up?" he asks, and I look around.

"Are you talking to yourself?" Maybe he *did* sustain a concussion when Charlie ran him over.

"Shut up."

"Real creative," I mutter, panic constricting my throat. Why did I have to say that? My brain must be short-circuiting from the wine and never-ending dangerous situations.

I have got to stop making things worse for myself.

He glares down at me.

"No, she'll cooperate. She's smart, aren't you, June?" A second man enters the room, and my blood runs cold.

Pierce. His skin is pale, with an odd greenish cast. Probably a side effect of losing who knew how much blood.

"You look like shit." My hand clenches on the neck of the wine bottle and I stand, holding it behind my back. "You both do."

"Shut up." Pierce pulls a gun of his own, a wild look in his eye. "Where are they?"

"Where are what?" I'm at a total loss.

"The fucking drugs, you dumb cunt."

"Wow. That's too far."

He raises the gun, clicking the safety off. "Talk or get shot, I don't fucking care."

There's no way out of this one. I'm outnumbered and outgunned. I look down at my robe. And way, way underdressed. How do they not know the drugs were confiscated?

I can use that.

It isn't much, but it's something. I've been lied to most of my life, by my father, by Charlie… it's my turn now.

There's no way I'm letting them abduct me; at this point, it's a matter of pride.

I screw my lips up to the side.

"Talk, now," Pierce says, wagging the end of the gun at me.

I narrow my eyes. Maybe it's less a point of pride and more red wine courage. My fingers clench the neck of the bottle.

"I can take you to them. But I'm not going there like this." I gesture to the hotel robe with my free hand.

"You'll go there how we want you to go. We're armed. We make the rules."

Despite my growing desperation, I nearly roll my eyes.

"'We make the rules'?" I repeat, scoffing. "I'll just attract attention in the lobby if you take me down there in a robe." I cup my free hand around my mouth. "Help, help me, I'm being kidnapped."

Pierce frowns and I slowly smile at him, wondering where the fuck I found brass balls.

My fingers are slick against the bottle of wine.

Oh. That's where I found them.

"Fine," Pierce final snarls. "Get dressed. But hurry. And don't try anything stupid. You're too smart to get yourself killed."

Am I really, though? Unclear.

Despite the wine and my false bravado, I shiver. I really don't want to die.

Seems unfair to get murdered by someone as annoying as Pierce, anyway. The wine bottle starts to slip, and the man in front, my hit-and-run and margarita-first-aid victim, squints at me.

"There's other ways of getting information, Pierce." His voice is thickly accented. "We don't have to take her anywhere."

I swallow, eyes widening.

"Nah, she's smarter than her dad was. I'm sure she wouldn't want to die like he did, do you, honey?"

Oooh, now I'm mad. Well, even more mad.

"Why?" The question slips from my mouth like someone else is speaking. "Why would you do this? Betray your country?"

Pierce throws the back of his fist against my cheek, and I stagger at his slap. "You know nothing about me or the work I do. Keep your mouth shut."

"You hit me," I gasp. I shouldn't be shocked. I am.

My face is numb, mind reeling from being hit. I blink rapidly, trying to focus.

"Why?" I ask again, my vision foggy. I'm not sure if I'm asking why he's a traitor or why he hit me.

I doubt there are good answers to either.

"Why? *Why?* Because I've spent years watching politicians take money, take bribes. Washington is a sewer. None of the work I've done matters, not when the corrupt assholes won't do anything real to stop it. We're going to change all that. We're going to change this country, change the world."

"So you gave in? Helped the enemy instead?" I touch a finger to my lips, and it comes away bloody. "Decided to make money for yourself?" Now that I've started, I can't seem to stop talking.

Even if he decided to hit me again, my mouth would probably just keep getting me in trouble.

"You think this is about money?" He stares, slack-jawed. "This was never about money, never about drugs. We're not going down without a fight."

"Who is we?" A fight? The bright coppery taste of blood slicks over my tongue, and I spit, trying not to gag on it.

"We're patriots. I haven't betrayed anyone." His eyes are wild, fanatic. "Now tell me what I want to know, or things are going to really get ugly."

"I don't feel so great," I say, reeling off the first excuse that comes to mind. Used to get me out of gym class. Sometimes. Once.

"You're going to feel worse if you don't start talking." Pierce glares at me.

"Enough talking, we need to get her out of here," the Russian says.

I shift, trying a new strategy. "Pierce, are you going to take orders from him?"

The Russian sneers at me. "You think he's in charge?"

He licks his lips as I squirm, panic cresting at the malevolence in his stare.

Time. I need time, need to keep them talking.

Any minute, the cavalry will come bursting through the door, I'm sure of it.

"I don't know," I tell him honestly. "Are you?"

The bottle slips in my sweaty grip, but I cling to it.

"What's behind your back?" The Russian clicks the safety off his gun.

"Put it down or we'll shoot you somewhere it'll hurt." Pierce says, enunciating slowly. "Sound familiar?"

My teeth clench firmer, and I put the wine bottle back on the table. *So much for that plan.* Head pounding, the side of my face where Pierce backhanded me throbs. It pisses me off, heightening my anger, keeping me from losing myself completely to fear.

I have to get out of this. No way I'll let them take me to a second location.

"Good girl." Pierce motions for me to step forward.

The words further incense me. "I'm not a dog."

"Smart bitch, then." Pierce grins, and I wish I'd been the one to shoot him instead of Charlie, or left him for shark food. "And if you're thinking about stalling, don't. Evans' little helper is a little tied up at the moment."

I glare at him. "You suck at being a villain."

"Get your shit on and let's go. Don't make me hurt you." Pierce motions with the gun, and I stumble over to the closet, retrieving the bag.

The phone. The cellphone is somewhere in the bag of stuff Dean bought. Maybe I can make a—

Pierce snatches the bag away, throwing a shirt and pants on the floor. The black plastic phone case catches my eye, bringing despair, panic and fury fighting for dominance. But Pierce misses it, distracted, picking up a pair of panties, dangling them in front of me.

"You're gross." I spit out. My face hurts where he hit me. "Am I allowed to pick out a bra or are you going to act like a pervert about that, too?"

He frowns, pushing his floppy blond all-American hair off his forehead with his gun still in hand. "Fine."

I roll my eyes. Of all the things to be offended about, it's that? Whatever. Maybe I can exploit it. Quickly, I reach into the bag, find a bra, shoveling the cellphone in between the cups, and hold it up.

"Get dressed."

"I need to pee, and my stomach hurts."

"Fine, then get dressed in the fucking bathroom."

I can lock myself in. Snatching the clothes off the floor, I press the bra and phone against my chest, then scramble inside the bathroom, pulling the door shut behind me.

It doesn't close.

Mother Frito.

The foot in the doorway allows their laughter in, and it echoes off the walls.

"Hurry up."

I shrug out of the robe, refusing to cry. Despite the waterproof mascara. These assholes will see my crying as a win. Anger surges through me, and my knuckles whiten on the clothes. I won't let these mother-fluffers think for one second I'm broken.

I'm not.

I take a long, ragged breath, pulling on the underwear with shaking hands.

But I found the *Santu Espiritu*. I'm right on the cusp of breaking my career into the next level. It's all I've wanted for so dang long.

I found Dean.

I tug on the shorts. Or he found me. *We found each other.* These two turd sandwiches can get stuffed.

Maybe I should try a hail-mary of a phone call. Maybe Dean can track the phone. Better that than try and have it ripped away.

I snap the bra in place, tucking the cellphone inside one cup, and slide the shirt over my head. One boob definitely looks bigger than the other, but it's the left one, and maybe that isn't too far from what's normally there anyway.

As long as nobody touches it. Gross. They better not touch me.

Cellphone safely tucked in my bra cup, I open my shirt, turn the volume down and dial 911. The operator picks up immediately.

"911, what's your emergency?"

"Are you really going to shoot me?" I scream, overacting, trying to keep them from hearing the woman's muffled voice on my bra phone.

"You're taking too long. I wanted to do this the easy way, like a gentleman, but if you don't hurry your ass up, I will knock you out and carry you out of here," Pierce responds.

God, I hope the woman on the line heard that, that she won't just assume this is some crank call.

A blinking light catches my scattered attention.

Next to the travel-size hairspray, the curling iron is still on. A new plan, hare-brained and ill-advised, forms in my head.

It'll probably get me killed.

But the stats about kidnapping victims moved to a second location are never good. I did some research after the *last* time I was kidnapped.

Gotta stay informed!

"Not doing that again," I murmur, and turn the dial up on the iron. Hot enough to burn hair. Hotter than I've ever set it.

The deliciously scented bubble bath sits on the counter next to it. The wheel in my head picks up speed, the hamster definitely drunk on power and adrenaline.

I squirt it across the floor, making a foul sound. I kick the handle on the toilet for good measure, and it flushes loudly.

"I'd really appreciate some privacy." The words fly out of me, sounding embarrassed. I'm not, though, I'm scared out of my mind.

The 911 operator asks several quiet questions to my boob. Outside the men are laughing some more. This time I join in, high-pitched and keening like a hyena.

I shift my weight to my left leg, the curling iron in one hand, hairspray in the other. It's been a while since I took self-defense, since I forced myself to learn something to protect myself, something my therapist in high school suggested.

I'm not leaving this damned hotel room without a fight.

"I'll get her." A frisson of fear curls through me.

I bare my teeth, the curling iron sending up waves of heat as the hotel AC blasts the room. The door squeaks open, and the man I wish I'd told Charlie to run over again steps into the bathroom.

A high-pitched scream tears out of my throat, and I aim the

hairspray straight into his eyes, managing to dust his whole body in it as I back away from him.

"That's super-strength hold. Who's the bitch now?"

The bitter scent of it coats my nose, my tongue. His scream joins mine, and for a moment, we almost harmonize as his fingers scramble against his eyes.

Stumbling, his foot connects with the bubble bath slicked across the floor. His eyes and arms go wide as he tries to catch his balance, and I aim a kick at him but miss, connecting with the doorknob instead, locking it and slamming it shut.

The gun goes off, and I forget how to breathe, paralyzed with fear.

The shot goes wide, taking out a chunk of the bathroom ceiling. Well, better here than my kitchen.

Another shot goes off and I duck, arms over head, curling iron clenched tight. He hits the floor, his head bouncing off the marble with a sick crack.

Blood spills out of the wound. He doesn't move.

The whole moment is over in less than thirty seconds. I eye the bubble bath on the counter and edge further away from the bloody bubbling mess on the floor.

Maybe I'll stick to Epsom salts and bath bombs after this.

"What the hell is going on in there?" Pierce pounds on the door, the handle twitching as he tries to open it. The door shaking as he kicks it.

"Ah, nothing. He just slipped. Everything's fine." I'm a terrible liar.

The door splinters as Pierce kicks it. I reach for the fallen gun, my hands shaking as I make myself aim at the door.

I sniff. *What's burning?* Oh shit. A seared chunk of hair falls from my head. *Who invented these things?* If it requires a glove to curl hair safely, it's too damn hot. The door moves as Pierce kicks at it, yelling. I drop the iron, and it sizzles against the sprawled Russian's leg, glossy with my overzealous application of hairspray.

"Oh, sorry." The apology comes out automatically. Did I really plan on burning the shit out of this dude only a minute ago? Bending over, I yank the curling iron cord out of the socket.

Safety first.

It's too late, though. The place where the curling iron smolders catches fire, and I watch in open mouthed horror as flames crawl up his body. I turn the hairspray can over in my hand. Highly flammable.

Okay. Well, that would have been nice to know before now.

Alarms start wailing, and overhead, sprinklers go off.

"Goddamnit, Legarde, this isn't over. This isn't over." The door shakes once more, and then the door to the hotel room opens and closes. Pierce is gone.

I sag, a ragged breath tearing out of me.

The 911 operator continues to ask questions. Fishing the phone out of my bra, I bring it to my lips.

"I think we need an ambulance," I say. "Or something. Fire truck. And if you could call the DEA, that would be great."

The woman peppers me with questions, attempting to verify my location. I sink to the floor, watching my would-be kidnapper bleed. For the second time in a week.

The sound of the hotel room door opening and closing filters through my shocked haze.

Maybe I'll switch to gel.

I think I've had enough hairspray for a while.

CHAPTER
FORTY-TWO

DEAN

THE SOUNDS of firetrucks and ambulances blare through the night, cutting through the sound of the Jeep's tires on the road. Fear spikes through me, accompanied by the one-two gut punch of guilt.

Please, please don't be heading for the Wildwood Hotel.

"He's still not picking up, Dean." Charlie holds her cell to her head, as anxious as I've ever seen her. "I'm calling it in."

"Fuck." I never should have left. As soon as I picked up the phone, I should have run the name, verified it.

Red and blue lights flood my car, momentarily blinding me as they speed past me. Turning off on the same exit as the hotel.

If anything's happened to her...

The gas pedal hits the floorboard, and the car screeches as it picks up speed. The needle pushing past eighty. I'm vaguely aware of Charlie on the phone, the bare details of the situation, her hanging up.

My knuckles are white on the wheel.

"She's smart, she'll be okay." I'm not sure if she's trying to convince me or her herself. "Dean, slow down. If you wreck us, it'll take even longer to get to her."

The car careens onto the off-ramp, and a muscle twitches in my temple.

"Dammit, Charlie." I'll never forgive myself for this. *Pierce will pay.* Anger rises in me like a tide, slipping from the mental shackles I worked so hard to forge.

"Dean, you need to calm down. Talk to me. What's going through your head?" Charlie asks.

I want to rip the goddamn steering wheel off, that's what. My therapist would not be impressed. But the person I'm angriest at isn't Pierce, or the cartel, or the US government, for once.

No. It's myself.

"You like June. Like, really like her, huh?"

"Shut up, Charlie."

"No, you need to listen. Your ex was horrible. We all knew it. Bad news. June's different."

"Of course she's different," I snap, glaring at her.

Charlie rolls her eyes. "You made a mistake, don't yell at me."

"Don't talk to me like that."

She sighs. "Will you listen to yourself? You're a mess."

"You're the last person to be giving advice on relationships."

She shifts in the seat, and I regret the barb. She's my best undercover operative.

It was a coup to even get her to work for me. Unfortunately, she's great at forging relationships with the turncoats, the get-rich-quick sell-outs, and the dirty cops.

And in this case, June.

June, who's worth more to me than anything we found under the green waves of the gulf.

"That's not fair," she finally says, breaking the quiet, watching me. "I do my job. We *all* do our jobs. But Dean, sometimes I think there should be more than the mission. Maybe it's time to put you first. What you want. And if that's June? If that's this town and a life with her? The mission will still be there even if you take a backseat for a while." Charlie turns away, sinking into silence. "We'll all still be here too. Me and Thompson and Thorne. Not like we have anything special waiting for us."

My teeth clench.

The hotel looms against the dusky horizon, lit up like Christmas with parking lot lights and garden lighting designed to make it look like a serene retreat. Cascading sirens and emergency lights ruin the effect. They spin relentlessly, all blue and red, converging on the hotel where I left June, left her after—I can't even think it.

Charlie draws a long breath.

Several paramedics are walking out of the hotel, a stretcher carried between them. Grief tears through me like a hurricane. The force of it skidding across my awareness, and yet, through some superhuman ability combined with years of training, I push it aside.

The Jeep screeches to a stop, and I don't know if I turn it off, sprinting towards the body in the bag, towards the paramedics.

"How did it happen?"

"You can't be here, this is an active crime scene." A uniformed policewoman bars my entry, the yellow tape proclaiming as much pressing against my legs.

"No, you don't understand, that's my, my..." I trail off, fishing out my credentials.

"He's not anybody's anything anymore," one of the paramedics says.

"Nasty business," a second adds.

My head spins so hard it takes a minute to latch onto what they said. He. *He.* Not her. I don't dare hope.

"Was there a woman, a woman, is she okay? Where's the woman?" I grip the officer's arm, and a look of pity crosses her face.

"Dean, Dean! You're okay!" June's voice cuts through the chaos, and relief nearly brings me to my knees.

She tumbles into my arms, smelling like burnt hair, but I don't care.

She's safe. Good god, she's safe.

I hug her close. Her arms come up around my waist, squeezing me back, and a sudden wetness coats my cheeks.

"Of course I'm okay, are you okay?" I manage, bewilderment prickling my awareness. I pull away from her, checking her perfect, beautiful face, eyes scanning the body I treasure.

"I'm—" she swallows, "I'm really tired. And somehow, hungry again. And tired of being shot at. Like, really fucking tired of being shot at. But I'm okay. I am." Her mouth purses, and she closes her eyes. Her body goes soft against me, and my heart swells. She still trusts me.

"You said fucking." Why is that the thing I latched onto?

"I did. Sorry." She winces. "Fudging adrenaline."

"Thompson?" I ask.

"They slipped something in his food, he's on the way to the hospital. He's going to be okay." Her throat bobs.

"You're okay, holy shit, you did great, June." Charlie appears next to the ambulance, relief clear on her face.

For a moment, June's eyes narrow, irritation leaking out of every pore. Charlie takes a step back, a look I've never seen on her face before—uncertainty.

I nearly intervene, but I stop myself. They need to work this out, and no way anything I say is going to help.

"I'm sorry," Charlie says. It comes out like a question and my brows shoot up.

I've never heard her say that before.

"I'm sorry," she repeats. "I used you. I did what I had to do, but I know you're hurt."

"Charlie…" June shakes her head, "it's okay. I understand why you did it. But you know you're buying the next round of margaritas. And the queso. And the fajitas. And you still owe me a whole girls' night. How am I supposed to browbeat the rest of the faculty once you leave?"

Charlie tips her head back, laughing, a real laugh, one I rarely hear from her. "You'll have the *Santu Espiritu* to hold over their heads now. They'll be lucky to keep you on staff."

June grins, radiant despite the glow of police lights.

I exhale a massive breath in relief. Lucky. I was so damn lucky. Should I press it? She nuzzles into my chest, and it tightens at her simple gesture, at how she finds comfort in my arms.

"Pierce got away. Pierce is gone." Her forehead scrunches up, and I smooth it out with my thumb.

"I'll deal with it later. Charlie," I call out, "Call it in. We need to let them know Pierce is still in play. Who's the stiff?"

"Russian. The one I hit the other day." There's a feral light in Charlie's eyes, and her phone's already at her ear. "Should have tried harder."

I make a mental note to stay on Charlie's good side before turning all my attention back to June.

"The important thing is that you're okay." I can't seem to stop touching her. She *is* okay. She's here, in my arms. I'm never letting her go. "You come first. Always, June. I never should've left. I'm sorry. If I hadn't left, they never would've gotten this close."

I capture her face, my mouth finding hers, pressing a kiss to it. Her fingernails dig into the fabric of my shirt before I break the kiss.

"Stop it." She holds up a furious finger, and her eyes sparkle with tears. "I took care of it. I can take care of myself."

"I know you can, June. You've showed me that so many times. So," I paused, staring into her beautiful eyes, "you're not mad at me? That I ran off and left you vulnerable?"

She throws her head back, a bark of a laugh sounding. "No, you left me as safe as you could while you went off to save the world. You don't control Pierce, you didn't make him do that.

You're going to have to work on this blaming yourself for everything nonsense if you want to be with—"

"June, I…" She needs to say it. I need her to say it.

Her eyes press closed, her mouth a thin slash. "I know I'm assuming a lot, but…"

"No, I want that. I want to be what you need." I draw her close, sealing her mouth with mine.

A rousing cheer goes up around us, and her hands fist in my shirt. When we pull away, there are a few whoops from the crowd. And Charlie's grin stretches from ear to ear.

"What I need right now is about three days straight of sleep."

I raise an eyebrow, a mischievous grin curving my lips. "Is that all you need?"

She stands on her tiptoes, breath ghosting against my ear. "No."

Picking her up, I swing her against my chest, and she gasps before laughter trickles out of her as I carry her to the Jeep.

CHAPTER
FORTY-THREE

JUNE

I WAKE, toasty warm, sun streaming through the cracks in the window. The smells of home hitting me, lemongrass and coconut, the tick of the clock on the wall in the living room a reassuring metronome.

Something prickles across my neck and I stiffen, then relax.

Dean. Dean is in my bed, in my house. The fan makes lazy swirls overhead, the white sheers on the widow billowing in the gentle breeze it creates. A large hand on my waist pulls me closer, and I snuggle into the dip in his arm. A strange moment of déjà vu passes over me, followed by a twinge of regret. The last few mornings have begun nearly the same way, and I was too out of my mind with stress and worry to enjoy them.

Not this time though.

"You awake?" His voice is a deep rasp in my ear.

"Mmm."

Small circles start across my stomach, and I arch into him.

"I think we need to talk."

"Oh." Lead fills my stomach, the happy, floating feeling disappearing. I squeeze my eyes shut, as though it can keep me from hearing whatever Dean is about to say.

"Not like *that*."

"Oh!" I gasp, my eyes wide open. Strong hands flip me onto his stomach, and Dean grins up at me.

"You're beautiful in the morning." He pushes a wayward lock of hair from my forehead, and I bite my lip. There's a but coming, I can sense it. And not the butt I want. "You're beautiful all the time."

"Dean, if you have something you want to tell me, please say it. I can't stand this build-up. I'm tired of being tense." I sag against him, burying my face in his neck, breathing in the delicious scent of him, fighting the thought that it might be the last time I get to be like this with him.

"June, no, it's not like that." He strokes the top of my head, the other hand grazing over my ass.

I squeeze my eyes shut even harder, as if that will somehow block the inevitable words from coming out of his mouth.

"It's about your," he clears his throat, "your father. I asked a few questions yesterday while I was in the secure area, finishing up the paperwork on what we found."

My fingers find his biceps, and I pinch a little, opening my eyes. "Get it over with. Tell me whatever it is."

"Yes, ma'am." A hoarse laugh follows, his eyes crinkling as he stares up at me. "When we informed them of Pierce's illegal extracurriculars, the DEA was very interested in what I had to say. In return, my classification was bumped up and I got read-in on the full file on the shipment and the long-term mission down here."

Anticipation knots my stomach. Sliding off him, I prop my chin up on my hands. Staring into his dark brown eyes, which now track the motion of the fan on the ceiling.

"There was something else I asked for, and Uncle Sam agreed to it."

"Dean…" Strings attached is the only way the government operates.

"Your dad wasn't just running drugs."

Teeth grind against teeth as I clench my jaw, stomach sinking. Dean turns his full attention on me, scooting back against the white headboard, his tan standing out in stark contrast.

God, I don't know if I can take this.

"He was our source. He was the informant on the whole mission, on the cartel, for years. He was one of the most important assets in South Texas for a decade. That's why he's dead, because Pierce knew, and the cartel found out. Your dad must've figured out Pierce was dirty and scuttled the drugs. Your father isn't the bad guy, June. He's the hero."

Air. I need air. Taking a huge breath, I expand my lungs, a cross between a laugh and a hiccup erupting from my throat. Relief and love war for attention. I can't move, paralyzed by the sudden shock of knowledge. Of gratitude.

"You okay?"

I nod, then curl up on Dean's lap. "Thank you. You don't know how much this means to me."

"I know how much it would mean to me." His words rumble against my chest. Fingers stroking down my legs, comforting. "But Pierce is still out there, June, and you saw what was in that sub."

I nod, and he tugs my chin up to look at him. His lips are a firm slash, his brown eyes steady on mine. Aha. This is where the other shoe drops.

"They've asked me and my firm to take the lead on the whole thing, to figure out the reach of the domestic terrorists, what they plan next. Where Pierce is, all of it. I need to get back to DC early next week. We don't think the cartel is a threat to you, but the domestic terrorists, they very well may be. We're setting up round-the-clock surveillance on you. It might be best if we find you a new place to live."

"Next week?" My voice is soft, and I quickly do the math. "So that means you'll be here for a few more days?"

His throat bobs as he swallows, not taking his eyes from mine. "I don't have to stay here, I'm sure you're ready for things to get back to normal. Well, as normal as they can be. We don't think the terrorists will try anything, but there is a small possibility that they'll seek to silence your testimony against Pierce and his associates. You may want to think about moving away from this town completely."

"I'm not giving up my research on the wreck, I'm not just going to walk away from my life here."

"I had a feeling you'd say that. So... you're ready for things to go back to normal, after all." It isn't a question.

A beat passes, and my fingers finally still against his skin, where I absentmindedly traced a tattoo on his chest.

"Back to normal?" My eyes meet his.

"If that's what you want, just say the word."

He isn't asking about normal... He's asking about him. About the possibility of an us, for something longer. More serious.

"Stay." It bursts out of me, full of hope and longing. "Please stay."

A genuine smile lights up his face, and my heart leaps. "If you're sure."

I straddle him, taking his face in my hands, planting a long, slow kiss to his lips. "I'm sure. I wouldn't want anyone else to watch over me, anyway."

I found him, I found the *Santu Espiritu*, and I'm going to hang onto both for dear life.

"What parts do you want me to watch over?" He pulls his lips away, and I reach back for him. A teasing smile playing across his lips before he presses a kiss to my jaw. "Here?" Another kiss, lower, across the top of my breast. "Is this where I need to watch over?"

"All of it," I breathe, and he brings his lips back to mine for a moment before staring down at me, smiling, that delicious dimple firmly in place.

"Know what the best part of being tasked with this is?"

Dark hair tickles my eyebrows as I furiously shake my head.

"It means I'll be back here as soon as I can."

"I like that."

"I'm glad, because you're the reason I said yes."

I stare at him, my mouth dropping open. "Oh?"

"Yep." There's a devilish glint in his eyes.

A few days. Dean will be mine, all mine, no boats or guns or henchmen involved, for a few more days.

I grin back at him. I'll make the most of it.

EPILOGUE

JUNE

I SURFACE, popping up on the aquamarine water like one of the porpoises I saw playing earlier in the day. The ocean around me is thick with frenzied activity; a research vessel equipped to haul up and process large archaeological finds hums as its dive team suctions sand.

The seafloor beneath me has transformed in the month since I first reported the *Santu Espiritu*, the sand carefully gridded and plotted. Dipping my mask back in the water, I take one last look at the ghostly remains of the ship then swim back to my new boat.

Grant money is good.

Throwing my flippers onto the deck, I climb up, carefully setting my tanks down. Warm terrycloth meets my skin and I smile, toweling off. My phone sits in the captain's chair cupholder, and my gaze dips to it.

Slipping a lightweight tee over my head, I pick up the phone and read the new text.

Dean: missing you

I haven't heard from him much since he's been in DC. Most of the month, not the few days we thought, unable to talk during the day or even have his phone on him, thanks to classified protocols. In the few snatches of conversations we've managed, he made it seem like he was headed back to South Texas soon.

Another message pops up.

Dean: see you soon

I frown at it, confused. Surely he would have said something sooner if he was coming into town. Excitement blossoms, spiraling into full-blown butterflies.

A new sound enters the already loud fray and I look up, shielding my eyes against the sun. Not another group of archaeologists. They don't drive anything like that. This boat is sleek, closer to a pleasure cruiser than a research vessel.

Damn. Probably some tourists in search of a great fishing spot.

I chew my lip. If they got too close, they'll kick up all kinds of debris and silt and ruin the progress we've made. The strains of Jimmy Buffett fill the air, and the huge boat slows to a stop, a safe distance away from the precious grid. I exhale a sigh of relief. Though it's still a little too close for comfort. Wake is a pretty serious thing, especially after the fate of the *Betty*.

Dark hair longer now, a broad, chiseled chest on full display has my heartbeat picking up speed. I squint, trying to make sure my heart isn't lying to me. Dean would've called first, would've let me know…

"June!" Dean throws back his head and laughs, an enormous grin on his face. His chest ripples as he springs off the side of the boat, diving into the water. My eyes dart back to the boat, where Thompson waves a few times before he turns the wheel and takes off into the gulf.

I don't bother watching him go. All my attention is now on the man cutting through the water like his life depends on it. A half second later, I'm in the water, swimming towards him. He pulls up short, dog paddling in front of me, so impossibly handsome. Even better than my memory can handle, his aggressive jawline and sensuous mouth nearly stopping my heart.

"June."

I crash against him and he catches me in his huge arms, pressing me to his chest, kicking hard enough to keep us afloat.

"You came." My hands can't seem to stop skating over his skin, his now wet hair. His cheeks. He turns into my palm, closing his eyes before opening them again, a huge smile on his face.

"I missed you."

"I know."

It's my turn to laugh. "You know? What kind of a response is that?"

His smile grows, but he doesn't laugh. "I know because I'm in love with you, and every minute I couldn't be with you this last month was a minute wasted. I'm taking a step back from work. Running admin instead of ops."

I hardly hear the last half of what he says. "You love me?"

"Hook, line and sinker."

"I love you too," I whisper. His lips meet mine, and I melt into him until my research team starts whooping from their boats.

"Get a room, Legarde!" one of them shouts, barely audible over the sound of the equipment.

Heat floods my cheeks, and I look back to Dean. "Well, it's not a terrible idea."

His thumb strokes over my cheek. "We're going to finally have that date. How it ends? That's up to you."

"I can think of a few ways we could end the date." I wrap my legs around him, and that rich baritone laugh rings out against my ear.

"I like where your head's at, Dr. Legarde."

"Then you'll love where it's at later." I draw back, heart hammering in my chest, and manage a saucy wink, ruined by the tears moistening my eyes.

Dean's eyes are soft, his cocky grin firmly in place. "Come on, June, let's get you something to eat. I know a place we can get some killer margaritas."

Another laugh. "Sounds perfect."

I finally untangle my legs from around him and we swim slowly, hand in hand, towards my shiny new boat, the *Father's Pride.*

THE END

scan to find me online

ACKNOWLEDGMENTS

This book was a labor of love, one I started writing nearly five years before pressing publish.

A lot of people loved this book along the way, and for that, I can't thank you enough.

To my early readers, all those years ago, who told me I had something fun and different: Kelly Andrew, JoAnna Illingworth, Tiffany White, Ashley Reisinger, Starla DeKruyf— your love of this book and these characters made me dust it off and rewrite it all these years later.

To my agent, Jessica Watterson, who read and loved and laughed with these characters and has always, ALWAYS had my back, thank you.

A pair of editors I feel unbelievably lucky to have in my contacts, especially Morgan Waddle, who did a massive amount of work to transition this from third past to first present— you're the real MVP. To Kaylin at Happy Ever Author, you put up with a lot from me and I don't tell you I adore you enough. You're a dream.

Thank you and best wishes to Lauren Cox for putting up with my shit on the daily, pew pew.

To Caitlin Baileyface Garafola, who has been dealing with me and this book from the start: it's finally here. Thank you for being my friend.

And to my little family— you make me want to be better every day.

Finally, to you, my readers, thank you for taking a chance on a book like this and on me. May we all find the Dorito humans we deserve.

ABOUT THE AUTHOR

When Brittany's not writing, she's usually keeping h
jumping off things they have no business jumping
daydreaming about going on a date with her husband.

For the latest updates, subscribe to her newsletter o
her on Instagram and TikTok.

Head to www.brittanykelleywrites.com for more!